THE BOMBS
BURSTING IN AIR

THE BOMBS BURSTING IN AIR

A Mike Elliot Novel

Book II

Lee Duffy

Edited by: Jennifer Word, EMP Publishing

Cover Design: Julia Gollbach, bioBLOSSOM CREATIVE

Published by: Lee Duffy

Rev. 1

ISBN: 978-0-9966053-2-8

Library of Congress Control Number: 2017902672

Also by Lee Duffy

The Dawn's Early Light, A Mike Elliot Thriller, Book I

The Prison Compendium, Contributing Author

A Life Interrupted and Other Stories

Serendipity and Other Stories

Choices and Other Stories

Angela and Other Stories

The Mongoose & The Iguana and Other Stories

The Grifters and Other Stories

Courage, above all things, is the first quality of a warrior.

Clausewitz

Prologue

Kirovskaya, Russia, 2:56 a.m.

The world was about to be changed forever—and not for the better. The windblown snow obscured the road, as well as the crime against humanity about to be perpetrated.

In a surreal, hazy blur, snow blew steadily past the headlights of the Russian Army Lynx, a sort of military Land Rover. The vehicle made its way along a gravel road deep in the remote and heavily forested southern region of Kirovskaya, some five hundred miles east of Moscow. Two army panel vans followed closely behind the Lynx.

Great fir trees, barely visible, lined the sides of the road, their broad arms sagging in heavy wet blankets of snow. Tiny slivers of moonlight highlighted the sparkling crystals of ice cascading down from the grand conifers.

Colonel Vladimir Grigor, dressed in a Russian army field uniform, rode in the back seat of the lead vehicle. His insignia was that of the elite Russian nuclear surety forces. He wore a black patch over his right eye.

His driver and the men riding in the two vans were all Russian Army special operations soldiers, or Spetsnaz. The colonel's men came from various Spetsnaz units, from several locations across Russia. What they had in common, besides being military special operators, was that they had all served under the colonel, then Major Grigor, in Chechnya.

The three-vehicle convoy arrived at a tall gate blocking the road. Colonel Grigor checked his watch. The computer network in the Moscow headquarters of the nuclear surety forces would crash in four minutes from a custom designed virus.

Ahead lay Grigor's target, a heavily fortified military compound—Nuclear Storage Facility 1677. The garrison troops protecting this facility were well-trained in post security operations, but unlike Grigor's men who were battle hardened special operators, the garrison soldiers were not seasoned combat troops.

From inside the gate, three Russian soldiers peered out from a lighted gatehouse. Beyond the second gate, massive, round, steel anti-crash bollards protruded up from the roadway blocking entry to the facility. Double perimeter fences stretched off to the right and left.

The fences were twelve feet high and topped with shiny, looping rolls of razor wire. Just inside the outer fence, a vehicular anti-crash barrier of three heavy cables extended from the sides of the entry road and ran the entire length of the perimeter. Motion sensors topped the fence posts, and anti-personnel and anti-tank mines filled the dead-man's zone between the two fences.

Two of the soldiers exited the guardhouse, passed through a personnel gate, and walked toward the vehicles. One of them stopped some distance away, a Kalashnikov AK47 assault rifle cradled loosely in his arms. The other walked up to the car as the driver motioned toward the back seat. The soldier stepped to the back door of the vehicle.

Grigor rolled down the window and handed the soldier an envelope. Surprise inspections were routine for nuclear storage facilities, but the security procedures were strict. The soldier returned to the gatehouse and rang the camp commandant.

The guard opened the envelope and read the inspection authorization code over the phone. Major Aleksei Ivanovich jotted down the code and then pulled a small notepad from his pocket. He compared the number he had just been given to the next listed code in his little book. It was authentic; it could only have come from Moscow headquarters.

Code confirmed, he approved the inspection team's entry. The gate slid open and the large steel bollards blocking the roadway lowered into their concrete housing beneath the road.

A soldier stepped out of one of the vans to conduct the gate inspection, and the three vehicles pulled forward into the compound. The inspector asked to see the gate records and access codes. Once he had the correct codes, he stepped back from the three young men, reached behind his back, and pulled a silenced pistol from beneath his uniform tunic. *Pop, pop, pop*—three muffled shots and three bloody bodies lay in a heap at his feet.

Colonel Grigor's vehicles drove into the compound and stopped. Four men, wearing white, winter camouflage, slipped from the trail van and disappeared into the blurry night toward the post barracks filled with sleeping off-duty soldiers. One of the four men carried a rectangular shaped backpack.

The three vehicles drove on to the post headquarters to find Major Ivanovich and his deputy Captain Kuzman waiting on the porch, standing at attention, saluting.

Grigor exited his car carrying a briefcase. Three of his men, wearing standard Russian field uniforms, exited the lead van. They all approached the two officers and exchanged salutes. Inside, the major led them to the control room, where two soldiers monitored the security systems. He then pointed out the training room, where they had assembled the four soldiers assigned to roving patrol duty. One of Grigor's men stepped into each of the two rooms and closed the doors to begin the inspection.

In the monitoring room, the inspector introduced himself. He held a clipboard with a checklist. He inquired about the cameras and data transmission. They informed him that everything was off-line due to a network outage. He stepped back and drew his silenced pistol. The two soldiers at the console stared, eyes wide. He shot them each in the face.

In the training room, the inspector found the four soldiers assigned to roving patrol. He instructed them to unload their weapons and field strip them. He readied his watch to start the timer. The soldiers scrambled to their weapons and began the disassembly. Standing over them, the inspector pulled his silenced pistol and shot each of them in the head.

The colonel and the camp's two officers reached the commandant's office. The prize was there. Grigor needed access to their high-security safe, without tripping the safe's self-destruct mechanism. Only the camp's two officers could do that—and *only* voluntarily with their unique memorized codes.

Grigor opened his leather briefcase and extracted a clipboard with a checklist on it. He also pulled out a portable radio and set it on the desk.

Pen in hand, he said, "Gentlemen, shall we get started?"

He began to ask the two officers questions from a checklist concerning the camp's security procedures. He continued down his inspection checklist.

~

Several hundred yards away, Grigor's four commandos arrived at the post barracks. Three of them pulled their pistols and took up security positions. One watched the door, where inside, forty Russian soldiers slept peacefully. The other two scanned to the rear.

The driving snow concealed the four Spetsnaz commandos lurking near the entrance of the barracks, a single-story, concrete and steel building housing the off-duty men.

The fourth commando reached up and unscrewed a single light bulb from a rusting metal fixture over the barracks door. Then he placed a small steel flange across the center of the two metal doors, down near the ground, and began to spot-weld it into place. Sparks from the pistol-like welding device illuminated his covered face.

A sleepy but curious soldier inside the barracks, returning to bed from the latrine and wearing white woolen long johns, ambled to the door. He cupped his hands to his eyes, pressed his face to the glass, and peered through the frosted window into the darkness beyond, squinting to see outside.

Pistol in hand, the commando covering the door fired one round. The gun's suppressor and the howling wind silenced the shot. The commandos continued to watch the door for a moment but saw no further movement. One of them pulled off a small patch of duct tape stuck to the outside of his shirt pocket and placed it over the bullet hole in the door's window pane.

The welder completed his task, and the door was sealed. He affixed a small glasscutter on the lowest windowpane, pressed a button, and a tiny electric motor spun the diamond blade. It cut a one-inch diameter hole in the glass.

He removed his backpack, stretched a hose from it, and stuck the nozzle into the hole in the window as the four commandos donned their oxygen masks. Then he opened a valve on the backpack, and gas flowed into the building. They continued to scan the windows and the terrain behind them. No other soldiers inside the barracks had stirred.

Within minutes, the soldiers asleep in their bunks quietly ceased breathing.

~

In the commandant's office, the colonel's portable radio crackled to life. "Colonel, barracks team."

"Go ahead, Grigor here."

"The barracks has passed inspection."

Three more reports came in rapid succession stating that the gatehouse, the control room, and the roving patrols had all passed inspection.

The commandant and his deputy beamed with pride.

Turning back to the two officers, Grigor said, "Gentlemen, the next exercise is the most important for the overall success of your inspection. It is timed." He adjusted his wristwatch to prepare the timer.

"When I give you the start command, you will have one minute to open the safe. Then we will inventory your bunker keys and codes."

He held up his watch, his finger on the start button. "Ready?"

The two officers nodded affirmatively.

"Go!" He started his watch.

Each officer pulled out a key hung on a chain around his neck and inserted it into a slot in each of the safe's two doors. The major counted down from three and they turned their keys together. They tapped their personal memorized codes into two keypads—lights turned from red to green. Each man turned his handle to open his side of the safe's double doors.

The two officers smiled with satisfaction.

Colonel Grigor stopped the timer on his watch. "Excellent."

Stepping back, he said, "Thank you, gentlemen, you have passed inspection."

The commando standing next to him raised his pistol and shot the two officers dead.

Grigor returned to the safe, found the key and combination for bunker number four, and walked out. His men set thermal grenades on the safe and followed.

As they drove away, a bright flash and a muffled explosion erupted from the headquarters. They drove to bunker four, where the men from the barracks team awaited. Grigor unlocked the gate and the bunker.

This bunker held tactical weapons called SADM—Special Atomic Demolitions Munition. They were banned by international treaty, but both the east and the west maintained them nonetheless.

Two dozen of the devices—RA-115s—were neatly arrayed along both walls of the bunker resting on wooden pallets. The compact bomb was designed to be emplaced by special operations forces.

Grigor inspected the serial number tag on each of the devices, comparing the tag against the numbers he had listed in a small notebook. He identified the exact five devices he wanted. As he pointed them out, his men scooped them up and loaded them into the two vans.

He relocked the bunker, and they drove to the front gate. When the vehicles were through, the gatehouse commando hit the gate-close button. He ran out through the closing gates, jumped into the trail van, and the three vehicles disappeared into the wintry night.

PART I

SURVIVAL AND OTHER MATTERS OF IMPORTANCE

1

The White House

The president's national security advisor, Stuart Anderson, stopped to admire a yellow heritage rose, though he wasn't actually interested in the flower. He was digesting what the deputy director of the CIA, John Striker, had just told him. The two men continued along the small path of crushed marble within the rose garden.

He turned and said, "So let me get this straight. An entire Russian army base was found murdered, and there are indications that one or more Russian portable nuclear devices are missing."

They started walking again. Striker had adapted well to his prosthetic leg, but he still had a slight limp. He had lost his right leg in a savage and bloody firefight with Hezbollah soldiers in Lebanon a year earlier. At six foot, three inches tall, he towered over the smaller man. His weathered complexion belied his many years operating in difficult climates under treacherous conditions.

"Yes," replied Striker finally. "The base was small, probably forty to fifty men. It's located in a remote region east of Moscow, called Kirovskaya. We believe it is a nuclear weapons storage facility. There are a dozen or so installations like it scattered around Russia. The men who were killed were part of Russia's nuclear surety force, a classified branch of the army."

"How reliable is your source, and how did he come by this information?"

"He's been reliable in the past. He talked with at least one family member of a slain soldier and confirmed that the soldier was part of nuclear surety, *and* that he was stationed at Kirovskaya. Classified information of course, but military families usually know what their loved ones are doing in the military. The Russian government issued a statement that the men were killed in a training accident. We don't think it was an accident, but we *do* think that it was an inside job."

"What do you mean?"

"We're picking up a lot of Russian electronic communications intercepts. They're in a real frenzy right now. Communications are off the chart. And *one* name keeps popping up again and again—Colonel Vladimir Grigor. They want him badly."

"Do we know anything about him?"

"He's known to us. We have a dossier on him, but we're working to fill it out. We do know that he was a Spetsnaz commander in Chechnya. Then he moved to nuclear surety, *and* he moonlights as an international arms dealer."

"How can *we* know that he's dealing in arms and the Russians don't? How could he stay in nuclear weapons."

"Oh, they probably did know. He probably kept hefty kickbacks going to all the right people. They just didn't expect him to do something like this."

"Any idea where he is?"

"None, except that it's probably safe to assume he's no longer in Russia. We have agents scattered across Europe and central Asia looking for him. You can bet the Russians are doing the same."

"So, if we find this Grigor, we find the nukes?"

"I hope so," replied Striker.

"What else are we doing?"

"We're looking at the major international arms dealers. There aren't many of them who could handle a transaction of this magnitude."

"Okay, good, keep me posted on your progress. So just what are these weapons capable of?" asked Anderson.

"A typical Russian man-portable device can yield one to two kilotons, enough to vaporize much of the center of Washington, or most of Manhattan, and kill hundreds of thousands of people. They are the size of a small roller-bag suitcase. That's why they're sometimes referred to as suitcase nukes. They can even be carried in a backpack."

Striker handed Anderson a file folder. Inside the front flap, a photo displayed an image of the RA-115 SADM. The dimensions, weight, yield, and other data were printed on the photo. The device consisted of a small drum, sixteen inches tall and eleven inches in diameter weighing roughly fifty pounds. An olive-green canvas container with heavy-duty nylon strapping encased the bomb. Mounted on the side of the drum, a rectangular box housed the electronic controls.

Anderson asked, "And we don't know if it was one device or ten. Maybe more, correct?"

"That's correct. For all we know it could be twenty, but I think it's less. Trying to move too many of these things would be difficult to conceal."

"Could it have been a nuclear accident?"

"We don't think so. We would have picked up on it."

"I assume we have people working on this."

"Everything we've got."

"So there could be enough man-portable nuclear devices floating around out there to destroy large sectors of ten U.S. cities."

"Yes. At this point it is still just speculation, but why would someone kill all those soldiers unless it was to procure some nukes."

"But they wouldn't have the codes required to activate the devices, would they?"

"Well, the activation codes are never kept in the nuclear storage facilities with the devices. They are kept in Moscow. But I doubt anyone would go to the trouble of stealing a device that would be useless without the code, another reason to suspect that Vladimir Grigor was involved. He worked in the headquarters where the codes are presumably stored."

"Just for the sake of argument, couldn't someone hack the devices and eventually figure out the codes anyway?"

"I doubt it. Los Alamos has tried on our own SADMs. Even under laboratory conditions, employing massive computing power, they couldn't break the encryption. The Russian devices are easily as good as ours. No, if these bombs are going to be worth anything on the market, then whoever stole them had access to the codes in Moscow."

Striker stopped and turned to face the National Security Advisor. "Stuart, the worst part is that if these missing devices *are*

RA-115s, we believe that model is capable of getting past our port cargo radiological screening undetected."

"Crap. Is this in the president's daily brief?"

"Yes, tomorrow morning. We'll continue working on this through the night and have a refined analysis by morning."

"Okay, I'm going to give him a heads up that this is coming."

"Fine."

"John," added Anderson, "there is one other matter."

"Yes?"

"Jameson is out as Director Central Intelligence. The president has lost confidence in him."

Striker stopped. His hazel eyes were wide, his thick eyebrows raised.

"You'll be named acting DCI in the next day or so. The president wants to make it permanent, but with this new crisis on our plate, I'm sure he'll want you focused on finding these bombs rather than on confirmation hearings."

Striker nodded.

~

Poti, Georgia

Genadi Meskhi stood by the entrance to his large, metal-frame warehouse. It was located in the industrial complex of Poti's bustling port facility on the eastern shore of the Black Sea. Four heavily armed bodyguards stood nearby.

This building was the primary headquarters of Meskhi's extremely lucrative import-export business. He made millions from it. In the distance, up and down the harbor's concrete quay in both directions, huge cargo ships lined the port. Gigantic cranes loaded and unloaded fifty-foot long metal containers.

Meskhi's rotund profile was exaggerated in the shadow he projected against the metal building. He wore a white linen shirt and an expensive vest trimmed in gold. A stainless steel, diamond-encrusted Rolex hung loosely on his left wrist. He opened a fresh Cuban cigar and lit it.

He was short, overweight, and in his sixties. He had gray hair and brown tobacco stains on his fat lips. His jowls hung in folds on the sides of his pale jaw and under his chin.

Nikoloz Donauri, Meskhi's lieutenant, came out of the building and greeted him. Donauri was a small man physically, but he had a talent for numbers and organization. He handled the hundreds of minor details that kept the operation running.

A flatbed tractor-trailer carrying agricultural implements drove slowly past. The company shipped electronics, auto parts, tractors, and other goods all over the world. Meskhi's Import-Export was quite lucrative by anyone's standard, but it was not enough for Genadi Meskhi. This business was merely a front for an exponentially more profitable international arms trade that he and his mob-like enterprise conducted.

Donauri said, "We have the Iranian weapons shipment." He nodded toward the warehouse. "Not much, a dozen mortars, mortar shells, a couple hundred cases of rifles and several tons of ammo. We need to get it to Hezbollah in Lebanon."

"How will you send it?"

"Usual route. We'll truck it through Turkey, then by boat around to south Lebanon. No problem. It'll go out tomorrow."

"And this so-called reporter from Tbilisi?"

"In the back," he replied, nodding toward the building. They turned and walked to the building's entrance.

The two men, followed by a cluster of bodyguards, entered the warehouse and walked the hundred and fifty yards past long rows of shelving and stacked crates toward the back of the building. They arrived at a metal door and Donauri punched a number into a cipher lock. They went through and into a smaller concrete room.

The windows were grimy and the light dim, but it was bright enough to see the man strung up by chains attached to his wrists near the back wall. Meskhi's enforcer, a huge, bald man wearing a leather apron, stood nearby. His biceps were the thickness of a normal man's thighs.

The reporter's head hung down, and his body was limp. A large amount of blood stained his shirt and pants. His bare feet just touched a metal drainage grill in the floor beneath him. He was a young man, with longish black hair, now matted with blood.

"What did you find out?" Meskhi asked his lieutenant.

"The guy at first just kept saying he was a reporter and was curious about a rumor he heard in Tbilisi about a major arms smuggling operation in Poti."

"And?"

"He finally admitted that a man paid him to gather information about our operation."

"Did you find out who that man was?"

"He didn't know."

"You're sure about this?"

"Completely."

Meskhi flicked his cigar away, walked to the chained man, and clasped his large hand over the man's jaw. He lifted his head. The man, in his twenties, moaned and slowly came around. He looked at Meskhi with vapid eyes.

"So, what do you think of Poti?" he asked.

The man tried to shake his head but could barely manage a slight wiggle.

Meskhi snapped his fingers and held out his hand behind him.

The bald man stepped forward and placed a folded tactical combat knife on Meskhi's open palm. He slowly unfolded the blade while looking straight at the young man. The man hanging in the chains shook his head, pleading.

Meskhi thrust the blade into the man's throat. He held the knife there as the young man's body shook, until he sucked in a final gurgling breath and went limp. He removed the knife and handed it to the big man behind him. A bodyguard stepped up and handed the boss a handkerchief. He wiped the blood from his hands.

Donauri said, "We'll make sure there's no trace of the body."

Still wiping his hands, Meskhi turned to face his lieutenant. "And do we have a secure location identified for our latest acquisition?"

"We have a smaller building we haven't used in a while. I have a work crew on it now. They are cleaning it out and checking over everything. They will install a new high-security alarm system that we will monitor from here. There will be on-site security and a quick-reaction force nearby. I'll also put a roving security patrol in that sector of buildings. It will be ready tomorrow."

"Excellent," replied Meskhi. He tossed the handkerchief to the side and pulled a fresh cigar from his shirt pocket.

~

DIA Headquarters, Washington, D.C.

Mike Elliot walked slowly down a long corridor in the Defense Intelligence Agency in Washington. He was starving. He had worked straight through lunch in the classified-secure room on his floor, analyzing a recent terror attack in Nigeria.

He always took interest in the many portraits and photos adorning the walls of this hallway. He made it a point to read the captions on one or two of them each time he passed by. It always reminded him that many men and women had sacrificed for their country. Mike knew that he had.

He read the caption beneath one of the pictures. As he did so, he ran his left hand back through his short, sandy-colored hair. His wife, Lynn, frequently teased him about that habit—he did it when he was concentrating on something. On the inside of his left forearm, was the sole physical reminder of his previous life. In faded green ink, he had a small tattoo in script—*De Oppresso Liber*—the motto of the Green Berets.

At six foot, one hundred and seventy-five pounds, Mike was trim, lean, muscular, and quick. His complexion was slightly dark, as though he were perpetually tanned. He had just turned thirty-six. His wife Lynn was twenty-eight and now in medical school. It seemed like their world might just finally settle down and let the two of them lead a quiet, uneventful life, and just be happy.

The last four years had been difficult for Mike, to say the least. Four years earlier, Mike lost his first wife and daughter, Margaret and Emily. They were kidnapped in Brazil where Mike was assigned, and then taken to Colombia. Mike and a CIA operative named Jonas Ward were wounded in a rescue attempt. Margaret and Emily were murdered. In the hospital Mike met Lynn, his second wife.

Mike and Lynn were eventually assigned to Tunisia where Mike worked in the U.S. embassy in Tunis. It was only a year ago, but it seemed like yesterday to Mike when Tunisia had exploded in violence. The North-African country was beautiful, and he and Lynn were having the time of their lives. Then suddenly, a Muslim Brotherhood uprising threw the nation into murderous chaos.

The Americans tried to evacuate the embassy's non-essential staff and their families, but before the flight could depart Tunis, brutal Hezbollah terrorists hijacked the plane. Mike and Lynn were among the hostages, and Mike knew he had very nearly lost Lynn on that flight.

He shuddered at the memory, turned, and walked on down the hall. That was history. He and Lynn were safe now.

He only managed a few steps before another photo on the wall caught his attention. An image of a soldier wearing a beret reminded Mike of his dad. From Mike's earliest memories, his father was a U.S. Army Green Beret. As a child, Mike wore his dad's beret around the house, playing soldier. He was Mike's idol. When Mike was nine, the first gulf war came along. To pave the way for the invading forces, his dad's SF team entered Iraq before the U.S. invasion began.

Mike remembered like it was yesterday when the two officers wearing dress uniforms came to their doorstep to inform his mother of her husband's death. Captain William Elliot died in heavy combat with a superior Iraqi force, they told her. She collapsed to the floor. The two officers, with Mike trying to help, carried her to the couch. When she recovered, they told her of his heroism. Mike remembered just sitting there shivering and feeling very cold.

Somehow, Mike felt responsible for his father's death. It was irrational, but to Mike it felt very real nonetheless. His mother used to tell him that he always tried to take the weight of the world on his shoulders when there was no reason to do so.

He was devastated by his father's death, but worse, he watched his mother, Ellen, spiral ever deeper into drug and alcohol abuse over the next twelve years of their lives. At twenty-one, Mike had completed college and was about to receive his commission into the army as a second lieutenant. His mother never made it to the ceremony. She died in a car crash on her way to the swearing-in ceremony. She was driving drunk.

Mike sat at home later that day staring at a photo of his mom and dad, and he cried. The photo showed William and Ellen Elliot at a backyard barbecue taken when Mike was six or seven. They were laughing and William had his arm around Ellen's waist.

Mike felt responsible for his mother's death too. She had no business out on the road coming to his ceremony. He should have foreseen it and prevented it. Picked her up. Called a cab. Anything.

In memory of both of them, it was at that moment that he decided he would become a Green Beret—no matter what it took.

He completed a three-year assignment in the 82nd Airborne Division at Fort Bragg with top-level ratings and was accepted into the highly competitive and grueling Special Forces qualification course. He completed the training with honors and was assigned to *Group*—the term the men who wore the Green Beret used to refer to Special Forces.

Reminiscing about his father always reminded Mike of why he had become a Green Beret himself. But thinking of his first wife and daughter, and of his second wife Lynn, reminded him of why he left Special Forces.

He passed through the swinging double doors into the cafeteria. At this time of day, it wasn't crowded. Moving through the serving line, he picked up some water, a salad, and a ham sandwich. He paid and carried his tray into the large seating area full of tables and chairs.

Mike spotted Max Hardwick and Jonas Ward sitting at a table across the room, coffee cups on the table before them. Both men were from the CIA.

At forty-two, Max already had mostly gray hair. He was a heavy-set man who obviously relished his share of fine dining and good wine. His large, bulbous nose had a hint of raspberry color; his complexion was pale and mottled. Max enjoyed far too many Martinis for his own good.

At this distance, and seated, it wasn't immediately evident that Jonas was almost crippled. He of course got that way saving Mike's life in Colombia. Jonas Ward was only forty, but his hair was also prematurely gray and already thinning.

Mike crossed the room and joined the two men, thinking they were at DIA for routine business not concerning him.

Max said, "Mike, you're looking good.

"And you're looking as ornery as ever, Max. Hi, Jonas, any improvement?"

"Still in physical therapy three times a week. I think I'm getting some movement in my arm," he said, slightly lifting his left arm. "And I've graduated from the crutches to a cane." He pointed to the cane hanging over the seatback next to him. Jonas had always been a large and muscular man, but he had lost considerable weight since his injuries, Mike noted.

"That's great," said Mike, taking a bite of his salad. "So who are you guys here to spy on?"

"You," said Max.

Mike stopped chewing and his shoulders dropped. *Here it comes*, he thought, *the pitch*.

A lifetime of painful memories flashed through Mike's mind in an instant. He saw images of Margaret and Emily, his first wife and daughter, kidnapped four years earlier by Colombian narco-terrorists. Mike had left Special Forces because he wanted a normal life for his family instead of him being away all the time conducting missions for the CIA in some remote jungle on another continent.

The DIA offered him an analyst's position at the U.S. embassy in Brasilia, Brazil. Mike moved his family there and set up household. They lived in a gated community with security guards at the entrance. Emily attended a private American school, and they were happy. Daddy was home every evening for supper.

At work, Mike assisted Jonas Ward, and several agents from DEA working with him, to locate and target drug cartels operating across the border in Colombia. And then one day Mike came home to discover that Margaret and Emily had vanished. They were kidnapped.

Jonas eventually got a clue where they were being held, along with three other western hostages. Jonas, Mike, and a team of Brazilian Special Forces conducted a helicopter raid over the border into Colombia to rescue them. They actually found them, but all the hostages were tied up and rigged with explosives. It was a deliberate trap. Both Mike and Jonas were severely wounded in the rescue attempt, Jonas permanently, and the hostages died. Jonas had shielded Mike from most of the blast with his own body.

Still, Mike spent almost a year in the hospital. Lynn was his nurse and helped to keep him alive, both physically and emotionally. When he finally learned to stop grieving, she would later become his wife.

And though he didn't want to, Mike could also see and feel the hundreds of spec-ops missions that he and his team had conducted for the CIA over a decade—all the people they had killed or maimed—his own wounds, the regrets.

"Mike?" asked Max.

Mike shook his head and dragged himself back to the present.

"We need you, Mike," said Max, sipping his coffee.

"Max, you know I'm out of the business. I'm perfectly content shuffling paper and writing reports for someone higher up to toss in the can."

"Mike, this is big."

Jonas was nodding his agreement.

"If it's so big, why haven't I seen an intsum on it here at DIA?"

"Only a select few in the CIA, a few cabinet-level officials, and the president know about it so far."

"Well, I'm certainly not part of that esteemed crowd, so why are you here?"

"Mike, some Russian portable nukes are missing. They were stolen from a base in a remote region east of Moscow called Kirovskaya. Everyone on the base was murdered, and an unknown number of the suitcase devices are missing. We speculate that they have already been transported out of the country. But we don't *really* know one way or the other."

Jonas said, "The heist was either commissioned, or it's a rogue Russian agent who will try to sell them to the highest bidder."

Mike looked at Max and then Jonas, his electric-blue eyes focused and penetrating. "You're right, guys, that is huge. But it doesn't concern me, other than going back upstairs and looking for clues in the data."

Jonas added, "Mike, I know well your concerns. I'm living them every single day right along with you. It still tears me up that we couldn't save your wife and daughter. And I understand that you don't want to go off and get yourself killed and leave Lynn alone."

Max said, "Mike, we're mobilizing every possible, viable asset that we can muster to put on this. You're one of the most viable. Mike, you're a linguist. What is it, four languages?"

Mike frowned. "Max, I know you don't have to ask. You don't come recruiting without knowing the resume."

"Right, *and* you're a martial artist, *and* an expert in just about every kind of weapon out there. *And*, you've got a lengthy and proven track record of successful spec-ops combat experience. You're a viable operative all right, and Striker wants you."

"Striker will just have to get over it."

"Mike," implored Max, "if they manage to get even one of those devices onto American soil, it could be a hundred times worse than 9/11. It could destroy our government. All they need to do is get one device into a van, drive it to some location between the White House and Capitol Hill, detonate it, and bring the government down. It could mean our collapse."

"Max, I appreciate the gravity of the situation. And I'm committed to serving my country, just in a different way than before. I'm not the tip of the spear anymore. I'm now a support guy. I have to stay here, stay alive, and protect my wife."

"Last word?"

"Yes."

"All right, I understand."

~

Washington, D.C.

Forty-eight-year-old Gerald Billings walked slowly along Tenth Street NW. He was nearly bald and thirty pounds overweight. He puffed slightly from the mild exertion. His bushy brown eyebrows splayed around the edges of his thick, horn-rimmed glasses.

He was generally inattentive to his surroundings, even though he had long imagined how his fellow CIA employees moved about the world undetected. He had no formal training in tradecraft, however, only his imagination and countless spy novels.

A jackhammer rattled the air from somewhere behind a plywood construction wall, and a siren wailed in the distance. He barely noticed. The weather was warm, he was nervous, and he perspired profusely. He felt damp and uncomfortable.

Twenty-five years ago, he had joined the CIA fresh out of Harvard. He had graduated at the bottom of his class, but because his father had been a career CIA officer, Gerald snagged a legacy position with the agency. He remembered how he had been so full of ambition. He harbored fantasies of roaming the world, spying, keeping America safe from its enemies, and being a hero.

Gerald had been eager to make his father proud. Fortunately, his dad had died many years ago and was spared seeing his son's stunning lack of success in the agency. It just hadn't worked out the way Gerald had imagined all those years ago. He was a flunky, and he felt his face flush at the thought of it.

After a stint in analysis, they had moved him to administration, and despite repeated requests for overseas assignments, they had kept him in headquarters shuffling paper all these miserable years.

He handled important paperwork, but only because he was the administrative assistant to Alan Berg, the CIA's Director of Operations, known as the DO. Not because of any particular accomplishment of his own. The field agents who passed through headquarters for the obligatory meetings with the DO, barely recognized his presence in the room as he took notes for Director Berg.

A ratty looking, longhaired teen on a skateboard brushed past, jostling Gerald. It startled him back to the present. He didn't yell out or make a gesture. He hated confrontation and conflict, particularly where there was potential for violence.

Gerald didn't have much of a career, but he did have access to critical information, at least that which passed over his desk en route to the director. He didn't seek out classified information on his own authority—he didn't have a need to know. He wasn't an analyst or an operative, not even a manager. But when the director requested something, Billings retrieved it for him, and could get a glimpse of it. Or, he would hear things in the director's meetings.

So far, he had learned of, and sold, the names of two CIA employees and their cover identities. They both worked in overseas embassies. That was probably some of the most highly classified information in the CIA, and Gerald would never have had access to it on his own. But the director relied on Gerald to handle even his most sensitive documents. Gerald had received fifty thousand per name.

He turned onto Randolph and went another block. Then he walked down a ramp into a parking garage. As he descended into the near darkness, he felt as if he were entering the giant open mouth of some beast about to swallow him up.

He made his way toward the back of the garage, feeling more nervous with each step. Maybe his bosses could just tell by looking at him that he was not cut out for the cloak and dagger stuff.

He cautiously approached a large concrete column near the back. There stood the man he had come to think of as the Arab. He was not black, but his skin was dark, like a deep russet. He wore a blue suit, red tie, and his usual black fedora. He had a neatly trimmed, jet-black beard. His deep-set eyes were penetrating even in the dim light. Gerald could smell the man's cologne. It was probably expensive.

"Hello, Gerald," he said in his deep, smooth voice.

"Hello," he replied timidly. He didn't care for the small talk. He wanted to be done, be paid, and be gone.

Gerald pulled a small white envelope from his rear pocket, but then hesitated.

"There is one more name here. That's fifty thousand, right?" he asked, fidgeting awkwardly.

"Of course, Gerald. That is our arrangement."

"This one works out of the Paris embassy," Gerald said.

The man reached out and Billings handed over the envelope.

"I'll be paid?"

"Of course, once I verify the information, your money will be deposited into your Grand Cayman account, just like the last time."

Gerald turned and left in a hurry as the dark man watched him walk away. It had taken him a full year of careful grooming to recruit Billings, and now he was starting to produce. Sadegh Mohsen was no Arab, though it suited his needs for the American to think that he was. He had even fostered this idea by talking about his *Arabic* heritage during the recruitment phase with Billings.

In reality, the proud blood of ancient Persia coursed through his Iranian veins—superior blood in Mohsen's opinion.

He shook his head in disbelief. In Iran, someone like Gerald Billings would never get close to the ranks of the elite Revolutionary Guard. Yet here was this small man located in the very heart of the American CIA. It was their weakness, and he would happily exploit it. As he always said: *In direct combat and great battles alike, discover your opponent's weakness, and you shall prevail.*

The Iranian walked away, quickly disappearing into the cavernous garage.

2

Poti, Georgia

Genadi Meskhi's Lear jet, carrying Colonel Vladimir Grigor, set up its approach coming in low over the dark waters of the Black Sea. At the stroke of midnight, it touched down gently at the small, one-runway airport in Poti, Georgia.

Following the attack on the nuclear storage facility, all but two of Grigor's men had switched vehicles and headed south to deliver the nuclear weapons to Georgia. The remaining two men had driven Grigor some two hundred miles to the east. Meskhi's jet had picked him up at a small airfield there.

He had to flee Russia immediately. He would quickly be suspected of orchestrating the theft, and he could *never* return to Moscow. If he did end up back there, he knew it would be either in shackles or in a coffin.

Moscow was alerted the moment the computer network came back up and NSF 1677 was not on it. The protocol for such an emergency was to summon everyone working in nuclear surety to the headquarters. When Grigor didn't show, he would fall under direct suspicion, though it didn't really matter. Once he had been paid, he would vanish, never to be seen or heard from again.

Normally, when doing his arms dealing in Poti and other locales, he would be away for only a few days at a time. He always carefully planned his movements to avoid coming to the attention of the federal security services. Now, though, those agencies would be turning Russia and its neighboring countries upside down trying to figure out what happened to Russia's nukes. And he knew that they would be looking for him.

Therefore, *this* trip to Poti was different. It was one-way, his final journey out of Russia.

As for his men, initially there would be no reason to suspect they were involved. He knew, though, that it would eventually leak and they would be found out. One or more of them would talk, which would lead authorities to the others. But none of that mattered to him.

Grigor was in Poti to meet with Genadi Meskhi, a man he had dealt with many times over the years. He didn't like the fat little bastard, but Meskhi was a necessary evil. Grigor would complete his final deal with the treacherous mob boss. Then, under a new identity painstakingly prepared over the course of many years, he would retire a very wealthy man to a warm climate far from the Byzantine politics of Moscow. He had already purchased a property in a remote location untraceable to his real name. But for the moment, he needed to evade Russian intelligence long enough to fully change his identity.

Through the porthole window, he could see a black Mercedes sedan parked under several glowing streetlights. A driver stood next to the vehicle. Grigor would not go through the small terminal, or immigration, of course. Meskhi owned everyone of any significant authority in Poti. Those he could not buy tended to mysteriously disappear.

Grigor stepped down onto the tarmac, feeling the warmth of the night on his face. Here in the south, in mid March, the temperature was perfect. Central Russia, however, was still in the dead of winter.

Once in the back of the Mercedes, his weathered, brown leather briefcase on the seat beside him, he watched the rugged, green terrain as it sped past the car's windows. Meskhi's compound on the outskirts of town was only a short drive from the airport.

The yellow glare of lights on poles spaced along the small highway provided illumination. He touched the soft briefcase. It had belonged to his great grandfather in the days when Russia still had a czar. Grigor carried the first installment of his deal with Meskhi in the satchel. The second was en route overland at this very moment.

The sedan soon arrived at the main gate to Meskhi's sprawling, fortified estate. Heavily armed guards stood by. Others, flashlight beams bouncing left and right, roamed the perimeter of the property in pairs, some with huge dogs on leashes. More men secured the brightly lit estate house. A guard looked into the car and waved the driver forward as the massive iron gates swung open.

They drove up the long driveway and came to a stop in front of a large, white-stone terrace. Meskhi stood there waiting, a huge cigar protruding from his mouth. His short stature and ample belly made him easily identifiable even in a group. He was dressed in slacks, a white shirt, and a silvery vest that probably cost a small fortune. Two large bodyguards flanked him.

In contrast, Colonel Grigòr looked every bit the hardened soldier that he was. He was slim with broad shoulders, a muscular build, and stood six foot two. At forty-four, his jet-black hair was trimmed to strict military standards with only the slightest tinges of gray at the temples. He had a long, jagged scar on his left cheek and his usual black patch over his right eye—both were souvenirs from Chechnya where he led Spetsnaz teams in vicious and brutal combat against Chechen separatists some years earlier.

Meskhi shook Grigor's hand and then ushered him through tall windowpane doors into a large office. A bodyguard stood just inside the glass doors, another on the opposite side of the room by the hand-carved wooden entry doors to the room. Meskhi waved at the two guards. One went out into the hall; the other left through the glass doors to the terrace.

"So, Colonel," said Meskhi, "have you completed your plan?"

"I have."

"This is an ambitious and dangerous undertaking. I haven't heard of any large thefts in Russia."

"And you won't. It is a very sensitive matter."

"Ten million is a sizable down payment for something I haven't even seen—not to mention the additional forty million in final payment. How do I know you can deliver?"

"In fact, they are on the way here now, and have I not provided you with thousands upon thousands of top quality Russian Army Kalashnikovs over the years?"

"You have, but this is different. Nobody cares about Kalashnikov rifles. With this one, the world will be watching. Half the nations on earth are probably looking for these items, *and* for you. They will also be searching for the one who handles this transaction."

"Yes, but you will make hundreds of millions in the process—provided we do this correctly."

"You realize, Grigor, they will quickly determine that you were involved."

"Of course they will. I will be taking all the necessary precautions for my personal safety. As for the bombs themselves, *you* should have no problems. We are leaving no clues as to where they are being delivered, and Russian intelligence has no idea where to begin," he lied, knowing that both the Russians and the Americans would eventually track the weapons to Meskhi. "If you take similar precautions, it will all work out perfectly."

"I have remained in business all these years precisely because I operate only with the utmost caution. Along with a heavy dose of force," he added.

"It will work then."

Switching his cigar to the other side of his mouth Meskhi said, "I am concerned about the possibility of detection during storage or transport."

"Do not be. I have direct experience with these devices. We in Spetsnaz trained with them. We conducted tests, and we developed deployment tactics and techniques. They would not be very reliable tactical nuclear weapons if they could be easily detected by the enemy."

"What about radiological detectors or explosive detection canines. Everyone uses these tools these days?"

"What you must understand, Genadi, is that these devices were painstakingly designed by Mother Russia's best nuclear scientists *not* to be detectable."

Meskhi jerked the cigar from his mouth and spat to one side. "Don't get me started about *Mother Russia*, Grigor," he hissed through gritted teeth, his face set in a heavy scowl. The history between Russia and Georgia had not always been pleasant.

"As I was saying, Genadi, yes, they have a slight radiological signature, but the fissile material is heavily shielded. It requires a sophisticated radiological detector placed almost on top of the device to pick it up. The portable detectors police and customs officials wear are not enough.

"And yes, the device contains explosive charges for detonation. But it is all completely encapsulated and sealed in a magnesium-carbide container. In our tests with canines, only one in twenty experienced dogs would alert, and then only after specialized training. No, this device is a masterpiece, Genadi. Do not worry."

Meskhi chewed his cigar for a moment, and then nodded. "Okay then. You brought me something?"

"Yes," replied Grigor, unbuckling the flap on his briefcase. He extracted six PDAs, small electronic devices that resembled smart phones. They had hardened, rubberized exteriors, and near shatterproof screens.

He held up one device. "This one holds your activation and deactivation codes for all five RA-115s." He turned it over and pointed to the five serial numbers etched on the back of the PDA.

He spread out five more PDAs on the desk next to the first one. They were labeled with the numbers one through five. "These five PDAs are each unique. They each hold the codes for one nuclear device," he said, shoving them toward Meskhi. "Each RA-115 has a unique serial number stamped on a metal tag, *and* etched on the bomb's housing."

Grigor flipped over one of the PDAs. "Each single PDA has one bomb's serial number etched on the back," he said, pointing to the number on the PDA.

"The PDAs are military grade, and they have solar panels as well as internal, long-duration batteries. The panels will recharge the batteries, and they in turn will hold a full charge for at least six months, even if they never see the light of day. They are designed to be carried by special operations troops under difficult conditions, and yet remain failsafe."

Grigor continued, "They also have step-by-step instructions if employed by someone not familiar with the devices. For someone knowledgeable, more complicated deployment methods can be accomplished."

"Do these PDAs have passwords?"

"Yes." He handed Meskhi a small card. "This is the PIN for all the PDAs."

"Won't these PDAs be missed in Moscow?"

"No. Nothing is missing in Moscow. These are duplicates. There is no indication that the codes in Moscow were ever accessed. They will conclude that whoever has the bombs does not have the codes to activate them. They will eventually write it all off and get back to business as usual."

"Excellent," replied Meskhi, raking the PDAs into his desk drawer with his arm. "How do you want the down payment?"

Grigor handed him a small piece of paper.

"The down payment, ten million, should all go into the first listed account immediately. Then upon delivery of the five packages to the transfer point, the balance of forty million should be paid. Sixteen million more into the first account. The remaining twenty-four million should be distributed equally between the next twelve accounts listed there.

"At the transfer point my man will receive an automated message from the bank verifying the deposits. At that time my men will release the weapons."

Meskhi nodded his agreement. "My man will call me from the transfer point once he has inspected the weapons and I will make the payments."

"Excellent," Grigor replied. "Genadi," he continued, "I assume you will be selling all five to the Iranians?"

"That is my intention. They *are* my best customer. *If* they are willing to pay my price that is."

"I think they will jump at the chance."

"So why do you ask?"

"It is safer for all of us. The Iranians are crazy, but not so crazy as to actually use one of the bombs. If one were to be detonated, it would complicate things for the both of us."

Meskhi nodded.

"Unless there is anything further that you require," said Grigor, "I will depart now. As I said, your items are en route as we speak and will be delivered to the designated contact point by truck. As we previously discussed, you will handle the border crossing into Georgia."

"Agreed."

Grigor extended his hand to Meskhi. "Genadi, to our mutual profit."

Meskhi gestured toward the glass doors and the waiting car.

~

DIA Headquarters, 6:00 p.m.

Mike walked out of the classified-secure area on his floor after a marathon stretch of searching the databases for any hint of the missing nukes. It hadn't taken long for a new tasking to arrive from DOD—*look for clues on the missing Russian nuclear devices.* Everyone was on it.

Thoughts of that morning, before he and Lynn left for work, however, kept intruding on his concentration. Mike had just stepped into the shower. He'd been there for several minutes when the opening of the shower door startled him. Lynn stood there with a sheepish grin on her face—and nothing else.

Her tawny-smooth skin demanded to be touched. Smiling and stepping into the shower, she whispered softly, "How about some company, lover." She pressed her silky body next to his. Mike slipped his arms around her slender waist. He closed his eyes and held her next to him as the warm water cascaded over their bodies. "I love you," she purred. He found her lips with his.

At times, their lovemaking could be feverish. But as the water traced their bodies, they made love slowly, tenderly. They savored fully the other's warmth and pleasure. Tender caresses had momentarily replaced the coming day's plans and worries. He had stared deeply into her loving eyes knowing he could look into those dark mysterious pools forever. "I love you, Doctor," he told her with a smile.

Someone walked by, and it dragged him back from his daydream.

Electronics were not allowed in the secure areas, where analysts could leave classified documents spread out on worktables while doing analysis, so he didn't have his phone. When he got to his desk, he saw that he had just missed a call from Lynn. He tapped the number and it redialed. She picked up immediately.

"Hello, sweetheart," she cooed, toying with her ponytail. She kept her long, black hair tied back and out of the way when she worked. "Thank you for this morning. It was wonderful."

"No, thank you, and as a matter of fact, I was just thinking about it. So how are you, hon?"

"Tired. Dr. Hamilton is riding roughshod over me." She sighed, and Mike could hear her frustration.

He could picture her. She would be standing there, one hand buried in her white lab coat pocket, or she would be playing with her hair. She had her French mother's mouth and lips, but her Vietnamese father's dark eyes.

"You're his star intern," said Mike.

"In my dreams."

"We both know it's true."

"Well, I had a quick break from the ER, and I wanted to tell you I love you. And that I'll be late, as usual."

"You know I'm proud of you."

"Yes, if I survive this internship."

"You will."

"Okay, hon, they're calling. Incoming car wreck with injuries."

"Call me when you get off. I'll pick you up."

"No, you won't. I'd have to leave my car. I'll be fine. See you later tonight. I'll text you when I'm leaving. Gotta go, love you."

"Love you, too."

~

Washington, D.C., 8:55 p.m.

A short distance from University Hospital, Ernesto Diaz stumbled down a dark trash alley between blocks of row houses. Reeking cans lined the narrow pothole-filled lane. He didn't smell much better himself. He had just awoken behind a dumpster, his face in a puddle of dried vomit. He needed a meth fix badly, but he had no money, and he knew his credit was shot with his regular dealers. He had to try though.

He checked and the long folding knife he carried was still clipped in his waistband. Even though it was warm, he wore a tattered, red-plaid flannel shirt that he noticed was hanging completely open. He fumbled with the buttons as he continued to walk. Several were missing. The shirt was wet with something that smelled awful. He briefly wondered what the hell happened, but he had no memory of the past twenty-four hours.

He was pale for a Latino. It came from rarely seeing sunlight and from often being ill. He couldn't get medical treatment, though, because he was in the country illegally, and he knew there were probably a half-dozen warrants out for him. He shuddered and felt queasy, like he might throw up. He couldn't remember when he had last eaten and knew that if he did retch, it would only be painful dry heaves.

He approached two young black men standing in the shadows at the intersection of another alley. They watched him approach. Diaz knew that several more just like these two were positioned out of sight with pistols in their hands, ready to gun down anyone stupid enough to try to rob these two.

Diaz was a regular with these guys, but the encounter didn't go well. He already owed them money, and they wouldn't front him any more dope. He wandered away toward the hospital. He had told them that he would be back soon with money.

He didn't have a problem with robbing someone; he did it almost every night. But he was feeling shaky. He checked the watch on his wrist that he had recently stolen. It was still early. He preferred catching a victim out late, when fewer eyes were about. He didn't have a choice right now though. He needed to score, and fast.

At 9:35 he entered the hospital's parking garage and walked down a car ramp until he was several levels below ground. He found a concealed spot. His back to the rough wall, he slid down and plopped onto the hard concrete floor behind a car, almost falling over. He was feeling desperate.

He quickly started to nod off, but slapped his own face. "Stay awake, asshole," he chided himself, "somebody will be along soon. Don't miss them."

~

Southern Russia

A medium-sized moving truck drove south on a two-lane highway in the Russian region of Rostov. Two men rode in the truck's cab. They wore civilian clothes and appeared to be ordinary workers for a moving company. *Belgorad Movers* was stenciled in Russian prominently on the truck's side.

Though appearing to be simple workers, they were heavily armed with concealed weapons—silenced pistols and submachine guns, combat knives, and grenades. They were Grigor's men, delivering five crates stamped as *Copy Machines*. Their destination—the Georgian border in the Caucasus Mountains.

A large, black SUV with four more heavily armed Spetsnaz commandos led the moving van a half mile farther up the road while maintaining radio contact with the truck. A similar SUV with another four men trailed the truck about a half-mile to the rear.

~

University Hospital, Washington, D.C., 10:00 p.m.

Lynn Elliot completed her eight-hour shift in the emergency room, which had stretched into fourteen. She made her way to the elevator. She was tired. Her purse hung on her left shoulder, and a small tote bag with her personal items hung on her right. Even at five-foot-four, barely a hundred pounds, she was quite strong. Still, her bags felt like they weighed a ton.

She punched the button for G-3, the lower level garage. She checked her phone. She had no cell signal in the elevator, nor would she have one in the underground parking garage, she knew, so she scrolled through unread messages and emails already downloaded.

She saw a text from Mike, but couldn't answer him. She would be home in a few minutes anyway.

She read an email from the cosmetics company she ordered from. They were having a sale. The door opened, and she walked into the garage still reading about the sale—her favorite makeup was 25% off. She had to stop for a second to remember where she had left her car. It seemed like eons ago that she had parked. The night air was warm.

Walking on, she thought she heard something behind her. She turned and scanned the dimly lit garage while fishing into her purse for the small canister of pepper spray she always carried. She knew Mike would not be happy to know that she had to search for it when she potentially needed it, *and* that she was looking at her phone and not paying attention to her surroundings.

She didn't see anyone, but she pulled out the pepper spray and her keys, and dropped her phone into her purse. She turned and headed toward her car.

"Okay, girl," she said to herself while looking over her shoulder. "Pay attention now."

She neared her BMW 320i and punched the button on the key fob. The car honked and the lights flashed twice, and then stayed on, adding additional light to the murky garage. Numerous employees had repeatedly complained about the dim light, and hospital management had promised to update the lighting. But a renovation had yet to begin.

Lynn opened the driver's door and tossed her two bags onto the passenger seat. She had both the keys and the pepper spray in her left hand. She stooped to slide into the car when someone grabbed her right arm and jerked her back.

She gasped. Adrenaline surged through her body like a tidal wave. Fear gripped her and she was terrified to the point of near shock.

The attacker wore a ragged flannel shirt, and his stench was strong.

"Give me all your stuff, now," he grumbled at her.

She thrust the small canister of pepper spray towards him and sprayed him in the face.

He swatted her hand away and screamed, "You bitch," as he rubbed his eyes.

He jerked out his knife and flipped it open. "You'll pay for that."

He swung at Lynn with the long blade. She pulled her head back and turned. The knife hit her shoulder and cut a long gash. She was suddenly aware that she was screaming. Her mind was in chaos, swirling with thoughts of pain and fear and regret. She felt helpless. She knew that she *was* defenseless.

Lynn fumbled with the keys and the pepper spray, trying to get the canister back into position. He had her trapped behind the open car door and the car parked next to hers. He slashed at her again, deeply slicing the palm of her hand that she had thrust out in protection. She screamed, "Stop! Stop!"

Diaz stepped forward and thrust the eight-inch blade into Lynn's stomach. She started to fall. He jerked the knife back and thrust again, ramming it into her side. She slid down the inside of her car door, smearing blood as she went down. She dropped to the pavement as the man stabbed her repeatedly.

Her white medical coat was now soaked in red. Lynn's dying thought was that she would never see her loving husband ever again.

He reached into the car, grabbed her purse and bag, and then slowly walked away toward the garage exit.

~

Alexandria, Virginia

Mike arrived home just after 10:00 p.m. He texted Lynn but didn't get a response. That was not unusual. If she was tied up with an emergency, it could be hours before she would be able to answer.

He took a shower then grabbed a snack and a glass of red wine. He settled into an easy chair with a book and his food. He turned on the lamp, still pondering the nuke crisis. Everyone in the intelligence community was scouring the metadata looking for the missing devices, but so far, no leads. Whoever did it was running a tight operation.

He managed to get back to his book, but in the corner of his mind, he wondered where they should look next. Just after 11:00, the doorbell rang. Thinking Lynn might have her arms full and need help getting in, he bolted to the door and jerked it open.

A female, blue-uniformed Alexandria police officer stood at the door. A male officer stood behind her. A police car was parked on the curb, its blue lights flashing. Mike's heart sank.

"Oh, God, it's Lynn, isn't it?" he blurted.

"Sir, may I come in?"

Fearing the worst, Mike staggered back, his head whirling.

The officer stepped inside and took Mike's elbow. She directed him to a chair. Mike sank down, terrified of what this woman had to tell him. Her partner stood at the open door. The female officer pulled over a chair and sat in front of Mike, her elbows on her knees, leaning in toward him. She reached out and put her hand on Mike's knee.

"Sir, I am so very sorry to have to tell you this."

Mike dropped his head to his hands. Years' worth of old wounds cut at him like a buzz saw, ripping and surging like electricity though his body.

"Sir, another hospital employee found Dr. Elliot's body in the parking garage at the hospital a short while ago. She was apparently robbed and killed."

Mike shook his head in disbelief. An overwhelming weight fell over him, as if he were deep under water. He felt a crushing pain in his chest as he tried to absorb this unbearable sorrow.

"H-How?" Mike stammered.

"How was she killed?" she repeated. She hesitated, not wanting to go on. Then she said, "It appears that she was stabbed. But the medical examiner will have to make that determination."

"Anyone caught? Any suspects?"

"No, sir, not yet. Sir, you'll need to come down to the coroner's office to identify your wife's body."

Mike looked at her. He was numb, but he nodded.

"Sir, you can ride with my partner and me, or follow us, whichever you prefer."

"I'll follow you. I'll just be a minute."

Mike went to the bedroom, slipped on his shoes, grabbed his wallet, and put a sweatshirt on over his T-shirt. Like some robot, his body seemed to know what to do.

The officer waited for him by the front door. Mike followed the police car to the medical examiner's office. He was on autopilot as he walked through the glass front doors, following the two officers.

In the examining room, a medical technician pulled back a white sheet on a gurney in the middle of the floor. Lynn lay on the table. Another cloth covered her from the neck down. Only her face was visible.

Mike leaned over, put his face against hers, and cried.

The tech put his hand on Mike's shoulder, and said softly, "Sir, there might be evidence. You could contaminate it."

Mike stood and looked dully at the young man. "Of course," he said, stepping back.

He somehow managed to look again at Lynn's face and identify his wife. He signed some papers for the assistant and the police officers. Then he left. The two officers wanted to follow him home to make sure he arrived safely, but Mike insisted he would be okay.

He drove aimlessly for at least an hour, and then finally went home. He called Lynn's sister, Claire, in Paris. She was Lynn's only living relative. Claire sobbed uncontrollably. They were both worn emotionally, and it was difficult to talk about Lynn. They eventually hung up. She would catch the next flight.

He called his boss, who wanted Mike to take a few days off. Mike said he wanted to come in. Work would be the only thing that would help him keep his sanity.

~

Bucharest, Romania

Vladimir Grigor walked cautiously out of the Henry Coanda International Airport. It was much cooler here in Eastern Europe, and the morning air had a mean chill to it. A leaden sky threatened nasty weather. He hardly noticed; he was concerned only with his immediate security.

He took a cab to a seedy and dangerous part of the city, verifying that no one followed. He had to pay the driver a bonus to venture into the neighborhood. He got out of the taxi two blocks from his destination and walked to a small, drab hotel. Its only advertisement was an ancient, rusted, metal plaque affixed to a brick wall.

A local mob boss owned the hotel. Grigor had sold him weapons on numerous occasions over the years, always at steeply discounted prices, and all in preparation for this day.

Grigor walked in and said to the front man, "Sobichevski."

The clerk didn't bother to take a key from the rack of room keys hanging on a large panel behind him. He opened a drawer, pulled out a key with a bronze metal tag, and handed it to Grigor.

"You know where it is, I believe," said the young man. "Remember to insert the key into the elevator key slot in order to access the fourth floor."

Grigor took the key, entered the elevator, and went to the fourth floor. There was only one door. He opened it with the key and went in. He knew the place well. He had stayed here many times when completing arms transactions with the Romanian mobster.

It was an exotic and luxurious penthouse suite, though the windows were darkened for security reasons. He walked to the dresser and pulled open the top center drawer. In the drawer was a Beretta 9mm pistol, a compact silencer, two spare magazines, a box of bullets, and a shoulder holster.

He slipped on the holster, adjusted it, and then set it aside. Next, he unloaded and disassembled the weapon, carefully inspecting each component. Satisfied that it was in good working order, he reassembled and loaded it, conducting a final press check.

He sat on the bed and placed the gun by his side. He let out a long, slow sigh. It had been a tense three days since he had left his dacha outside Moscow. He snuck out of the capital, assembled his team, stole the nuclear weapons, completed the deal with Meskhi, and successfully made his way to Bucharest, all without encountering Russian intelligence agents.

When he left Meskhi's compound, the driver took him to the airport. Then he caught a cab into Poti, rented a car, and drove to Batumi. From there he took a flight to Bucharest under his temporary alias, Rens Sobichevski, using a fake Russian passport.

The identity was only temporary, because once he reached Prague, he would undergo surgery to alter his appearance. Then he would assume his final identity. But getting to Prague was the trick. He knew that the FSB, Russia's internal security agency, would quickly determine that he was the culprit. He held a high position in nuclear surety and then suddenly disappeared at the same time five of Russia's finest tactical nuclear weapons mysteriously vanished.

Russian intelligence services, both the GRU and SVR, would be frantically searching for Colonel Vladimir Grigor from the Baltic to the Aegean. If they could find Grigor, they could find their missing weapons and end this embarrassing situation. He was also sure that the American CIA would be looking for him as well.

The flight to Bucharest had been tense. His hope was that they wouldn't be fast enough to intercept him there, and he was right. The remainder of the journey to Prague, however, would be more dangerous. He would travel by train to avoid airport security. How fast his pursuers could cover all the major train stations in Europe was uncertain, but the clock was undoubtedly ticking.

Once in Prague, he would go to a medical clinic that catered only to underworld kingpins, wealthy fugitives, or spies with no country but plenty of money. He would undergo plastic surgery and remain there for one week. In this guarded, private facility, he would receive around-the-clock care from a plastic surgeon and his nursing staff. Such service did not come cheaply.

The doctor had assured him that the necessary incisions would be minimal, but the change in appearance would be remarkable. With the addition of facial hair and a change of hair color, he would have an entirely new appearance.

The surgeon was confident enough in his ability to assure Grigor that after six or seven days, the swelling and redness would be almost invisible. They would take a photo and prepare a new passport with his final identity.

He scooted back on the bed, pulling the pistol in close beside him. He quickly fell asleep and slept soundly for five hours. He rose, showered, and dressed in clean clothes. He put on the shoulder holster, mounted the silencer to the pistol's barrel, and tucked the gun into the holster. The silencer protruded through the hole in the bottom of the hostler.

He threw away his eye patch and donned a pair of glasses with one lens dark and the other clear. Then he applied makeup to conceal the jagged scar on his cheek that he had gotten in combat. The surgeon would remove the scar, but for now it was an identifying attribute that his pursuers would certainly be looking for.

He donned a brown felt Homburg, pulled on his wool overcoat, grabbed his treasured leather briefcase, and left the room. He was not a sentimental man, but of all his worldly possessions, only this old case had special meaning.

He made his way by bus to the north Bucharest train station. It was nearing 8:00 p.m. He planned to take the 11:00 p.m. express train to Vienna. The train would make one stop in Budapest, Hungary.

In a café across the busy avenue from the station, he observed the promenade and terminal entrance for an hour. He saw no one he suspected might be either a Russian or foreign agent. At a small general store next to the café, he purchased a newspaper and a walnut cane. Walking with an affected limp, he crossed the street and entered the station.

He observed the bustling terminal from several locations while seemingly reading his paper, his new cane hanging over his arm. Then he made his way to the ticket window and purchased a first-class berth to Vienna, departing at 11:00 p.m., though he would be slipping off the train in Budapest. From there, he would take another train to Prague.

Verifying that no one took any particular interest in him, he left the terminal and crossed back over the street. He stopped at a different café, where he could continue to observe the terminal, and took a seat.

At 10:00 p.m., he paid and walked back to the station, carefully scanning his surroundings as he did so. From a concealed position, he watched the inside of the terminal until 10:50. The station was busy, even at this late hour. There were twenty-one platforms, half of them filled with trains either arriving or preparing to depart.

He walked toward number fifteen, the cane supporting him in his left hand, his leather satchel slung over his left shoulder. His dark brown overcoat was unbuttoned, and his right hand was in the coat's pocket. But there was no liner in the pocket. He held the silenced 9mm by his side, concealed by the topcoat.

He spotted two men standing at a news kiosk browsing magazines. As he continued toward the platform, they followed. One of them spoke into a lapel mic, confirming Grigor's suspicions that they were agents. But whose agents? He expected Russian intelligence, but his gut told him that these men were not Russian.

Grigor walked out onto platform fifteen. His train to Vienna was on the right, and to his left, train number 1714 to Sofia,

Bulgaria was boarding for departure. He crossed the platform and climbed aboard the train for Bulgaria, looking back through the train's window at the approaching men. One of them spoke into his lapel mic and again reported over the radio.

In the train car, Grigor turned right, tossed the cane onto an empty seat, and stepped through double, automatic doors. He crossed over the breezeway and passed through into the next car. It was crammed with people trying to find seats and settle in. The two men followed some thirty feet back.

Grigor continued through the car to the next set of doors at the front of the car. He entered them, stepped into the darkened passageway between the two cars, and let the doors close behind him. Then he stepped to the side.

Seconds later the two men reached the doors. The first man stepped through. His focus was straight ahead, looking into the next car for his target. The second man stepped through the door behind him.

Grigor shot them both—two quick, silenced rounds to the temple. They crumpled to the floor just as the doors closed behind them. Grigor quickly checked their pockets but found no identification. They had pistols and portable radios. Their clothes were local but had no tags. He stuck his thumb into each man's mouth, twisted the head toward the light, and inspected their teeth. The high-quality dental work was definitely not Russian. His gut was now telling him that these men were American agents.

He rose, continued through the next car, and climbed down from the train. He crossed the platform and stepped aboard the train to Budapest and Vienna. An instant later, the doors closed and locked. The train's whistle sounded, and he felt the first slight jerk of the train pulling forward.

3

Southern Russia

The small convoy of Spetsnaz commandos reached the Caucasus Mountains, not far from the border with Georgia. The black SUV carrying four of the men parked on the side of the narrow, two-lane highway.

The area was remote and not well traveled; they had not seen another vehicle in the past hour. They were approximately twenty miles from the linkup point, which was a mile or so inside Russia from the border.

Three of the commandos from the lead SUV had deployed a short distance up the slope beside the road, into a cluster of boulders, to provide security for the convoy. The driver of the SUV waited beside the vehicle.

Soon, the truck and the trail SUV arrived. The men gathered beside the cab of the truck to confer. They studied a map and finalized their plan. Then the four commandos who had arrived in the trail SUV got back into their vehicle, pulled out onto the road, and sped away toward the border.

Ten minutes later, and about a quarter mile from the linkup point, the lone SUV pulled off the road and parked. Three of the men, carrying weapons, moved up the rocky hillside next to the road and made their way to a bluff overlooking the linkup point with the Georgians.

One of them pulled out a pair of binoculars and studied the scene below. Two vehicles were at the linkup site. The other two commandos took up prone positions, leveled their Dragunov 7.62 mm sniper rifles, and sighted in on the men below.

Eight men milled about near the two vehicles—the expected number. The commandos carefully scanned with their riflescopes and binoculars as far around as they could see. No other vehicles or persons were in sight.

The man with the binoculars pulled out a portable radio, called their companion waiting at the SUV, and said in Russian, "Overwatch position set. Linkup site secure."

"Affirmative," came the reply from the radio.

The moving truck and the remaining SUV drove forward toward the rendezvous with Meskhi's men.

Within a moment, the snipers spotted the black SUV, followed by the truck, as they came around the bend and into their field of view. The truck stopped on the side of the road several hundred yards short of the Georgians.

The SUV proceeded toward the men ahead, stopping about fifty feet from the two parked vehicles and the group of men. One of them got out, and holding his jacket open, walked straight ahead.

As the Russian approached, one of the Georgians stepped forward, his hand thrust out offering a handshake. The Russian walked up to him and offered his hand as well.

In Russian, the commando asked the Georgian, "Who was Stalin's mistress?"

The Georgian replied in Russian, "Mother goose."

The Russian smiled and waved his two vehicles forward.

The Spetsnaz snipers watched the scene intently for any sign of treachery but saw no suspicious moves. The Georgians all appeared to be relaxed.

The truck and SUV drove to the Georgians. The men got out of the truck and opened the rear sliding door of the truck's cargo bed.

Three of the Georgians climbed in. They found five crates and pried the tops off, removing the straw-like packing material. The objects they saw matched the photo the boss had given them. They compared each serial number tag to a list of numbers one of them had in a small notebook. The numbers matched. The man nodded, they resealed the crates, and climbed down from the truck.

One of the Georgians pulled out a cell phone and hit a speed-dial number. An instant later Meskhi answered. They had a brief conversation and then he put the phone away. He nodded to the Russians.

One of the Russian commandos took out the smart phone Grigor had given him and stared at the screen.

They waited.

Six minutes later a message appeared on the screen: *Full payment has been confirmed.*

He nodded to the Georgians.

One of Meskhi's men held out his hand.

The Russian driver of the truck dropped the truck's keys into the man's palm.

The eight Russians crowded into their SUV, drove back the way they had come, and linked up with the returning snipers. They then headed north and back toward central Russia.

~

CIA Headquarters, McLean, Virginia

Gerald Billings sat in his small office. It was just off the entry area where the director's two secretaries had their desks outside the director's spacious suite. It reminded him of his station in life as he looked around his closet-sized space, while the man he served occupied a large office with a private bathroom and windows that looked out over manicured grounds.

It made the acid in his stomach churn. He popped two antacids and chewed them with a clenched jaw.

Looking over his notes, he reflected on what he had just learned in a meeting the director had with several department chiefs. He would type up the notes in memo format, have the director sign it and assign a classification level to it, and then file it in the director's classified storage vault.

He had learned about the two dead American agents in Bucharest, and that the DO was convinced it had to be the Russian colonel named Grigor. The last report from the CIA agents trailing him had said they believed it was Grigor, and that he had boarded a train bound for Sofia, Bulgaria to the south. Grigor wouldn't have stayed on that train after killing the two Americans, but the CIA was still concentrating its search in Bulgaria since they had no other leads. Grigor's trail, however, had gone cold.

Gerald had also learned that the CIA's plan of action was to figure out which of the major arms dealers would be handling the stolen nuclear weapons. If they could figure out who was selling them, maybe they could then get their hands on them. They might even try to buy them.

He set his steno pad on a stand next to his computer, adjusted his keyboard, and began to type. His mind soon wandered, though. This was important information and would be worth a lot. Should he give it to the Arab? Maybe.

~

DIA Headquarters, 9:10 a.m.

Two days after Lynn's murder, Mike sat in the DIA cafeteria. He drank coffee and tried to eat some breakfast, but he had to force it down. He knew he needed it. He hadn't eaten much in the last couple of days.

He looked up to see Max and Jonas standing in front of him. They took seats across the small table.

"Mike, I'm sorry," said Max. Jonas just hung his head. He knew better than anyone how Mike felt right now. He of course had been with Mike when his first wife and daughter were murdered in a bomb blast only a few short years earlier.

Max added, "Mike, I asked a friend of mine with the FBI to keep tabs on this case and let me know the minute something broke on it. He just called me. The DC police tried to arrest a guy named Ernesto Diaz this morning on a drug charge. He attacked them with a knife, and they shot him dead.

He was an illegal from Honduras, a drug addict with a long history of arrests. He had Lynn's credit cards and cell phone on him. Looks like it was random street crime. Mike, I'm sorry."

Mike looked up slowly and said, "At least justice was served, and it was swift."

Max and Jonas nodded.

Mike dropped his head into his hands.

"Mike," said Max, reaching out and touching Mike's arm, "I know this is a tough time right now, but I *have* to talk to you about this crisis. If even one of those nukes ends up on American soil, not to mention perhaps all of them, then we've lost the fight and the terrorists will have won. We can't let that happen. Striker wants you on the team."

"We need you, Mike," added Jonas. "Everybody we've got is on this, and it's not enough."

Mike looked up at Jonas and said softly, "Jonas, you saved my life in Colombia. And you paid a heavy price for it. And I suppose I owe you. But you did me no favors. I should have died with Margaret and Emily."

"You have work to do, Mike," said Max, reaching out and putting his hand on Mike's. Mike gripped Max's hand as he fought back tears.

Mike got himself under control and looked up at the two men sitting across from him. "You know I'm on active duty. The Army is going to have something to say about all this."

"No, it won't," replied Max.

"How's that?"

"Striker took it to the White House. It's already taken care of. As of about an hour ago, you are no longer on active military service."

"Pretty sure of yourself, aren't you?"

"Like I said," Max answered, "you have work to do, important work, like helping us save our country from possible ruin."

"Okay," Mike whispered, nodding. "Let's go."

~

Poti, Georgia

Behdin Khorasani's plane landed in Poti. After crossing the border from Iran into Turkey by land in his usual manner, he had taken a commercial flight on Izmir Air from Ankara, Turkey to Poti, Georgia.

Meskhi's man waited beside one of the many black Mercedes sedans that Meskhi owned. The car was parked curbside directly in front of the entrance to the small Poti air terminal.

Georgian immigration ushered Khorasani through the terminal like a VIP. He was soon in the back seat of the sedan headed for a meeting with Genadi Meskhi. The Iranian noticed that they were not driving in the direction of Meskhi's compound, but toward the port. He said nothing.

At five-foot-eight, one hundred and forty-five pounds, Khorasani was not a large man. Nevertheless, he was quite lethal. He had close-cropped, jet-black hair and a short beard with a full mustache, stylishly trimmed. He had dark, intelligent eyes, and wore black, plastic-frame glasses with rounded lenses, giving him a distinctly intellectual appearance. If seen on a college campus, one would assume that he was a handsome, young, brilliant professor.

But he had been a member of the elite Iranian Quds Force since he was twenty. At thirty, he was now a senior operative. Also called the Jerusalem Force, his unit was the special operations element of the Iranian Revolutionary Guard, responsible for extraterritorial operations. The Quds commander reported directly to the Supreme Leader.

Khorasani had come to the attention of his Quds leaders early on. His superiors had used many words to describe this promising young agent over the years—intelligent, resourceful, relentless, cunning, ruthless, and loyal, to name a few.

At twenty-two he had begun specialized training for foreign undercover operations—intelligence, sabotage, assassination. He spoke four languages fluently—Farsi, English, Arabic, and Russian. His language skills, and the fact that he was already a master of several martial arts disciplines, made him a perfect candidate. With Quds Force training, he also became skilled with a multitude of weapons, such as sniper rifles, pistols, garrotes, and knives.

The Mercedes arrived at a small, one-story building inside the industrial zone next to the port. The concrete building was tucked in behind several large warehouses and not easily visible from the main road.

The sedan pulled up and stopped. Meskhi and his entourage stood in front of the building, waiting. Meskhi had a cigar in his mouth and laughed heartily at something one of his men was telling him.

Khorasani got out and walked over. The two men embraced. Meskhi did not speak Farsi, and even though the Iranian spoke multiple languages, Georgian Kartuli was not one of them. They always spoke in English.

"Genadi," said the Iranian, with a low voice into Meskhi's ear, "I am hoping that the reason you summoned me here is because you have something very special to offer me."

"You seem well informed," replied Meskhi.

"My dear friend, the intelligence services of practically every nation on earth have only one thing on their minds right now. They are talking and thinking only about this one thing. And I suspect you know what that *one* thing is."

Meskhi nodded. "As a matter of fact, I do have something special."

"Are there other bidders?"

"Not yet. And there *is* no bid. I have set a price, and it is non-negotiable."

"What do you have for sale, Genadi?"

Meskhi pulled the Iranian closer and whispered into his ear. "I have five Russian RA-115 tactical nuclear bombs."

The corner of Khorasani's lip twisted up in a sly, almost evil grin. The Iranian seemed stunned, even though he had already suspected this was why Meskhi had summoned him here. "You have them under your direct control now?"

Meskhi signaled to follow, and they entered the building. In the rear of the warehouse was a concrete, bunker-like room with a thick metal door. He motioned for his guards to wait outside. One of them pulled open the door. Meskhi and the Iranian went inside. A guard closed the door behind them.

Spread out on the concrete floor, sitting on wooden pallets, were five cylinders encased in army-green canvas containers.

Khorasani's mouth hung open.

"Beautiful, aren't they?" asked Meskhi.

The Iranian walked through them, caressing each one, almost salivating at the mere thought of getting these incredible weapons back to Iran.

"And you have the codes as well?"

"I have both the activation and deactivation codes for each one of them."

"Of course, you know I must have these. Name your price."

"Fifty million immediate deposit. Two hundred million on balance."

Khorasani knew that he referred to dollars. They always dealt in U.S. currency. That sum would be difficult for Iran to come by these days, but he knew that his country would find a way to do it. This was too important for the strategic future of the Iranian Republic.

"No other buyers will be involved?" asked Khorasani.

"Behdin, Iran has been a good customer for many years. You have first opportunity. If you meet my price, they are yours. Besides, it is much better not reaching out to other potential buyers. The fewer people who know of this the better. This transaction is a highly sensitive matter."

Khorasani nodded. He desperately wanted these weapons for his country, and that would happen. Nevertheless, he was already simultaneously hatching a plot to fund his own retirement from this transaction as well. He walked to Meskhi and extended his hand. They shook on the deal.

"I will return to Iran immediately, and I will arrange for the down payment within forty-eight hours. The usual account?"

Meskhi reached into his shirt pocket and pulled out a folded piece of paper. He handed it to the Iranian.

"No, use this new one. We must take every possible precaution with this transaction."

"Agreed."

~

CIA Headquarters

Mike walked off the elevator on the executive floor of CIA headquarters. This was where the brass plotted the demise of America's enemies.

He had just completed two bruising days of briefings from seemingly every analyst in the CIA, several chiefs of station from overseas posts passing through headquarters, as well as a half-dozen department heads. Then he had endured hours of briefings on the latest technology for use in the field. He *did* pay close attention to the CIA-issued smart phone. This he would need.

He had thrown himself into the work. It helped not to have too much down time right now.

Wrapping up his headquarters orientation, Mike had spent a half hour with the director of operations, Alan Berg, and his assistant, Gerald Billings. Berg resembled a washed out prize fighter while Billings came across as totally out of his element. Mike couldn't quite peg him or his role in the meeting other than to take notes.

Now, Mike was on his way to his last meeting. The acting DCI had summoned him for his final briefing at CIA headquarters.

Mike stood in front of the desk of a pretty, smiling secretary. She was the gatekeeper. She verified that the director was ready, and then ushered Mike into John Striker's spacious office. It had nice views of the Virginia countryside.

Striker rose from behind his mahogany desk and walked around to greet Mike. He took Mike's hand in both of his and shook it. He looked directly into his eyes and said, "Mike, I am so very sorry about your wife. It's a terrible tragedy. I lost my own wife to a similar attack many years ago. She worked for the CIA. I'm sorry to say, it never fully goes away. You just try to bury it and carry on."

Mike just nodded. He had ample experience with trying to bury grief.

Striker pointed to a stuffed chair in front of his desk and then went back around to his own chair and sat. Mike took a seat.

"Mike, we're facing one of the biggest crises in modern history, but I think you already get that."

"I do."

"Well, I'm glad you are on board with us. I wish it were under better circumstances, but at any rate, we need everyone with talent that we can muster."

Striker leaned back in his chair. "Mike, I believe Berg has already filled you in on the details, but I want you to go to Beirut and interview a Russian defector named Oleg Baskov. You'll work with the chief of station there, Doug Andrews.

"A Lebanese asset brought Baskov to our attention. He's been talking openly about the nuke heist. We're told that Baskov was Russian Spetsnaz. He has been telling people that he has information to sell, and he has claimed that Spetsnaz soldiers were involved in the heist. For some reason, he had to flee Russia. At any rate, he's the only lead we have. I know that you were fully briefed on Colonel Vladimir Grigor. If Baskov can give us *anything* that gets us closer to Grigor, then maybe we'll have a shot at getting our hands on those weapons."

"I'll do my best," Mike answered.

"So, anyway, Doug will set up a temporary safe house for the interview."

"Wouldn't Andrews normally handle something like this?"

"Yes, and I trust Doug Andrews completely. He was my deputy in Beirut. But you speak Russian, and I want you involved. Depending on which country this leads us to, you may have to follow a trail somewhere else. And I want Doug in place in Beirut."

"Okay," Mike nodded.

"Sergeant Major Scott Barrington and Master Sergeant James Palmer from Delta Force will meet you there."

"Protection?"

"Yes and no. But if you do end up needing help, is there any better?"

"None."

"When we find the stolen nukes, we're probably going to need Delta to capture them anyway. So I want to get them on board up front. But first, we have to find the devices. From what we're hearing out of Beirut, this Russian guy is a pretty rough character. And if he really does know something about the nukes, or Grigor, and if Spetsnaz was really involved, then I suspect that his Spetsnaz buddies would like to keep him quiet and will be actively looking for him too. So be careful. And if you think he has value, you are authorized to extract him."

Striker paused and then said, "Mike, one more thing. As you also know, we lost two agents who had briefly located Colonel Grigor. So if we do catch up with him again, remember, he's skilled and deadly."

"Got it."

Striker rose, leaned forward, and reached across his desk, extending his hand to Mike. They shook. "Welcome aboard, Mike, and good luck. We're going to need it."

~

Fort Washington, Maryland, 5:00 p.m.

Mike entered his room at the Marriott not far from the Potomac Airfield. That night he would board a CIA 737 and fly to Beirut. He dropped his bag, and after clearing the room, stripped down to his T-shirt and shorts.

He knocked out a quick hundred push-ups and another hundred sit-ups. Then he practiced a dozen different karate kicks and punches. He wrapped up with some shadow sparring, working on a few jujitsu moves. He was a little winded and realized that he had not been working out enough since settling down as a paper-pushing intelligence analyst. That would have to change.

He turned on the TV to CNN, grabbed a bottle of water from the mini-fridge, and plopped down on the bed. He pulled a folded map from his bag and spread it out before him on his legs. The map covered the Middle East and western Asia.

At 10:00 that evening, Mike would depart for Beirut. From there, he had no idea. On the map, he traced the borders of Lebanon and Turkey. It was a rough neighborhood—Syria, Iran, Azerbaijan, and Georgia.

He would meet Sergeant Major Scott Barrington and his partner in Beirut at the U.S. embassy. Then they would interview the Russian informant. The CIA had no real clues as to the whereabouts of the missing Russian nukes, but maybe this defector would give something up. More U.S. operatives scoured eastern and southern Europe, from Estonia to Bulgaria, regions near Russia that might serve as a transit point for someone trying to move stolen nuclear weapons.

It had been a whirlwind four days since he learned of Lynn's murder. The night of her death, Mike had packed a few clothes and moved into a hotel. When Max and Jonas succeeded in recruiting him, he went straight into briefings at the CIA.

Lynn's sister, Claire, had arrived. Mike gave her power-of-attorney, and she had agreed to handle things for him. Claire made the funeral arrangements. The coroner released Lynn's body, and yesterday, they'd had a small funeral service and laid Lynn to rest.

Mike had also asked Claire to take care of the house. The only thing he kept with him was a photo of Lynn.

"Put everything in storage and sell the house. I can't go back there," he had told her.

She had agreed.

Mike didn't think that his longevity would be that great anyway. What were the odds of surviving more than a couple of years working in hostile regions of the world as a non-official-cover operative, or NOC, for the CIA?

Thinking back on all the missions he had conducted for the agency with his Green Beret team, he knew it was a miracle that he had survived this long. He also knew that this new work would be even more treacherous—he wouldn't have his teammates covering his back.

Mike had a new passport, driver's license, social security card, and several hotel and airline cards, all in a new name and identity. He was now Steve Holt—at least for the moment.

He also had the latest CIA smart phone. The device could display his encrypted CIA credentials, send or receive CIA messages, disguise its location, and safely handle classified intelligence summaries.

He lay down on the bed and finished reading an intel report on Beirut, but he was having difficulty concentrating. He had placed the small photo of Lynn on the nightstand by the bed. He picked it up. She was smiling her beautiful, radiant smile.

He tried to swallow the lump in his throat, but couldn't quite manage. A single tear ran down his cheek and he wiped it away with the back of his hand. Her smile was the light of his life. How would he be able to live without it. He could still see her standing in the kitchen, a dishtowel in hand, telling him about something absurdly funny that had happened at the hospital that day. They would laugh.

He knew she saw terrible things in the ER, but she never talked about any of that. Only the good. That's the way her heart was; she focused on the good in every situation. But there was *nothing* good in this situation.

Why didn't I pick her up as I said I would? he asked himself for the hundredth time. But he had no answer. Just like he couldn't answer the questions he asked himself about why he took Margaret and Emily, his first wife and daughter, to Brazil and let them be kidnapped and murdered.

What would Margaret, Lynn, and my dad expect of me now, Mike wondered. *I guess, just stay alive. Do the right thing. Keep my country safe.*

He set Lynn's picture back on the nightstand. "Just try to do the right thing," he said. "That's what they would want."

4

Prague, Czech Republic

Colonel Grigor's train arrived in Budapest without further incident. He remained there for three days, changing hotels each day. He put on as much of a disguise as he could manage and spent most of those three days watching the train station from various locations.

For his plan to succeed, he had to be certain that his enemies did not see him depart Budapest. He would be incapacitated in Prague for a time, and therefore vulnerable if his adversaries knew where to find him.

At 1:00 a.m. on the third night, he took a train to Prague. He was cautious and observant, but detected no other agents en route. He couldn't be sure, but he hoped that the last transmission from the agents trailing him in Bucharest reported that he had boarded the train heading south to Sofia, Bulgaria, instead of north to Budapest. With any luck, his pursuers were concentrating their search in the south.

The train arrived in Prague at 9:20 a.m. A drizzling rain fell from a slate-gray sky. The air was cold, but not frigid like Moscow in winter. It felt refreshing.

The plastic surgeon he had arranged for ran a very specialized practice. For the surgery and a week of intensive care, new identification documents included, Grigor had paid one and a half million dollars.

The doctor maintained a completely secure compound with state-of-the-art surgical and recovery facilities. The private rooms, and the service that accompanied them, would rival a five-star hotel. The facility had its own security force, a complete medical staff, and a hospitality team, all of whom were extremely well paid and very discreet. He was headed there now.

Grigor left the central train station from a less busy side entrance and walked for thirty minutes, changing directions randomly. A car from the medical facility would pick him up, but not in public view at the train station.

When he was confident that he was not followed, he made his way to the rendezvous point. A driver in a black limousine waited there. As Grigor approached, the chauffeur got out and stood by the car. Grigor walked up to him and nodded. The man opened the rear passenger door and Grigor slid in.

Several minutes later, the car pulled up to a gate, which swung open to the side. Standing by a guardhouse next to the gate, a security guard waved the vehicle through. The driver pulled the big car forward to a large, four-story, red-brick building. He hit a remote and a double garage door lifted upwards. He drove in, parked, hopped out, and ran around to open the passenger door.

A man, wearing a white lab coat, waited by the limo. He gestured toward the elevator and walked toward it. Grigor followed. No discussion was required. He had made the arrangements, and payment, months ago.

They exited on the third floor. An attractive nurse waited there holding a folded hospital gown and a pair of disposable slippers. She handed them to Grigor and gestured toward an ornate, salon-style bathroom.

"Please shower and put on this gown and slippers. Your belongings will be cleaned and placed in your room, along with new clothing."

"I have a weapon."

"It will be in your room. Would you like it cleaned?"

"No, thank you."

Grigor did as the woman instructed and soon emerged wearing the gown and slippers.

A different nurse gestured to a hospital gurney. He lay on it, and she expertly started an IV.

"This will make you relax," she murmured.

"I am relaxed," he replied.

She completed checking his vital signs and placed an oxygen mask over his face. He quickly faded into oblivion.

When he awoke some seven hours later, he was in a private intensive care room. A male nurse stood next to the bed. He carefully scanned Grigor's vital signs on a bank of monitors positioned next to the bed.

"How do you feel?" he asked.

"Mirror please."

He handed Grigor a mirror, and he stared at his reflection. All he could see were his eyes and lips. Otherwise, bandages completely covered his head. But seeing two eyes was startling. There was once only a ragged scar where his right eye used to be, but now a perfectly matched glass eye seemed to stare back at him.

The doctor entered the room. "Ah, you're awake. Very good. Everything went *exactly* according to plan. In six or seven days, as I promised, you will be ready for a photo and a new passport."

The doctor ran a one-stop shop for those needing to change their identities—a new face and identification documents to go with it. Grigor would walk out a different man, and the former Russian officer that so many were searching for, would no longer exist.

~

Over the Arabian Sea

Behdin Khorasani sat in first class on a Qatar Airways 757, flying from Riyadh, Saudi Arabia to Islamabad, Pakistan. As usual, he had first driven into Turkey from Iran, avoiding any Turkish border checkpoints, thus ensuring that no record existed of him leaving Iran.

Once inside Turkey, he hired a small plane from a criminal organization he had dealt with on many occasions, and flew to a tiny dirt airstrip outside of Ankara, Turkey—no questions asked, no record maintained. He then took a commercial flight from Ankara to Riyadh using a Saudi passport, and an assumed identity. Now he was on his final leg of the trip to Islamabad.

He sipped champagne and nibbled smoked salmon while alternately gazing out the window and watching the amazingly attractive flight attendant. She had been flirting with him since boarding.

His trip back to Iran after meeting with Meskhi had been successful. The Quds Force commander had approved Khorasani's plan to acquire the devices, and in turn, the Supreme Leader as well.

The commander not only enthusiastically approved it, he assured Khorasani that should he succeed in this unexpected, yet vital mission, there would be a significant promotion for him, and the highest honors of the Revolutionary Guard would befall him.

Khorasani had told his leaders that the price for four devices was two hundred and fifty million, and that a fifth bomb had already been sold to an unknown buyer. They of course wanted all five, but eagerly agreed to buy the four. Iran would gladly pay the price for the four devices—they would easily save that much in research and development alone.

Khorasani reflected on Sadegh Mohsen's mission. He was a rival in the Revolutionary Guard, but Khorasani welcomed the cover that Mohsen's efforts might provide. He had informed his commander that Genadi Meskhi was the broker. The commander decided to task Sadegh Mohsen to activate his mole in the CIA in an effort to keep the Americans away from Meskhi, at least until Khorasani could get the nuclear weapons safely into Iran.

Khorasani hoped Mohsen would help buy him the extra few days he needed to set up his own plan. With all five paid for, and only four going to Iran, one device remained for Khorasani to sell.

In Pakistan, he would set in motion a scheme that would make him a wealthy man. If his plan played out properly, Al-Qaeda terrorists would buy the fifth bomb, thus funding Khorasani's retirement, and the bonus, he would see the very soul of America shattered to rubble. He knew that his superiors in Iran would never initiate such a bold attack against America. But he would.

More important even than his own personal wealth, the plan, he hoped, would do irreparable harm to the United States of America—the Great Satan. Best of all, neither he nor his nation would be implicated in the attack. If Al-Qaeda did manage to detonate a bomb in America, his leaders would naturally assume that the terrorist organization was the buyer of the fifth bomb and had acted alone.

Behdin Khorasani smiled as he closed his eyes for a much-needed nap.

Lee Duffy   **61**

~

Fort Washington, Maryland, 9:45 p.m.

Mike waited in front of his hotel. He had a black nylon backpack slung over his shoulder. A Walther PPK .380 was tucked into his waistband in a clip holster. An unmarked, white CIA sedan pulled up in front of him. The driver got out, walked around the car, and opened the back door without a word. Mike slid onto the back seat.

Five minutes later, the sedan arrived at Potomac Airfield, a small, private runway near the tiny hamlet of Fort Washington. The car drove along the narrow apron, toward a white Boeing 737. The jet had no markings except a tail number painted on the vertical stabilizer.

The single runway on this unsecured airfield was much too short for a commercial model 737 to land or takeoff. This plane, however, had mil-spec capabilities that commercial models did not possess. The ability to make short takeoffs or landings was just one of them.

The forward portside door was open. It folded down toward the tarmac and had a ladder that extended to the ground. The jet could accommodate mobile stairs, but the crew didn't have to rely on someone to bring stairs planeside.

The sedan came to a stop next to the aircraft's ladder, and Mike got out with his bag. The car pulled away. Not a word had been spoken. Mike walked over to an agent standing by the ladder. The man wore a Glock in a shoulder holster under his left arm. Mike pulled out his CIA phone and opened an app. A QR code appeared.

The agent held up a similar device, tapped in a six digit PIN, and scanned the code on Mike's phone. Mike's CIA credentials were displayed on the agent's phone. The agent nodded and put away his device. Mike did the same. "Welcome aboard, Mike. My name is Jim," he said, extending his hand. They shook hands, and then Jim gestured to the ladder.

Mike climbed up and entered the jet. Several other agents, including two women, moved about the plane taking care of various tasks on the aircraft. All of them were armed. Jim stuck his head into the cockpit and said, "Got him." The pilot and copilot both waved over their shoulders without looking up from their checklists and instruments.

Mike had flown many thousands of miles on military aircraft—mostly C-130s and C-17s—but this was a civilian aircraft modified for paramilitary operations and prisoner movement. Jim gave Mike a quick tour.

The plane had everything a well-equipped spy team might need—automatic weapons in a rack, passenger seats, a conference table, a galley, bunks, showers, a medical station, and prisoner cells. Jim opened one of the cell doors. It was utilitarian, just a metal bench with arm and leg shackles, and an open toilet.

"We like to take real good care of our passengers," said Jim.

Mike laughed and said, "Nice." The plane was impressive. "Doing much prisoner work," he asked Jim.

"Yeah, we run a lot of errands, like getting you to Beirut, but we also hop around the world picking up America's enemies when they've been scarfed up. And we've never been busier," Jim added, grinning.

The plane began rolling forward.

"Better grab a seat and buckle in," Jim said. "Twelve hours and nine minutes to Beirut. We'll arrive at 5:00 p.m. or so, Beirut time."

Mike grabbed a bottle of water as he passed the galley. He settled into a seat and fastened his seatbelt.

As the jet roared seemingly straight up into the sky, Mike slipped Lynn's photo from his shirt pocket and looked at it for a moment. It was too painful, though, and he slid it back into his pocket.

Concentrate on work, he reminded himself, pulling out his phone and opening the latest intsum on the hunt for Colonel Vladimir Grigor.

~

Falls Church, Virginia

Gerald Billings made his way through the rows of tall bookshelves, browsing the many tombs as if he were searching for a particular book. He worked his way toward the back of the cavernous

Tysons-Pimmit Regional Library where he eventually spotted the man he came to meet at the far end of the last row.

Sadegh Mohsen, or as Gerald considered him, the dark man or the Arab, didn't look up as he casually flipped through the pages of a large hardbound book. As usual, Gerald felt anxious to the point of near panic. His armpits dripped, even though it was a comfortable seventy-three degrees in the room.

He glanced around, saw no one else, and then made his way to the dark man, his feet shuffling, almost resisting. He arrived at the man and stopped. After what seemed an eternity to Gerald, Sadegh Mohsen looked up and smiled.

"Relax, Gerald. You look so tense."

Gerald realized in that instant just how tense he really was. He was committing treason. Suddenly he was confused as to why he had started down this path to begin with—revenge, money, some kind of strange fantasy adventure? Yet here he was, face-to-face with a foreign agent at a clandestine meeting.

"So, Gerald, what do you have for me?"

"Well, nothing really new. Nothing specific."

The Iranian furled his thick, black eyebrows for just an instant but then smiled again. "Gerald, we have had such a good relationship. You have provided me with information, and I have paid you well. So don't patronize me. We both know that there is a lot going on right now."

"Ww-what do you mean," Gerald stuttered.

"Gerald, I need to know about the stolen nuclear weapons, what the CIA knows about them, and what it is going to do about them. Believe me, we are just as concerned about this problem as you are. We want to help resolve this before they fall into the hands of some terror group that will harm us all."

Gerald's shoulders dropped, and he felt the tension flowing from his body. Maybe this wasn't so bad after all. He was collaborating to solve an international crisis, not committing treason.

Gerald reflected for a moment on what he knew about this matter, and it was quite a bit, actually. "Will I be paid?"

"Of course, Gerald."

"They don't know where the bombs are located or who stole them, but a Russian named Vladimir Grigor is high on the list of suspects. They think he's the one who killed two of our agents in Bucharest five days ago."

Sadegh Mohsen just looked at Gerald without expression.

Gerald fidgeted for a moment and then continued. "They think the devices will likely be sold through a high-level international arms dealer, and there are only five or six such dealers in the world who could handle something this big. They are trying to check out each one of them. There is one in Poland, one in...."

The Iranian interrupted him, "Yes, I know who they are. Tell me about the one from Georgia, Genadi Meskhi."

"Yes, he's one they are interested in. Two different agents have meetings set up with informants to see what they can find on him. One is going to Tbilisi; one to Istanbul. Oh, and there's a new agent, non-official cover. Just came on board. Guy named Mike Elliot. He was some kind of military special operations guy. He's going to Beirut to interview a Russian who says he knows something about the missing weapons. I have a photo of him because there was one attached to his file."

"And do you have the details of all these meetings?"

Gerald nodded and provided the specifics on the meetings.

"Send me the photo by the secure messaging app I provided you."

"Okay," said Gerald meekly, unsure why he had snapped a picture of Elliot's photo or even brought it up.

"Is there anything more?" asked the Iranian.

"That's all I know."

"That's fine, Gerald. You've been very helpful. You will soon see a new deposit into your Grand Cayman account. Now keep your eyes and ears open. This is a very fluid situation. I expect you to contact me immediately through the message app should you learn *anything* new. And don't worry, the messages vanish once read."

Gerald nodded sheepishly, slowly turned, and walked away.

Already deep in thought, Mohsen watched Gerald for a moment until he rounded the end of the row and disappeared. He needed to deal immediately with the two meetings looking into Meskhi's operation. That was the most immediate threat to

Khorasani's mission. He would dispatch the Nigerian to deal directly with those two.

As for the Russian in Beirut, he didn't have an asset there that he could quickly mobilize. At any rate, it would take the Americans a day or two to act on anything they learned there, and he might be able to counter their next move then.

He pulled out his phone and messaged instructions to the Nigerian.

~

Islamabad, Pakistan

Khorasani stepped through the doorway of the 757 into the bright Islamabad sunshine. He wore a simple, white, short-sleeved shirt and cotton slacks—very nondescript for the locale. He carried a small briefcase containing fake business contracts between several Pakistani companies and a Saudi Arabian company.

He had arrived at the New International Airport on the southwest side of Islamabad, adjacent to Rawalpindi. The two cities, with a population of over four million, were often referred to as the twin cities.

He slipped on his sunglasses and looked up at the blue sky. It had been a long trip. First to Turkey, then to Saudi Arabia, then to Pakistan. He followed the passengers in front of him slowly down the steps to the tarmac below. The weather was warm but felt good. He concentrated on pleasant thoughts of women and carefree days—maybe in Paris or somewhere else chic and rife with decadence and good times. Even though he was a devout Muslim, he *did* enjoy the pleasures of the flesh—particularly with western women.

What he did *not* think about was his mission. Never while traveling. Khorasani was well aware of behavioral observation techniques. He himself was an expert in such methods. An agent somewhere, probably several, including possibly computer software, would be watching the passengers. A person with something to hide would display some form of sign, or tell, in their expression or movements.

He followed the other passengers and the instructions of the Pakistani agents to proceed into a doorway. This was where the passengers would undergo the scrutiny of the Pakistani immigration services. He had a legitimate Saudi passport under the name of Memud Al-Yasin, as well as business papers and business cards from an office supply firm in Riyadh. If inquiries were made, the firm would check out, and so would he.

Khorasani was not worried. He had done this sort of thing a hundred times traveling around the globe doing the good work of the Iranian Revolution and the Shiite Islamic world. He just continued thinking happy thoughts, and smiled. He was next and stepped forward to the immigration officer's booth.

"You seem happy," the officer said gruffly.

"Oh, I was just thinking about my little daughter. She's three. The love of my life. Her first word was *father*. You should see her...."

"Okay, okay, enough," muttered the agent, stamping the passport and ushering him along.

"Thank you, sir. Have a good day," said Khorasani, still smiling and moving on as ordered. He exited the terminal to the taxi stand. Khorasani was very good at what he did, and as he traversed the terminal, waited in the taxi line, and departed, he counted seventeen surveillance cameras observing him and the other passengers. He had spotted at least six covert Pakistani agents conducting surveillance of the terminal area.

He determined that no one took any special interest in him, and no vehicle followed his cab from the airport. He had to take every possible precaution. He was coming to Pakistan to meet with a terrorist organization that the Taliban protected. Both organizations were enemies of the Pakistani government. Pakistani intelligence was one of the most efficient, ruthless, and corrupt intelligence organizations in the world. He did not want them to know that he had ever been in their country.

Once the event that he was about to set into motion actually occurred, there could be no possible record or trace back to him. If he left a single clue, the American CIA would eventually hunt him down and kill him, and he would not live to enjoy the money he planned to make from this operation.

The drive from Rawalpindi toward its sister city of Islamabad was speedy and reckless. The taxi driver weaved from lane to lane, zooming past the other vehicles, yelling curses and blaring his horn at those he passed.

The driver swung north onto the Kashmir Highway, a multi-lane road running straight through Islamabad. The capital city rested on the Pothohar plateau and was flanked by beautiful, lush-green mountains shrouded in mist.

Islamabad was Pakistan's most futuristic city as well. Much of the modernist-style architecture had a near whimsical quality to it. In jarring contrast, many older, mud-brown brick buildings were wedged in between the more fanciful structures with their soaring spires and colorful cubes.

Miraculously—at least that's how Khorasani felt about it— they safely arrived at the Hilton Royale. The Iranian paid the driver and gave him a nice tip, but not too nice as to be memorable. He would check in and rest for a few hours before meeting his contact.

Soon, he would be traveling west with the contact to the tribal region.

~

Approaching Beirut, 4:30 p.m.

Mike Elliot sat in his passenger seat thinking about the Russian interview to come. A pilot approached and sat on the armrest on the opposite side of the aisle facing Mike.

"Joe," he said, reaching out and offering his hand. They shook.

"Mike," he replied, thinking that no one on this plane but him had used his or her real name.

"We're thirty minutes from Beirut," he said. "The U.S. has an arrangement with the security agency responsible for the airport. We can come and go hassle free, most of the time. But we don't dally here. Once we stop and open the door, we will remain parked for about sixty seconds.

"There will be two cars waiting for you. When we takeoff, we're going to Incirlik Air Base in Turkey. We'll be on standby there in case you need to exfil this guy you're coming here to see. Headquarters will reach out to us if we're needed."

Incirlik was a joint U.S.-Turkish air base in southern Turkey east of Adana. U.S. forces staged aircraft there for missions to hotspots in the region. Special Operations Command also maintained a secure, fenced compound on part of the flight line of the base to support U.S. special operations forces from all branches of the U.S. military.

Joe patted Mike on the shoulder and said, "Good luck," as he stood and headed back toward the cockpit.

Mike checked his gear and prepared to exit the plane quickly. He realized that he felt right at home being back in the regimentation of a well-oiled paramilitary organization.

Soon, they began their descent into Beirut. The jet touched down and decelerated fast. The pilots ran out to the end of the runway, turned right onto a taxiway, and fell in behind a *Follow-Me* truck. A short distance later, they came to a halt in a secluded ramp area near several large, rusting hangars. Two black Mercedes sedans waited there. Several men in tactical vests stood by the vehicles.

An agent lowered the cabin door, pushed a button on a control panel, and extended the door's ladder to the ground. Mike quickly descended and gave a wave over his shoulder as his feet hit the tarmac. When he let go of the ladder, an electric motor kicked in and the ladder retracted. By the time he reached the car just off the port wingtip, the jet began to roll forward again.

Sergeant Major Scott Barrington from the Army's Delta Force gestured toward an open door and the back seat of the second car. Mike slid in followed by Barrington. He handed Mike a holstered Glock 17.

"Just in case," he said. "It's locked and loaded."

Mike had his Walther but took the Glock from Barrington— just in case.

Riding shotgun, Master Sergeant James Palmer turned and introduced himself to Mike as the two sedans drove away. A Lebanese airport police officer opened a gate for the two vehicles, and the cars pulled out onto a side road and sped away into the southern outskirts of Beirut leaving the Rafic Hariri International Airport behind.

Barrington said, "I remember the first time I saw you, you were a bloody mess lying on the cockpit floor of that hijacked airliner. The cockpit was filled with gore and dead bodies. You had just killed three heavily armed, desperate terrorists—and you began the fight bound and unarmed. My team was impressed with what you did."

"Yeah, and I managed to save my wife's life that day, only to let her get murdered in a brutal mugging once back home."

"Yeah, heard about that. Really sorry, Mike."

Changing the subject, Mike asked, "When did you get here?"

"Couple days ago. Master Sergeant Palmer and I were in Germany doing some coordination with the GSG9, their federal police counterterrorist unit. Then we were told to get our asses over to Rhein Main and get on a C-21 to Beirut. So here we are.

"Had a little down time the last few days so we reconned the route to the meeting place and the hotel itself. We've also been doing some training for the embassy's Marine security force in close-quarter combat drills. It's been productive."

Mike watched the shattered, war-torn city of Beirut speed past the window. They drove north on Avenue General De Gaulle. The multi-lane highway traced the shoreline around the western edge of the city.

Dozens of cranes topped the taller buildings. There seemed to be construction underway everywhere, hinting that Beirut might have entered a renaissance phase in the aftermath of a lengthy, brutal, and destructive civil war. Perhaps, though, the cranes were just permanent fixtures and nothing was really happening. Hard to tell.

Beirut's jagged skyline also seemed thrown together without much of a plan. Many of the multi-story buildings looked like someone had stacked concrete boxes together haphazardly. Some buildings had cinderblock walls with no plaster. Many of the walls, even entire buildings, leaned precariously, defying gravity and looking like they might topple over at any moment. With little or no government oversight, unskilled people built their own homes and apartment buildings, and it looked like it.

Beirut was obviously facing another crisis as well. They had driven past dozens of huge mounds of rotting trash waiting to be hauled away.

"My, how Beirut has changed," Mike said.

Barrington laughed, "Yeah, but some things here haven't changed a bit. It's still as dangerous for Americans as ever."

The two vehicles arrived at the rear gate to the U.S. embassy compound in El Metn, several miles north of Beirut's center.

The lead driver pulled up to the outer gate, and since the two-inch thick polycarbonate windows didn't roll down, he opened his door. The passengers followed suit and opened all the doors on both cars for inspection.

A federal agent stuck a small device into the car and took an iris scan of the driver. They knew each other, yet followed protocol nonetheless.

He asked the driver, "How's your mom?"

"She's good," he replied.

Had he responded with, "She passed away," the security agent would have known something was wrong. Maybe the driver had a pistol pointed at his ribs, or a bomb was in the car. But in this case, he had signaled all secure.

He moved on to the second car and went through the same routine. While he did so, several uniformed federal officers and embassy Marines checked the trunks and under the hoods. They slid long mirrors under the vehicles to inspect the undercarriage.

The agent came back to the first vehicle and waved at a guard in the security booth. Both gates rolled open to the right, and the bollards lowered into the pavement. The agent waved the driver forward and into the U.S. embassy Beirut compound. They were home.

~

Islamabad, Pakistan, 5:45 p.m.

Khorasani walked out of the elevator into the plush lobby of the Hilton Royale. He had a small brown satchel with him.

He picked up a local newspaper, got a cup of coffee from a stand, and took a seat in one of the many overstuffed chairs that dotted the lobby. He had set up this meeting through his contact via encrypted messaging. The contact would take him to the Federally Administered Tribal Area, or FATA, to meet with

Sheikh Amir Halabi, an Egyptian cleric who had been with Al-Qaeda from the beginning.

The sheikh was reputed to be a deputy of the terror group, but Khorasani suspected that he was now actually the supreme leader of the movement, what was left of it.

The Americans had killed many of Al-Qaeda's members in drone attacks. He knew that once in the FATA, his own vehicle might be watched from the sky and could even be targeted by the Americans. He did not believe, however, that the Americans would have the ability to know his identity. He was too cautious in his movements to have been detected.

Khorasani did not have to wait long. A clean-shaven young man in his twenties, dressed in jeans and a blue, long-sleeve sport shirt, walked into the lobby. He picked up a newspaper and took a seat in an easy chair next to the Iranian.

Khorasani said to the man, "There seems to be no interesting news in the paper today."

"There is one article of interest."

"Ah, yes, gas prices have risen."

"Yes, they have. Are you ready?"

Khorasani nodded and got up. He followed the contact outside to the street. The man led him to an old, battered, white Suzuki sedan. He opened the back door and Khorasani slid in. The contact got into the front passenger seat. A second man, middle-aged, with a short, gray beard, sat behind the wheel. He eased the car into traffic onto the Kashmir Highway.

As always, the traffic was a chaotic mix of buses, vans, cars, trucks, motorcycles, bicycles, mule-drawn carts, and even people walking in the road. They all drove everywhere in the road, back and forth between lanes in a mishmash of humanity and vehicles.

Multitudes of gaudy, highly decorated, every-color-of-the-rainbow buses plied the streets haphazardly, carrying throngs of workers and travelers about the city. Khorasani just tuned it all out and reviewed his plan. His mission was too important for sightseeing.

They soon turned north onto Route N5 toward Peshawar. Beyond that city, they would travel on small, treacherous back roads though the mountains into the Bagh region, along the Afghan border, a largely ungoverned part of Pakistan. The journey would take three to four hours, maybe longer, depending on the security precautions his two escorts employed.

~

Tbilisi, Georgia, 10:20 p.m.

Ingrid Holman had arrived in the capital city of Georgia two hours earlier. Now she sat in her hotel room at a small, granite-topped, mirrored dressing table combing her long blond hair. Her 9mm pistol, provided by a CIA asset in Georgia, lay on the night stand by the bed.

The thirty-five-year-old stood six feet tall in her bare feet. She was trim and muscular. She was also an accomplished martial artist. In fact, she had begun her career in the CIA as an instructor of self defense at the Farm, the CIA's training facility at Camp Peary in Virginia.

Her superiors quickly recognized her potential and she soon became a CIA officer. Since, she had served in Iraq, Afghanistan, several embassy posts, and now as a non-official-cover agent. She was a CIA trouble shooter, and a reliable one at that.

The CIA had become aware of an informant located in Tbilisi who wanted to sell information about Genadi Meskhi. Her mission—meet the informant, assess his reliability, and determine if Meskhi was handling the stolen nukes. At midnight she would meet this man at a boisterous night club several blocks from her hotel.

She planned to be particularly cautious with this one because the CIA had recently paid a Georgian asset to go to Poti, Georgia to gather information on Meskhi's operation. The op was routine intelligence collection, back before Meskhi had become potentially important because of the nuclear heist. The asset had not been heard from since.

In the hall outside Ingrid's door, Chinwe Okeke pulled a master electronic key card from his pocket. Its former owner, one of the housekeepers, lay dead in a broom closet two floors above. A siren wailed on the busy street below. He carefully slipped the key card into the slot on the door and the light turned to green as the door unlocked, the siren masking the clink of the lock.

He gently twisted the door handle and quietly opened the door just a crack. He waited, and listened, checking left and right up and down the hall. He stood silently for a moment.

Okeke was a large man—six-foot-four, a solid two hundred and forty pounds, thirty-four-years-old. His skin was dark and he bore the tribal scars of manhood from his native Nigerian village—three scars under each eye.

He knew that the inside security bar would be in place on the door to prevent it from opening, and he knew that his target would be armed and trained. None of this mattered to him, of course. In fact, it made his assigned task more enjoyable.

He looked up and down the hallway one more time, lifted his leg, and kicked the door with a solid forward thrust kick sending the door flying open, the metal bracket formerly securing the door bounced off the wall with a clang.

Ingrid lunged toward the night stand and her gun, but seemingly from nowhere the intruder produced a large, heavy dagger and launched it with an overhand throw just ahead of her path. She slammed her leg and foot against the bed and rolled back. She could hear the swoosh of the spinning dagger and feel the air pushed out by its propeller-like motion as it zoomed past, brushing her hair and missing her face by less than an inch.

She continued her roll backward and came up in a crouch facing her attacker, but she was astonished by the speed of such a large man as he quickly closed on her. He reached for her, but she swept his arm to the side with a block and threw a kick toward his groin. He easily blocked it. She threw a rapid flurry of kicks and punches, but he parried every strike she made as if he knew in perfect detail each move she was about to make.

Ingrid felt fear for perhaps the first time in her life. He seemed to be toying with her, and enjoying it. She launched a fierce spinning back kick. She had taken down many a man with it. Okeke dodged the kick, and before she could complete the full spin, his hand shot out and he grabbed a fistful of hair on the back of her head. He jerked her violently into his grip.

He had full control of her now, and Ingrid knew that she was in trouble. She continued to try new maneuvers and thrusts, but nothing worked and she couldn't free herself. Okeke pushed his body against hers and pinned her against the dressing table. She could do nothing. Her attacker was too powerful. He gradually forced her upper body slowly down to the hard, cold granite of the table, and then twisted her head until the side of her face was flat on the table.

Her eyes watered and through her tears, she could now clearly see his reflection in the mirror. There were neat rows of scars just below each of his calm umber eyes. She tried to move her arms, but couldn't. She was terrified. She watched him in horror in the mirror as he placed a long ice pick in her ear.

He slowly pushed all seven inches of the metal prong into her ear. Her body twitched several times and then was still. He stepped back, released her, and Ingrid slid off the counter and collapsed in a heap on the floor, the ice pick still protruding from her ear.

5

U.S. Embassy Beirut, 5:30 p.m.

Mike and the others entered a building toward the back of the sprawling compound. One of the CIA agents led Mike, Barrington, and Palmer up to the top floor. As the men exited the elevator, Doug Andrews, the CIA chief of station for Beirut, came out of his office.

Mike was meeting Andrews for the first time. After the introductions and handshakes, Andrews led the men down the corridor to a large room with some beds and showers. Barrington and Palmer were already bunked there, and each had a single backpack on one of the beds. The dorm had a small kitchen with two large refrigerators, a stove, sink, some cabinets, and a table with chairs.

Andrews pointed to an open door at the end of the room. "Showers and heads that way. There's also a clothes washer and dryer. I'll let you settle down a bit, and then we'll grab some dinner in the cafeteria downstairs. Afterwards, we'll go to my office to discuss the plan."

Mike thanked him and picked out a bunk. He showered and changed clothes. After a copious meal in the embassy cafeteria, Andrews, Mike, Barrington, Palmer, and one of Andrews' agents retired to his office.

Andrews had a nicely stocked side bar. It had just about everything one could imagine. He offered drinks and each of the men mixed something—some just had juice, some a highball. They settled in on a sofa and easy chairs arranged around a coffee table.

Andrews began the discussion. "Tomorrow, we have a meeting set up with a Russian named Oleg Baskov. If that's his real name. He's former Spetsnaz, and from what we can gather, he's a really nasty fellow.

"There's an ethnic Russian, Coptic Christian community here in Beirut. He's staying there. That's where all the chatter is coming from about this guy. A Lebanese asset in the Christian community told us about him. Said he could set up a meeting.

"Anyway, Baskov apparently wants to talk, for payment in return. Word is, he's been blabbing about the Russian nuke heist. Nothing specific, just a lot of allusion, except for the part about Spetsnaz operators being involved in the theft. But we know that Grigor was previously a Spetsnaz commander, so it stands to reason that he would recruit some of his former soldiers for the attack on the nuclear storage facility.

"So we want to find out why this guy is in Beirut? Why did he leave Russia? Is he hiding? Why is he on the run? Did he actually participate in the heist and have firsthand knowledge, or is he just regurgitating rumors? And if he doesn't know where the nukes are, then does he know where Colonel Vladimir Grigor might be?"

Mike said, "Striker's instructions are to bring Baskov out if we think he's got further value."

Andrews added, "Yeah, I know, the rendition team is on alert at Incirlik. They'll be on station off the coast over the Mediterranean during our meeting at 10:00 a.m. I will have a team at the airport ready to meet us. But I'll tell you now, as far as I'm concerned, just plan on extracting him. This guy is our only lead. And if he doesn't show, we're going to have to go find him. If he does show, we're keeping him."

Everyone nodded.

Mike said, "Striker also thinks that Baskov's friends will be looking for him as well."

Barrington spoke up for the first time. "Just remember, these Spetsnaz guys are some bad dudes."

Mike laughed. "Aren't you guys just as bad?"

"We like to think so, but we have a conscience. These men are like machines, like terminators. If we come across these fellows, they will be seriously armored and heavily armed. Shoot for the face or legs. It's likely the only way you'll stop them."

Andrews got up, mixed himself another drink, and returned to his seat.

Barrington asked, "Just what do we know about the nuke theft, anyway? And this guy Grigor."

"About the heist, not a lot," answered Andrews. "The base was a small Russian NSF—Nuclear Storage Facility. It had forty to fifty men, all of whom were killed. We think some nukes are missing."

"Some?"

"We have no idea. Five. Ten. Twenty. That's why this Russian guy is so important. If he knows *anything*, it'll be more than we've got right now. As for Grigor, we think he's the mastermind. He was already on our radar. Former Spetsnaz commander, then nuclear surety. He's also an arms dealer."

"Wow," said Palmer, "nice combo."

Mike added, "We lost two agents in Bucharest a few days ago. We think it was Colonel Grigor who killed them."

"Yeah," added Andrews, "they had just reported sighting him, *and* that he was headed to Bulgaria."

"Then he ambushed them on the train," said Mike. "Shot each of them through the temple at close range."

"I knew both of them," Andrews said. "Very experienced and capable men. We'll need to be careful if we catch up with Grigor. We have teams scouring Bulgaria, especially Sophia where he was supposedly heading, but so far nothing. If he stole the nukes, though, then he knows where they are."

"Where are we meeting with Baskov?" asked Mike.

Andrews answered, "The Commodore Hotel downtown."

"We looked at it," added Master Sergeant Palmer. "Pretty straight forward. On a side street called Neheme Yafet. Not much traffic. Good visibility on the street. Highest rooftop right around it is three stories. Columns all along the front of the hotel. We have to watch the windows and rooftops on the buildings opposite."

The men finalized the details of the mission, and the conversation moved to small talk.

Andrews said hesitantly, "Mike, I was really sorry to hear about your wife."

"You know," replied Mike, "I told her I was going to pick her up after work, but she refused. She didn't want to leave her car at the hospital."

"Mike," said Andrews, "you can't blame yourself."

"Yet I do," replied Mike. Getting up, he said, "See you guys in the morning. I'm beat."

~

Western, Pakistan

The trip was long and the ride uncomfortable, but well before dawn, the Suzuki sedan arrived at a large compound with high stone walls. Khorasani was impressed with the security measures the driver had taken—frequent switchbacks, stops in locations concealed from aerial view. They had learned the hard way that the American drones never slept.

The contact hopped out of the vehicle, unlocked a heavy wooden door, and swung it open. They drove in. Inside the wall was a three story white house constructed of concrete. The contact showed Khorasani to a room on the second floor. It had a comfortable bed and a small bathroom. The window was covered with a black cloth, as were the windows on the first floor.

Soon, a veiled female, accompanied by the contact, brought a tray of food filled with meats, grains, vegetables, bread, and hot tea. The contact told him to rest, and that he would meet with the Sheikh in a few hours. Khorasani took the tray and nodded.

Soon, he hoped, he would learn several important things crucial to his plan—was the Sheikh the decision-maker for the organization, did he have the resources to finance a major operation, and did Al-Qaeda still have the ability to execute a bold and dangerous plan?

~

U.S. Embassy Beirut, 7:30 a.m.

In the basement of an annex building near the rear of the embassy compound, Mike Elliot, Sergeant Major Barrington, Master Sergeant Palmer, and several of Andrews' CIA men, prepared for the 10:00 a.m. meeting with the Russian defector, Oleg Baskov.

The men were in the CIA's arms and equipment room. Barrington and Palmer had brought their weapons and equipment. Mike was selecting his.

Mike watched Barrington checking his two Colt Model 1911-A1 pistols. He wore a double, black nylon shoulder holster over his body armor. When he was satisfied that the pistols were ready, he tucked them neatly into the two holsters, one under each arm. He was ambidextrous and could shoot equally well with either hand, and he trained constantly in doing so.

Barrington had a worn, leather slapjack stuck in his right rear pocket. Shaped like a flat spoon, it was two pieces of sturdy leather sewn together with a piece of lead in between. It could knock a man senseless with just a tap. He slipped on a lightweight, tan, cotton utility shirt that he left unbuttoned. It concealed the guns. He stuffed several cable ties into a pocket of the shirt and buttoned the pocket.

At six foot, one hundred and seventy pounds, Barrington was lean, wiry, and compact. He was a man who exuded energy. He wore a short black beard and medium length black hair. Only thirty-six, and he had already been a Sergeant Major for three years.

At thirty-two, Master Sergeant Palmer on the other hand, was a huge man. Mike estimated him to be at least six foot three, and probably two hundred and twenty pounds. He was a burly, muscular man.

He obviously had some Irish in him—ruddy complexion, green eyes, wavy reddish hair, and a short beard of the same color. According to Barrington, Palmer was the best recon man Delta Force had. Despite his size, he could sneak up on anyone or anything, undetected.

Mike closed the Velcro strap on his own body armor, thinking that Barrington and Palmer would both be at home in 1860's Dodge City. They were gunslingers. True warriors. Mike, too, was of that same warrior spirit. It was a life he had tried to leave behind more than once, but was never able to escape it.

Mike kept his .380 as a backup. The lightweight pistol fired a smaller round, but at close quarters, Mike was quite deadly with it. Plus, it suppressed nicely.

Today, however, he wanted more firepower. He picked the same pistol Barrington carried, a 1911-A1. Compared to the .380, this gun was a cannon. He hoped he wouldn't need it, but if he did, he wanted the extra stopping power of the .45 ACP. He slid the pistol into a shoulder holster under his left arm. He also carried four spare mags.

Mike had his black backpack on the floor at his feet. He would put it in the car because he would not be coming back here. Barrington and Palmer were doing the same. They all wore comsets and lapel mics, all on the same channel. Mike adjusted the earpiece in his left ear.

The lead security team of eight men was already on site at the hotel. They would secure the street, the hotel front and rear, and the interview room. If all went according to plan, the Russian and the Lebanese asset would be waiting in the room when Mike's team arrived.

~

Istanbul, Turkey

Ronald Nelson stepped into the elevator in the lobby of the Hilton Hotel. He was on his way to the fourteenth floor to interview a local informant who was supposed to have information about Genadi Meskhi.

A very large, dark-skinned man wearing an expensive suit stepped into the elevator with him and pushed the button for the sixteenth floor. He turned and faced the door and stood beside Ronald Nelson. The wide brim of his hat concealed his face from the surveillance camera, but Nelson got a glimpse of him as he walked in. He had three rows of inch-long scars under each eye. *They were obviously done on purpose*, he thought, *perhaps tribal.*

Nelson took a step back so that he was slightly behind the larger man.

Nelson's job title was first secretary at the American consulate in Istanbul. That was not his real job; it served as his official cover. He was an officer of the CIA. He, like everyone else in the CIA, was beating the bushes trying to pick up even the slightest hint of who might be trying to move a handful of tactical nuclear weapons. His focus for the moment was on Genadi Meskhi, but so far, they had nothing to go on.

Nelson was alert and cautious. Ingrid Holman had been brutally murdered just the day before in Georgia, only a few hours flying time from here. He knew that her assassin was formidable because it would not have been easy to take down Ingrid.

The difference with this meeting, however, was that Nelson knew this informant, having met with him several times already on various intelligence matters. Ingrid was going in blind and it was obviously a set up. Nevertheless, he was proceeding with caution. He had his right hand in his suit coat pocket. The pocket liner had been removed, and his hand rested on the grip of a .40 caliber Glock pistol.

A moment later, the doors opened on the fourteenth floor and the dark man stepped off the elevator. Fortunately for the guests of the Hilton, no one was waiting for the elevator on that floor. As the Nigerian walked up the hall, he slid his long dagger back into its sheath in the small of his back. He had cleaned it on Nelson's trouser leg.

In the elevator, Ronald Nelson's body lay slumped in a corner, his throat cut so deeply that he was almost decapitated. Nelson's hand still clenched the grip of his pistol, still resting in its holster.

~

Western Pakistan, 8:40 a.m.

Khorasani heard a light tap on his bedroom door. He opened it, and the veiled woman with the contact at her side stood there. Khorasani had already bathed and put on fresh clothes.

She came into the room and took away the food tray.

The contact said, "You may now meet with the sheikh. We will depart for Islamabad immediately following your meeting."

Khorasani followed the man downstairs, through the house, and out a rear door. They walked over a dark stone pathway, through a flower-filled garden, to a cottage tucked away in a corner of the compound wall.

The door was open and they entered. The contact gestured toward an elderly man wearing white robes. He had an ivory beard and a turban of sorts. The man sat on a pile of cushions. The contact bowed and left.

Khorasani bowed, lowering his chin to his chest. As he straightened, the sheikh gestured to a low chair before him. Khorasani sat. He waited for the elder to speak first.

The man sat, silently taking stock of his visitor. Then he said in Arabic, "Welcome. You may begin."

The Iranian nodded and said, "I am humbled to be in the presence of someone who has sown such devastation on America. I consider the nation, along with Israel, an abomination, a curse that must be eradicated from the face of this earth."

The sheikh nodded. "And whom do you represent?"

"I come here from Saudi Arabia, but I do not represent the kingdom itself, only a select few powerful men, who feel as I do about the Great Satan."

"As do I," replied the sheikh, "but it seems that all we can manage these days is to hide from the American drones. Even hiding is not enough. They still kill us from the sky." The old man looked up at the ceiling as if expecting to see an American drone there.

"We still have dedicated, idealistic disciples of our cause, spread across numerous countries. They are willing to die for that cause, but we are not as great as we once were. It was a glorious achievement when we successfully attacked America on that fateful day in September, but I worry that those days may have slipped away forever."

"And if you had the means to attack America in a manner one hundred times grander than September 11, would you do so?"

"I would destroy them and spit on their ashes."

"I can furnish you with a two kiloton, man-portable, state-of-the-art, Russian nuclear bomb that is virtually undetectable without specialized scientific equipment. With it, you could destroy the new World Trade Center and kill untold thousands of Americans. You would rock the very foundation of their country, perhaps even cause it to disintegrate entirely. You would once again be the world's foremost organization for the liberation of Islam from western tyranny. *You* would once again thrust a dagger into the heart of the Great Satan while it slept."

The sheikh's eyes were wide in surprise and excitement. He sat up straight and gazed at Khorasani with an intensity that startled even the Iranian.

"You have this device now?" demanded the sheikh.

"Yes, I have access to it," replied Khorasani, "but I must pay for it. I do not seek to profit financially from this transfer. The money you pay will go to the broker possessing this device. My reward will come from seeing it detonated in the new World Trade Center in New York City."

The sheikh leaned back on the cushions piled behind his back. He felt a little short of breath, and his heart palpitated in his chest. He had not felt this way since September 11, 2001. He cared not if the Americans succeeded in killing him once he brought down the tower they put up in defiance after Al-Qaeda's glorious attack. The sheikh realized that he had been hiding, cowering, sleeping, anything but attacking. Every nerve in his body was awake and alive.

"What is the price of this device?"

"Fifty million dollars."

The sheikh did not respond immediately. He appeared to be deep in thought. Then he said slowly, "Our man who is responsible for external operations is in Iraq. I won't say where, of course, but he would be the one to develop and implement the plan. He must see the device to verify its authenticity and availability, before money is paid."

"Of course. This can be arranged."

"Your idea to place it in the World Trade Center is an ambitious one. How can this be achieved? How could one possibly get such a device past the American security services?"

Khorasani nodded. "I have given this problem considerable thought. I would use a trusted operative with European citizenship. He would contact an American lawyer to form a U.S. corporation. Then, in the name of the company, the attorney would lease a suite in the new World Trade Center.

"I would move the device first to Venezuela. There is a man, a Jamaican, who specializes in transporting packages of all types into the U.S. from South America. I would hire him to move it from Venezuela to New York.

"Once the package is delivered to the new office suite, just like any other regular delivery, I would have a skilled person, also with a European passport and able to travel easily, to set up the device. It is not complicated to do so. It was designed to be emplaced on the battlefield and activated by soldiers.

"The device has a built-in anti-handling function. It would be set up with this capability activated. Then I would leave the country before it detonated. It all carries a certain risk, of course. But I believe that it can be done."

"You make it sound so easy," replied the sheikh with a skeptical tone.

"No, not easy, but the Jamaican can do it. I assure you. They will use the Americans' own regulations against them."

"In what way?"

"As I understand it, the Jamaican uses a variety of legitimate companies which regularly ship items to the United States and have long track records with the U.S. Customs agency. I also know that the shipments will be scanned for drugs and radiation. But I am confident that this device will not be detected by their scans."

The sheikh's eyes were now bright and alert. "How would the money be paid?"

Khorasani pulled a folded piece of paper from his shirt pocket and opened it. It contained two numbers: one was ten-digits, the other twelve. He handed it to the sheikh and said, "The numbers are the bank code and an account number. When your man confirms the authenticity of my offer, fifteen million should be paid to this account. When the transfer of possession is ready to occur, thirty-five million should be paid to the same account. When the money is verified, the transfer will be completed."

The sheikh thought for a moment.

"Can *you* deliver it to Venezuela?"

Khorasani thought for a few seconds. This would complicate matters somewhat, but he could do it. "Yes," he replied.

"The man who brought you here will arrange contact with two men—Hamadi Hassan and Yousef Amad. Hassan will act on our behalf. Both men have British passports and are able to travel freely, at least, so far."

Khorasani leaned forward, once again bowing his head. The sheikh reached out, placing his hand on the Iranian's head. He said, "Young man, with happiness in my heart, I will stand in this yard, my arms raised to the sky, my eyes to the heavens, and watch with contentment at America's drone as it sends its fire to strike me dead, if only I can fulfill this holy vision you possess."

The sheikh removed his hand. Khorasani rose, turned, and left the small building. He waited in the flower garden while the contact entered the sheikh's apartment to receive his instructions.

Smiling, Khorasani leaned in toward a large purple and white iris and took in its wonderful aroma. His plot was in motion, and his retirement assured.

~

CIA Headquarters

Gerald had suspected for days that something big was up. Director Berg had been constantly running back and forth between his office and Striker's. None of the other working stiffs had any idea what was going on, but the senior staff were in and out of constant meetings. Fear was in the air, and Gerald suspected the worst.

In ten minutes, the CIA's Chief of Station for Ankara, Turkey would arrive for a meeting with the director of operations. The director's two secretaries prepared his conference table with pens, pads, glasses, and ice water. There was a pot of coffee brewing on the dais.

Gerald sat in his small office. He watched the bustle through his open door with trepidation, certain that this hubbub was all about him. *They know!* he realized, as that thought rattled through his head in a never-ending loop.

He popped another antacid and chewed it slowly. His armpits stank. He closed his door, unbuttoned his shirt, and applied a heavy dose of deodorant under each arm. He straightened his shirt and opened the door just as Max Hardwick and the Istanbul chief arrived in the outer office.

The senior secretary led them directly into the DO's office. An instant later, she was back and leaning into Gerald's door. "He wants you," she said, nodding toward the boss's office.

Gerald rose robotically, grabbed a pad and pen, and walked into the DO's office, sure his fate was sealed. He sat several chairs down from Max Hardwick, toward the end of the table, an indication that he was not really part of the meeting. He was just there for administrative support. As usual, Gerald's job at such meetings was to create a classified record of the conference and file it. The director didn't care for audio recordings.

The DO sat opposite Max and the Ankara chief. The DO, sixty-year-old Alan Berg, was short but stocky. He had a pug nose from boxing in his early years.

He asked the station chief, "What happened?"

"We're still trying to piece together how Ingrid was compromised. Georgian intelligence notified us that she was found dead in her room by hotel staff where she was staying in Tbilisi. As you know, she was following up on a lead on Genadi Meskhi. She was going to meet with a paid informant who supposedly had information for sale about the arms dealer. She never made it out of her room, and the informant was also found dead.

"The hotel called the local police. What we *have* learned is that she apparently put up a good fight, but lost. She was killed by an ice pick in her ear."

The DO grimaced in anger and disgust.

Max just shook his head and said, "Ingrid was a tough cookie. I sure wouldn't want to face her in a fight."

They all nodded in agreement.

"And Ronald?" asked the DO.

"Ronald Nelson was in an elevator going to a meeting, also with an informant, at the Istanbul Hilton. He never made it to the meeting. He was murdered in the elevator, throat horrifically slashed. And I personally know that he was armed and wary. With Ingrid's murder in Tbilisi just twenty-four hours before, everyone was on edge. None of us made a move without a weapon close at hand.

"And you know Ronald. He was an experienced agent, a phenomenal shot with a pistol, and very good at hand-to-hand. He could best any of us. But it obviously didn't help. Whoever is doing this is a real piece of work. Local authorities, just like Tbilisi, also found the informant in his room—dead."

Gerald was in shock. His mouth hung open. He had just learned that the last two agents he had given up were dead!

"Gerald?" the DO asked.

"Sorry, sir. It's just shocking, that's all."

The DO turned back to the chief of station. "So we're back to square one as far as the nukes are concerned it seems."

Gerald of course knew about the missing nukes from previous meetings. Now, he wondered if he was somehow mixed up directly with the stolen nuclear weapons. This was far worse that he could have ever imagined. And he had a very vivid imagination.

"Maybe not," said Max. "Maybe Mike Elliot will find something in Beirut."

The DO nodded and said, "Yeah Elliot should be wrapping up there today, and I hope you're right, Max, but unless something comes up in Beirut that points in a different direction, Striker wants him to move on to Istanbul after Beirut. He can try to pick up where Nelson left off. Maybe one of the dead contact's associates knows something. Elliot will need to see if he can pick up a trail, and not get killed in the process."

Max said, "We've got him set up at the Istanbul Marriott East downtown. I'm working on getting a security plan in place just in case our killer is still around."

The Istanbul chief asked, "Need any support from us?"

"Yeah, I want Mya."

"You got it."

6

Beirut, 9:00 a.m.

Mike's team departed the embassy in two armored Mercedes sedans. The Commodore Hotel was only five miles from the embassy, but how long the drive might take was unpredictable.

Mike had a black nylon bag with a shoulder strap. It contained bundles of counterfeit hundred dollar bills. They didn't intend to risk any real taxpayer dollars on this op, but the fake cash made for a good prop.

The streets of Beirut were chaotic, at best. Most intersections were uncontrolled—no traffic lights or stop signs. The traffic somehow melded together in a strange symbiosis. Cars, buses, and trucks—horns blaring—inched forward into tiny gaps between other vehicles. Somehow it worked, though it wasn't pretty. Neither were the hordes of scraped and dented vehicles.

They entered a tight, one-way street as they neared the hotel. Sewage ran down the middle of the street, and the odor was strong even inside the car. Hundreds of electrical and telephone wires crisscrossed the street just overhead in a drunken weave-like pattern.

At 9:55 a.m., the two CIA sedans turned north onto Neheme Yafet. The Commodore was ahead on the left. Barrington, riding shotgun in the lead car, scanned the passing rooftops and windows.

They drove past the first vehicle of the advance security team where two CIA men stood near their car. Mike's team parked across the street from the hotel. The second security car was farther north on the street. Two more CIA men stood near that vehicle.

One of the advance team agents stepped out of the big glass doors of the Commodore and spoke into his lapel mic. The security teams reported all clear. He nodded to Andrews. They exited the two cars and crossed the street to the Commodore, keeping a close watch on the buildings around them. The two drivers remained on the street.

Inside the Commodore, Andrews' man informed him that the Russian soldier and the Lebanese asset were in room 315. They crossed the near-empty lobby and climbed the once ornate staircase covered in threadbare carpet to the third floor. The hotel had seen better days.

Mike, Barrington, Palmer, and Andrews entered room 315. The other agents remained in the hall. Two men sat waiting in the room.

Mike said, "Good morning," in Arabic to the Lebanese man and then repeated it in Russian to Baskov.

He just grunted.

Palmer led the Lebanese asset out to the hall, pressed a folded wad of bills into the man's palm, and said in Arabic, "Thank you, go now." Palmer returned to the room.

Oleg Baskov sat in an easy chair by the coffee table. The man was exactly what Mike had expected—large, brutish, and muscular. He had a three-day stubble of a beard with several prominent scars on his face. This was certainly not a man to trifle with. Mike could only imagine how many men, women, and children this man had killed with everything from his bare hands to a bayonet, or explosives and booby traps.

Mike stood across the table from him. Barrington stood behind him near a side bar. Palmer took a seat next to Baskov. Andrews sat across the table from him.

"Do you speak English?" Mike asked him.

He shook his head no.

Mike asked him in Russian, "What's your name?"

"Baskov."

"Oleg Baskov?"

"Yes."

"Where are you from?"

"Minsk, but what difference does it make. I am not here for small talk."

"Fair enough," Mike answered. "You have something to tell us?"

"I want payment."

"We know, and we are prepared to pay." Mike dropped the cash satchel onto the coffee table and opened it.

Baskov reached for it, but Mike pulled it back. "Information first."

The big man scowled for a moment, and then said, "A couple of men from my unit were away when the nuke base was hit. I was supposed to go too."

"Why didn't you go?"

"I don't know. They decided to leave me out of it. I didn't know what the mission was when they left. But when I heard about the hit on the base, and all those men killed, I knew it was them. No one else could have done that."

"Spetsnaz?"

"Yes. When one of them returned, I started asking about the mission. He warned me not to talk of it. I don't like to be warned, about anything. I pressed the issue. Then I heard that they were planning to kill me. So I left."

"That's it? You want me to pay for you to tell me that Russian Spetsnaz did the attack? We figured that much out for ourselves. What else?"

"Nothing more."

"Do you think your friends are still looking for you?"

"Probably."

"Would they know you're in Beirut?"

The Russian thought for a moment. "Yeah, they would probably figure that out. Some of them know I have friends in Beirut. I come here sometimes when I'm off. But I've been mostly staying out of sight in case they show up."

Mike glanced at Barrington and could see in his eyes that this was a troubling development. Barrington knew enough Russian to get the gist of what was just said.

Mike said to Baskov, "Tell me about Colonel Vladimir Grigor."

A crooked grin snaked across the Russian's harsh face. "Oh, you've heard of him. He was our commander in Chechnya."

"Was he involved in the operation the men went on?"

"I heard his name mentioned, but I don't know for sure if he was involved."

"Tell me about him."

"He was one of the toughest, fiercest men I have ever known. And you should hope that you never encounter him."

"I'll keep that in mind, Oleg. Now, one more time, *what* was stolen and *where* was it taken?"

"I don't know. Look, I'm telling you it was an inside job. Members of the Russian army hit that base. That's worth knowing."

"It's not enough."

Baskov tamped his foot and clenched his teeth.

"What did they steal?" Mike asked more forcefully.

The Russian looked up at Mike with an icy expression that would have sent a cold chill up most men's spines. Mike was not most men.

Baskov said, "No one but me knew *who* was involved, but it was soon common knowledge in Spetsnaz that five RA-115s were missing. We trained with the devices many times."

"SADMs? Man portable?"

"Yes."

"What kiloton?"

"Two."

"Any special functions?"

"Anti-handling trigger. Delayed detonation—one minute to five days. Also detonation by cell phone, but not just any phone, a special one designed for the device."

"Are the phones kept with the bombs?"

"No. In Moscow."

"Codes?"

"Yes, required. Separate activation and deactivation codes. Also never kept with the device. Maintained in Moscow central headquarters."

"How are the codes stored for field use?"

"On a small electronic PDA."

"How detectable are the bombs?"

"What do you mean?"

"Radiological signature."

"The scientists demonstrated this to us. Very small chance they can be detected."

"Where did they take the nukes? And where is Grigor?"

"I said I don't know."

"Oleg, I've got a bag *full* of money here," he said, patting the satchel, "and I would really like to give it to you, but you've *got* to tell me everything."

Baskov growled under his breath, "You know, little man, I would kill you in a heartbeat, and not think twice about it."

"Where, Oleg?"

"Turkey, maybe."

"Where in Turkey?"

"I don't know," he yelled, jumping up and reaching for Mike.

In a blur, Barrington's hand shot out and grabbed the Russian's collar. He whacked the man on the back of the head with the leather slapjack.

Baskov tumbled forward, unconscious, shattering the coffee table to splinters.

In the next breath, Palmer had the man's wrists zip-tied behind his back. He searched the Russian and removed a folding tactical knife and a 9mm pistol.

While giving Andrews a rapid recap of what Baskov had said, Mike zipped closed the moneybag. Andrews was already dialing Striker on a secure sat phone. He answered on one ring. Andrews relayed what they had just learned.

"Good work," said Striker, "that's a *lot* more than we knew five minutes ago. Take him to the airport," he ordered. "I'll bring the plane in. Give me Mike."

"Will do," responded Andrews, handing the phone to Mike.

Baskov was coming to, moaning, and struggling against his bindings. Barrington leaned down and gently tapped the big man several times on the back of the head with the slapjack. He lay still.

"Elliot here," Mike said into the phone.

"We're pulling this guy out. You, Barrington, and Palmer, fly with him to Incirlik Air Base. We're having Delta Force position an assault team with helos there. Barrington will be heading up the team. Tell him he'll get his orders when he checks in with his unit.

"Mike, I want you to go on to Istanbul from Incirlik. See if you can pick up a lead on who killed Ronald Nelson there. We don't know if these murders are connected to the nukes or not, but maybe he had stumbled on to something. We'll have another plane for you. Max is making the arrangements and will get the details to you. That's all."

"Got it," replied Mike, disconnecting.

Andrews said, "Okay, we're taking this guy to the airport."

Mike added, "Scott, James, we're going to Incirlik. Scott, you'll be heading up Delta's assault force there. I'm moving on to Istanbul."

Barrington nodded and said, "Okay, remember what I said, if we run into this guy's friends on the way out of here, don't fuck around. Unless you pop 'em between the eyes, or from the knees down, you're wasting time and government ammo."

He turned to Master Sergeant Palmer. "James, you hang onto our friend here. I don't want to lose him. Mike and I will clear the street before you bring him out."

Palmer jerked Baskov to his feet.

"Let's go," said Andrews.

The men hit the stairs with the Russian in tow. Andrews called over the radio for the inside team to converge on the lobby. They went down to the first floor, crossed the foyer, and reached the large glass front doors of the Commodore. Hotel guests stared at them wide-eyed. Barrington raised his hand, and the team stopped. Palmer shoved the Russian off to the side of the doorway by the wall.

Pulling a Colt from its holster, Barrington told Andrews, "Wait here until we clear the street." The other men drew their weapons. Barrington pointed at Mike and two other agents, and the four of them headed out through the doors.

Outside, Barrington tapped Mike on the shoulder and pointed to the right. Barrington turned left. The two agents started across the street toward the two CIA vehicles parked there.

Moving to the left, Barrington scanned the windows and rooftops. Nothing unusual. The street seemed calm. Little traffic and no pedestrians. Barrington and Mike could see the two agents to the far left and right. Barrington was about to signal all clear over the radio when he saw one of the security men to his left suddenly drop. It was silent. No shot rang out. In the same instant, the second man disappeared from view.

Barrington glanced right and could no longer see the two agents on the right flank. Out of the corner of his eye, he caught a glint of light above and to the left. He raised his .45 and fired one round. The echoing boom of the .45 ACP rattled the surrounding windows as it reverberated up and down the street. The bullet hit the lens of the ten-power riflescope perched on the rooftop and entered the sniper's right eye. The rifle barrel fell away from the edge of the roof.

Inside the Commodore, the Russian said in perfect English to Palmer and Andrews, "You have only minutes to live. Say your prayers."

"Shut up, asshole," grumbled Palmer, slamming the man's face against the wall. Blood poured from Baskov's nose.

Barrington said over the radio, "Lead and trail security teams down, one sniper eliminated."

At that moment, the two agents now halfway across the street, guns oriented outward, came under fire from both ends of the street. The attackers' weapons were suppressed.

One of the agents was hit almost immediately and went down. The other agent fired in one direction, then the other—hitting his targets, but to no effect. Still firing, the attackers slid behind parked vehicles and disappeared from view.

Ricochets sparkled off the street and concrete buildings. The agent dragged the wounded man toward the CIA cars ahead. Another agent dashed out and helped him pull the man to safety between the cars. He was bleeding badly. One of them began first aid. The other two returned fire.

The attackers then stood and began a moving assault. Two to the left. Two to the right. They began jogging toward the center firing rapidly. The scene was surreal, as if they were invulnerable and had no fear.

Barrington had drawn his other .45 and was already moving to the left. He used the big columns in front of the hotel as cover. Mike was halfway down the row of columns to the right. Barrington had a pistol in each hand, held down by his sides. Mike moved in a combat stance, his pistol thrust forward in a double-handed grip.

On the left, Barrington stepped between the columns, facing the two gunmen in the street not twenty yards away. The attackers quickly oriented their weapons, but Barrington already had his pistols up. He fired both guns at once.

He got a headshot on one. The man collapsed to the street. He hit the other in the chest, slamming his body armor. The .45 caliber round rocked the man back, but he quickly recovered and returned fire. Barrington ducked behind a column. Several rounds went through the hotel's facade, and the huge plate glass windows exploded. Slabs of glass crashed down in a ferocious thunderclap. The attacker backed away and slid around the corner of a building into an alley.

On the right flank, Mike closed on the other two gunmen. They shot at him as he moved randomly from one column to the next. Bullets zinged off the concrete wall to Mike's right.

From a position behind a column, Mike fired a single shot at the feet of one of the men. The man dropped to the ground screaming. The second attacker tried to close the distance on Mike, running forward at a fast trot, pistol extended, firing rapidly.

Mike stepped out in a crouched position, fired, and hit the attacker just above the left eye. The man flipped over backwards from the impact of the heavy round and hit the pavement, already dead.

Mike moved toward the wounded gunman. He wanted him alive, but as he approached, the man rolled over and fired. Mike twisted, and the round whizzed past his left ear. He returned fire, hitting the gunman under the chin and killing him instantly. Mike dropped the magazine from his pistol and slapped a new one into place.

On the other end of the street, Barrington stepped around the corner of the building into the alley following the attacker. His pistols hung down by his side. The gunman was twenty-five yards down the alley, now facing Barrington, his pistol also at his side.

The two men walked toward each other like old west gunfighters. Both raised their weapons simultaneously, but Barrington fired first with both guns from a low arm position without aiming—both rounds hit the attacker's face knocking him off his feet. He hit the pavement with a heavy *thud*.

Barrington spun around and scanned the area. Nothing moved. He ran to the two downed CIA men. Both dead. He called on the radio for help, and two agents bounded toward him.

Mike checked the two agents on his end of the street. They were also dead. He called for backup and two more men sprinted to him.

Barrington and Mike covered the agents on both ends of the street as they moved the bodies of their fallen comrades to the cars. Barrington said to the two agents with him, "I'll give you the signal when to move out."

Barrington then called over the radio, "All hands, we're moving to the airport." To Palmer, he said, "James, bring 'em out." To the agents out front, he yelled, "Get the car doors and one trunk open."

The drivers of the two middle cars sprang into action opening the car doors. One of them popped the trunk.

Palmer shoved the Russian out the front door and directly across the street to the two waiting cars. Andrews, pistol drawn, covered them as they moved. Palmer literally rammed the man headlong into the trunk. He pulled off the Russian's belt, hog tied the man's legs together, and slammed the lid. He jumped into the back seat.

Andrews hopped into the lead vehicle, and the drivers started their cars. Mike stood next to the front sedan waiting for Barrington. They were the last two men on the street.

Barrington walked toward Mike. Suddenly, Mike saw movement behind Barrington and shouted a warning. A round hit Barrington in the back slamming his body armor and knocking him sprawling face-first onto the pavement.

Mike raised his gun to engage the new attacker who had just stepped out from behind a car and shot Barrington. But before Mike could pull the trigger, Barrington flipped over onto his back and fired both pistols, shooting between his feet—*boom, boom, boom*—alternating back and forth between the two guns in rapid succession. It sounded like automatic weapons fire.

The gunman went down, screaming, wounded in both legs. In an instant, Barrington was up and closing on him. On the run, he holstered his left-hand pistol, dropped the magazine from the other, and rammed in a fresh load. He approached the attacker, weapon at the ready. The man was bleeding badly as he writhed in pain on the pavement.

The two agents from the lead car jumped out, guns drawn. They ran to Barrington. One of the agents kicked the man's gun away. As the attacker grimaced in pain, they rolled him over and bound him with flex cuffs. One of the agents ran back to the car and popped the trunk.

Barrington and the other agent dragged the downed man to the car. The three of them hefted him up and into the trunk. Barrington checked him for weapons and removed a knife and another pistol. He pulled two field-dressing packs from his left leg cargo pocket, ripped them open, and tied them tightly around the wounds on each of the man's legs. He moaned loudly as Barrington did so. He pulled a syringe from a pouch on his belt and jabbed it into the man's leg.

They slammed the trunk. Tapping on the car's top, Barrington yelled at the two agents. "Move out. Airport."

Over the radio he said, "Palmer, go." Palmer's driver peeled out and sped past Barrington following the lead car. The third sedan sped past. Andrews' car pulled up next to Barrington, and he leapt into the front seat. The car took off behind the other three vehicles.

The small convoy raced north on Neheme Yafet. They crossed over Baal Bak and continued straight. In the back seat, Mike watched to the rear for any further threat behind them.

Barrington said over the radio, "Left on Hamra, at normal speed. Merge onto General De Gaulle south. Airport everyone. Tight formation and stay alert."

The other three drivers responded in turn, "Roger."

Andrews dialed Striker. "How many attackers?" he asked Barrington while waiting for the connection.

"Six."

"Spetsnaz?"

"I would bet on it."

Striker answered, "Striker here."

"Andrews here, we were hit. Spetsnaz, six of them. We lost four men, one wounded but alive. We have the Russian and one of the attackers, also wounded."

"I'll alert the med team," said Striker. "The plane will touchdown in nine minutes. Doug, I'm sorry about the casualties. This second Russian, though, is a huge bonus. He may have actually been on the nuke heist. He could be a goldmine."

"By the way," said Andrews, "we would not be having this conversation right now if not for Scott and Mike. The two of them killed all five Spetsnaz and captured the sixth."

"I'm glad they were there. Okay, check in when you are back in the embassy. I'll get you some replacements as fast as I can. Anything else?"

"Negative, out," said Andrews, disconnecting.

Barrington twisted around and said to Mike, "You know, Mike, it's not going to take long for the Lebanese to figure out the guys we left back there are Russian. They'll notify the Russian embassy who'll quickly figure out that somebody snatched two of their soldiers. So watch your ass in Istanbul. Russian intelligence will be everywhere."

Mike nodded and looked back out the window. It had already been a long day.

7

Poti, Georgia

Forty-eight hours after his first meeting with Meskhi, Behdin Khorasani had just landed back in Poti. With his plan to sell one of the bombs and pocket the money now in motion, he was on his way to see Meskhi to finalize the deal. He arrived at the compound and was escorted into Meskhi's office.

"I have approval for this acquisition. My country will meet your price of two hundred and fifty million. I am prepared to transfer fifty million in down payment immediately, but I need to take possession of one device in return."

Meskhi considered whether he should release one of the nukes for only the down payment. Then he realized that the first Iranian payment would completely cover his initial investment. Everything else would be profit.

"Okay," replied Meskhi.

Khorasani pulled out a smart phone and took a seat in front of Meskhi's desk. He tapped out an encrypted message to his Quds Force commander. Meskhi sat down behind his desk. He opened an app on his laptop computer, logged in, and watched the numbers on his account.

The two men sat patiently, waiting. Within ten minutes, Meskhi saw the numbers on his account change. The money had transferred. He smiled and closed the computer, leaning back in his chair. "When will you take the first device, and what is your plan for the remaining four?" he asked.

"This is what we have decided to do. We want to move the first one to Venezuela to a research facility we have there," he lied. "When that is accomplished, I will have a small convoy of vehicles come from Iran to pick up the remaining four and transport them back to my country."

"The four will be moved upon full payment," interjected Meskhi.

"Of course," answered Khorasani, "but first we need your assistance to move the one device to South America. I know that your Lear jet has special capabilities and highly skilled Russian pilots. We would like to fly it there on your jet."

Meskhi frowned.

"I assure you, it will be untraceable to you, or to me for that matter. Your plane will land on a remote, cartel-controlled airstrip. It will unload, refuel, and immediately takeoff for its return leg. There will be no record of the aircraft ever having been in Venezuela. My country has shown good faith by paying fifty million up front. We ask you to do the same by assisting with transport."

Meskhi considered this for a moment. "For such a long trip, the airplane would need to refuel in the Cape Verde islands. But I see no problem, as long as you can assure that there will be no record of the flight. I do not want any trail back to me."

"I can assure you without reservation."

"And, you will pay for the trip," he demanded.

"Agreed," said Khorasani.

"I will release one nuclear device and its codes on a PDA as a show of good faith."

"Excellent, thank you, Genadi. I will need to bring two men to Poti to see the one device."

"Okay, when?"

"As soon as possible. Tomorrow if I can arrange it."

"When will you make final payment and move the remaining four? I want to wrap this up and get them off my hands."

"Before one week."

Meskhi nodded.

~

Georgetown, Washington, D.C.

At the back booth of a small, out-of-the-way Italian restaurant, Gerald Billings took a seat opposite the Arab. At least he thought the man to be Arab, but he couldn't be sure. The man spoke perfect

English. Gerald tried to control his shaking. It occurred to him that he didn't even know to what foreign government he had sold out his country.

"You promised me months ago," Gerald said in a strained and trembling voice, "that you were just going to watch the agents I gave you. Now two of them are dead. I can't do this anymore," he whimpered, shaking his head. He could feel his eyes tearing up and his pulse racing.

The Arab said slowly and with meticulous diction, "Gerald, it is *far* too late for that. You are in *much* too deep, and the fellow I use to take care of things for me, is a *very* bad and *very* efficient man. He learned his killing skills in the African jungle, and I assure you that you do not want to meet him. You would just wake up one night, and he would be standing by your bed looking down on you.

"Or, perhaps, evidence of your treachery could mysteriously show up at the Washington Post. You would spend the rest of your life in prison being sodomized by whatever gang owned you that particular week. And, of course, *I* would just disappear. I'll have to decide which option I would enjoy most."

Billings couldn't be sure if he was about to vomit or not. He swallowed hard. The smell of the pasta primavera on the table in front of the Arab was almost overwhelming.

"Gerald, I need the next location of the new agent. The one who went to Beirut. Find out where he is."

The Arab smiled warmly. "Just relax, Gerald. Everything will be fine. I will continue to pay you, you will remain a free man, grow wealthy, and continue breathing. The world will move on nicely."

He got up and dropped two twenties on the table. "Remember, I want his next location." He donned his fedora, and started to walk out.

"Wait," Gerald uttered.

The Arab sat back down but didn't remove his hat.

"He's on his way to Istanbul. Marriott East."

"He?"

"Elliot."

"Well now, see how easy that was," he replied in a friendly voice. "Who is he meeting there?"

"He's trying to pick up the trail the last agent was following."

Mohsen's tone stiffened. "Don't hold out on me again, Gerald." He stood and walked out.

Gerald Billings dropped his face to his hands. *What have I gotten myself into?*

In eighteen months, his next routine agency polygraph would come due. With the extra money he was making, he had planned to retire before that date. His intention was to acquire a million and retire, thoroughly enjoying every cent of his ill-gotten gains from an ungrateful agency that had failed to recognize his worth.

Could he still retire? If he remained at the agency, he would eventually be discovered by CIA internal security. If he tried to retire, the Arab might have him killed. His stomach churned with acid. He chewed the last antacid in the roll he had just bought an hour before.

~

Istanbul, Turkey, 4:30 p.m.

Mike's plane touched down at the Ataturk International Airport. He felt drained. Just a few hours earlier, his team had been in a gunfight that would have rivaled the O.K. Corral.

At Incirlik Air Base, before departing for Istanbul, Mike had showered, put on new clothes, and eaten a meal. A CIA car dropped him at a hotel in nearby Adana. He took a cab from the hotel to Adana International Airport. His weapons remained with Barrington at the air base, and even though new ones would be waiting in Istanbul, he was now undercover and strictly on his own. He was traveling as Steve Holt.

What would turn up in Istanbul was uncertain. Max had booked a room at the downtown Marriott East. He was also setting up a meeting with an Israeli agent from Mossad. Israel was even more terrified of the missing nukes than America. He would also try to meet with an underworld connection on the CIA payroll, an associate of the murdered informant. No one knew for sure, but maybe Ingrid Holman and Ronald Nelson were onto something big enough to get them killed. Mike would try to find out what that was and if it was related to Genadi Meskhi.

Would any of it pan out? Or would it just lead to more trouble? No way to know.

His arrival in Istanbul was uneventful. Mike didn't detect any airport surveillance directed specifically at him, only the normal airport cameras and roving police patrols. He caught a cab at the airport and gave the driver an address that was six blocks away from the Marriott.

He walked a meandering route from the drop off point toward the hotel, carefully observing for any surveillance. He entered a bookshop and flipped through old books, keeping an eye on the street through the window.

Mike walked another block and approached Istikal Avenue. The street was wide, and he timed his movement with a large group of tourists also crossing. They walked over twin pairs of tram rails running down the center of the road. Crowds of people filled the sidewalk cafés, tony restaurants, and expensive department stores.

As he approached the far side of the avenue, Mike froze. He saw his wife, Lynn, walking away from him on the sidewalk to his left—same size, same hair, same walk. For an instant he truly believed it was her. He shook his head and quickly resumed walking. He chided himself. He needed to focus. This kind of weakness would get him killed for sure.

He was soon back on side streets and better able to monitor his surroundings. He made his way to the Marriott but continued past. At an intersection thirty yards farther up the street, two sidewalk cafés sat on opposite corners with entrances on both streets. He crossed over and took a seat at the café across from the hotel.

He had a coffee and read the paper for thirty minutes, studying the street and hotel entrance for anything unusual. If *any* information about the Beirut operation got out, Russian intelligence would be looking for him. Mike had just snatched two of their men. Plus, someone, possibly with inside information, was killing experienced CIA agents. He wasn't taking any chances and was conducting careful counter surveillance. His life depended on it.

He paid for his coffee and walked across the street to the hotel, checked in, and went up to his room. In an hour or so, he would conduct another sweep.

His room safe held the items Max had promised—a silenced, compact Ruger LC9 9mm auto with two loaded spare magazines, each holding seven rounds; a multi-tool pocketknife; a portable door alarm; a master key card for the hotel; and a packet of wooden shims. Carpenters used the wooden wedges in construction, but they had other clever uses as well. He tossed the packet onto the credenza next to his weapons.

He went to the window and nudged the curtain back slightly, just enough to see out, yet not enough to alert anyone watching the window from another building. The room was on the tenth floor, and the Bosporus stretched out below.

Istanbul sat on a peninsula jutting out into the Bosporus Straight, a narrow waterway that linked the Sea of Marmara to the south, with the Black Sea to the north. Dozens of ferries crisscrossed the dark water, while armadas of commercial vessels sailed both north and south over the channel that linked the two seas.

He carefully scanned the adjacent skyscrapers for signs of an observer but didn't detect anything unusual. He checked the sliding glass door to the balcony. It was screwed shut. Probably just a precaution by the hotel to prevent jumpers or accidents, but Mike wondered. He would remove the screws later. Satisfied that his room was secure, he stripped down to his boxer shorts.

He spread a towel out on the carpet and did some stretches. His muscles were tight. Then he knocked out his usual push-ups, sit-ups, and martial arts practice. He had worked up a sweat but had also worked off some tension.

He picked up the multi-tool, opened the screwdriver bit, and got down on the floor. Without disturbing the curtain, he removed all but one screw securing the sliding glass door. The balcony was small, but it had a metal railing that an intruder could climb. In an emergency, he could remove the last screw, but in the meantime, it would slow down someone trying to enter from the outside.

At 6:15 p.m., Mike showered and dressed. He wanted another look around the hotel. He slipped on his holster and pistol, grabbed his phone, room key, wallet, and passport, and walked out into the hall. Each end of the hall had stairs. He checked out both stairwells, verifying where they led and then exited the second one.

He walked through a long, wide corridor past some conference rooms and into the sprawling lobby of the hotel. Grabbing a bottle of water and a newspaper from a side bar, he found a seat in an easy chair with good visibility of the lobby and front doors. After watching the lobby for twenty minutes, he walked to the front entrance and stood in a concealed position to the side of a floor-to-ceiling window with good visibility of the street.

The activity in the hotel's pull-through drive, the street traffic, and the pedestrians on the sidewalks all appeared routine. He could also see the café across the street, with its rows of tables and chairs aligned along the sidewalk where he had stopped earlier. Nothing out of the ordinary.

He picked up a couple of sandwiches from a lobby café and returned to his room. He placed the alarm on the inside door handle and tested it. If someone jiggled the handle, it would ring. He ate, read a while longer, and then turned in for the night. Sleep was much needed.

~

Istanbul

Chinwe Okeke sat quietly in a dingy, sixth-floor hotel room situated in a dilapidated and dangerous part of north Istanbul. The earthy scent of musty carpet reminded him of rotting vegetation thick on the jungle floor. He focused on his breath, the rich ebony of his bare chest rising and falling in rhythm with his breathing.

The uninitiated would say that he was meditating, but Okeke would disagree. He was once again ten years old, asking the animal spirits to fill him with strength and courage as he prepared to go into the African bush with only a spear and a knife.

He was known by many names. In Nigeria, his tribe called him the Lion Slayer. In Holland, in his teens, the other students called him Chin. Today, professionally, he was called the Nigerian, but only by one man.

The Iranian, Sadegh Mohsen, had spotted young Chinwe in Europe when he was twenty-three and struggling to find his identity amongst the Westerners surrounding him. Mohsen saw potential in the young African and took him under his wing.

Chinwe had eventually recounted to the Iranian the story of his youth and his eventual revenge on his father's killers. Mohsen assessed, correctly, that the young man had the potential for special work, and he groomed him to become an assassin. He assigned him a code name—the Nigerian—and took him to Iran for training.

Chinwe Okeke was a natural and far surpassed Mohsen's highest expectations. His work gave him purpose. Of course talk of a shadowy assassin called the Nigerian eventually got out, but no one knew who this legendary and deadly killer really was. Those who had encountered him directly, where no longer around to talk about it.

Okeke settled into his trance. He took in a deep breath and focused on the images of his older brother and his beloved father. When Okeke was nine, he followed his father and the tribal elders through the jungle to the savannah. His thirteen-year-old brother led the elders. He wore a loincloth of soft hide and carried a spear and a knife, both of his own making. The older brother was facing the sacred test of manhood—he would kill a lion, alone.

Okeke hid and watched as his dear brother marched bravely to his death. He would not be a man that day, or any other. A year later, poachers shot to death Okeke's father. Ten-year-old Chinwe was with his father at the time of his murder. The leader of the poacher gang shooed the boy along. "Go home," the man ordered harshly.

Okeke did so.

The next day, he donned his brother's beaded headband and smeared colorful dyes made from berries in stripes on his face and chest. He picked up his brother's spear and knife and walked through the village. Several elders observed him and followed at a distance.

He killed the male lion that had mauled his brother to death. When the lion charged at Okeke, he calmly held his ground. He planted the butt of his spear into the soft dirt, the stone tip tilted toward the bounding lion. The beast impaled itself on the spear in its haste to have the brash young intruder for a meal.

Chinwe became a man that day. In the evening, around a large fire, the tribe danced feverishly and chanted ancient songs of bravery. He sat on a stool facing the fire, and the chief slowly cut three, one-inch lines under each of his fierce dark eyes. Chinwe did not flinch at the biting blade. He was now a warrior. The cuts would heal and become permanent scars. They were the tribal symbols of bravery and manhood. The chief presented the young warrior with an ear cut from the dead lion.

It was at this time, that his mother's sister, who had immigrated to Europe as a child with other relatives many years earlier, insisted that his mother and he join her in Holland. They did, and he eventually became a Dutch citizen. He had already learned English in the Catholic school in Nigeria. He learned Dutch and German next, and he excelled in his studies and in sports. He was especially talented in martial arts and even became his team's captain.

He trained and worked hard and grew to be a large man. He had a powerful build, enormous strength, and great agility. He was proud that his skin was markedly dark. He considered his skin tone to be born of the blackest night of the darkest jungle. It was his heritage. He wore a short black beard and close-cropped black hair. His tribal scars blended with his complexion and were not prominent at a distance. Face-to-face, however, they were unmistakable.

At twenty years old, he had returned to Nigeria and hunted down the seven poachers who had killed his father. He tracked them for days, and then one night, very late, as the men slept in their encampment near the glowing embers of a dying fire, he quietly slipped into their camp. One by one, he cut their throats. Except for the leader. He was saved for last. Okeke wanted to look into the man's terrified eyes before he killed him. He wanted the man to know *who* was about to kill him.

He dragged the begging, crying man to the fire pit and shoved his face into the red and yellow embers. Despite the pain from the heat on Okeke's bare sole, he held his foot on the back of the man's head until he stopped flailing and lay still.

Okeke's buzzing cell phone interrupted his reverie. He picked up the device and looked at the screen. It would be from Sadegh Mohsen. The message read: *Mike Elliot, Istanbul Marriott East. A* photo of Mike Elliot accompanied the message. Additional instructions followed: *acquire target, observe; Russians tipped off and should eliminate target; if not you may do so.*

The Nigerian studied the picture. The man in the image appeared lean and fit. He also had intense blue eyes. Okeke would be cautious with this one, but tomorrow they would meet.

~

Poti, Georgia

Behdin Khorasani anxiously checked his phone. He waited for a reply from the Al-Qaeda chief in Iraq, Hamadi Hassan. He was using the encryption app and code number provided by the Sheikh's man in Pakistan. If this didn't work, he would be back to square one.

Khorasani's phone vibrated, and he snatched it up from the table. The app showed one message. He quickly opened it.

In English, the message read: *The great leader has instructed me to meet with you to conclude transfer of a special gift. HH*

Khorasani smiled and tapped out a reply: *Can you travel to Georgia?*

Yes, came the reply.

Khorasani: *Poti, Georgia, tomorrow?*

Hassan: *Yes, in Turkey now. Travel tomorrow a.m.*

Khorasani: *Message when you will arrive airport. Will arrange pick up. Driver will have a sign for Mr. Mamud.*

Hassan: *There will be two of us. What will the driver ask me?*

Khorasani: *Where can I buy some oranges?*

Hassan: *Will answer: They are on sale today.*

Khorasani: *Agreed.*

The Iranian leaned back in his chair and sighed. "This will work," he said to no one. "This will work."

~

Istanbul, 7:15 a.m.

Chinwe Okeke placed his belt and daggers on the bed. He considered firearms to be evil and only for the weak of heart. He had a lion's heart, and preferred to use his hands. On the belt was a double, black leather sheath, holding two daggers with eight-inch, razor sharp, serrated blades. The handgrips were fashioned from rare, polished rosewood. The weapons were identical in every way—particularly in weight and balance.

The double sheath was one flat piece—one dagger on top with the grip to the left, one dagger on bottom with the grip to the right. He wore it at his waist in the small of his back. He inspected one of the blades, turning it over in his hand. The quality was exquisite. A knife maker in Nairobi, Kenya had fabricated this pair for him. The two weapons were befitting a Nigerian warrior.

He donned the belt and adjusted the sheath, checking the reach and feel. He pulled on an expensive, black silk, button-up shirt with a straight, untucked hem. He wore black pants and black shoes with rubber soles. Okeke left the room and walked the dark hall to a filthy stairwell. He made his way to the ground floor, encountering no other hotel guests on the way out.

He walked out onto the sidewalk and turned right. The street of worn and chipped red brick was narrow. Scattered trash lay strewn about. Two emaciated dogs, their snouts covered in mange, raced past him up the street as if they had somewhere to be.

He turned left into a narrow alley. He would walk in random directions for a while to ensure that no one followed him. He crossed a street and continued into another alley.

Above his head, clotheslines ran between the buildings. Clothes, sheets, and towels of all types and colors, flapped and popped in the breeze at various heights above, producing a somewhat melodious refrain. The warming aroma of baking bread floated on the air.

He sensed that someone was behind him. He continued straight ahead but casually glimpsed about, like someone admiring the ancient architecture. Two large Turkish men followed him. They were not professionals. He knew that they were simple thugs out to rob him. Then they would get drunk on the takings. He briefly wondered how these drunkards were up and about so early.

He let them close on him. They called for him to stop in Turkish. He continued to walk. Then one of them yelled in English, "Stop, mister."

The Nigerian turned, and pointing to himself, asked, "Me?"

The two men walked up to Okeke. One of them had a short, heavy piece of lead pipe in his left hand. He slapped it against the palm of his other hand. Among other foul odors, Okeke could smell the man's sour breath.

"Give us your money, your watch, and your phone, now. Or I'll bash your fucking head in."

The Nigerian looked about to ensure that no one was watching. He made a move so fast it was difficult to follow. Then he stood there in front of the two Turks, a long dagger hanging by his side in his right hand. Blood dripped from the blade.

The Turk with the pipe dropped it, and it clanged noisily to the concrete at his feet. The man's eyes were wide. He didn't actually know what had happened, but frothy pink bubbles oozed in and out of his neck as he tried to take his last few breaths before collapsing to the ground.

The second Turk recovered, turned, and dashed away up the alley. The Nigerian drew his arm back over his head, and with great force launched the dagger. The blade entered the fleeing Turk's back with such energy that it knocked the man forward. He went sprawling onto the concrete, face-first, his heart pierced.

The Nigerian walked the twenty feet to the dead Turk and extracted the dagger. He carefully wiped the blade clean on the Turk's clothing and then replaced it in its sheath. He scanned the area around and above. He was alone. He continued on his way.

Soon, the Nigerian cautiously approached the Istanbul Marriott East on foot. Still a hundred yards down the street, he leaned against the wall of a building and observed. As was his habit, he would reposition every twenty to thirty minutes. After twenty-five minutes, he walked up the street and took a seat at a café across from the hotel. He sat in the back row of small café tables arrayed on the sidewalk in front of the café. He would continue to move regularly.

He ordered a double espresso and a newspaper as he casually scanned his surroundings for any sign of surveillance, and for his assignment.

~

Ankara, Turkey

Thirty-two-year-old Hamadi Hassan was the operational chief for Al-Qaeda in Iraq. Yousef Amad, age forty-six, was his chief engineer and bomb maker. They had traveled to Ankara, via an unsecured crossing over the Turkish border with Iraq, in anticipation of the meeting with the Saudi man.

Both men were British citizens and had British passports with entry stamps into Turkey, arriving from London a month prior. The two men wore casual business attire, and their beards and hair were neatly trimmed.

They were well-educated men. Hamadi Hassan had an honors degree in business from the University of Birmingham. Yousef Amad had an advanced degree in chemical engineering from the University of Bristol. They appeared to be British businessmen of Middle Eastern descent.

They boarded their flight from Ankara to Poti, and an hour and twenty minutes later, they landed in Poti, Georgia. They quickly spotted the sign for Mr. Mamud held by their driver. They exchanged codes in English and then followed the driver outside to one of Meskhi's black sedans. Khorasani waited beside the car.

As the men approached, Khorasani said in English, "Welcome, I am the Saudi Arabian. We will go now and have a look at what you have come for." He gestured to the open rear door of the vehicle.

Hamadi Hassan nodded. He and Yousef Amad climbed into the back of the car. Khorasani closed the rear door and got into the front passenger seat. They drove to the Poti port complex in the harbor, winding through various turns and side roads. Tall cargo cranes lined the harbor's waterfront like a thick forest of metal arms reaching for the sky.

They finally arrived at a small concrete building tucked away behind several large warehouses. Along with three of his men, Genadi Meskhi got out of his sedan in front of the building. More men wandered about the outside of the building on security patrols.

Without speaking, Meskhi and his top lieutenant entered the building, followed by Khorasani and the two British Arabs. The lieutenant closed the door behind them.

In the center of the large room, on the concrete floor, was a single object about the size of a small trash bin. A musty, old canvas tarp covered the object.

Meskhi nodded to his lieutenant who pulled back the tarp.

Khorasani said, "This, gentlemen, is a Russian military RA-115, man-portable, two kiloton nuclear device, complete with activation codes."

Both Arabs were stupefied, but Yousef Amad looked as if he might be in shock.

"It is beautiful," muttered Hamadi Hassan under his breath.

Yousef Amad, the engineer, walked to it and stroked the device as if it were a pet. He ran his hand around the contours of the weapon, taking in every detail.

"How are the codes maintained?" Amad asked Khorasani.

"On an electronic PDA. There is an activation code and a deactivation code."

Amad turned back to the bomb and extracted from his pocket a small device that resembled a battery-powered portable radio. He took out a coiled white wire that had a jack on one end and a small tube-like device on the other.

He plugged the jack into the radio, and with what appeared to be a small microphone, he scanned over and around the nuclear bomb while watching a digital gauge on the device in his hand. He frowned. His small radiological detector registered nothing.

Amad said to Hamadi Hassan in Arabic, "I thought it would have at least *some* radiological signature. There is nothing. It is either a fake," he said, pausing and looking back at the bomb, "or it was manufactured with great precision and highly advanced technology. I believe it is the latter."

Yousef Amad nodded his approval to Hamadi Hassan.

Khorasani was frowning, but his scowl quickly morphed into a broad grin.

"Is there a problem?" asked Meskhi in English.

"None whatsoever," replied Khorasani.

Hassan said to Khorasani, "Shall we make final arrangements?"

The three men left together in the black sedan headed back to the airport.

Hassan said to Khorasani, "I am authorized to approve the first payment of fifteen million."

He handed Khorasani a slip of paper. On it was a ten-digit and a twelve-digit number.

"Please confirm that this is where you want the money deposited."

Khorasani knew the numbers intimately. It was his personal Swiss account.

"Yes, I confirm."

"The money will be deposited within two hours. And you are prepared to deliver the weapon, and the codes, to Venezuela?"

"I am," said Khorasani, pulling a folded piece of paper from his shirt pocket and handing it over the seat to Hassan. "This contains the contact information for the man who will facilitate our transfer on the ground there. I have already paid for his services. He will take you to the airfield where I will deliver it.

"Get a room in Caracas and then notify this man by text. He speaks English. When the time is right, he will take you to meet my plane and provide a truck. Neither he, nor his organization, will know what the item is."

"I am informed," said Hassan, "that you know of a man who can move it to New York."

"Yes, he is Jamaican." Khorasani handed him a second slip of paper. "This is how you contact him using secure messaging. Be prepared to meet his price, he does not haggle, but he will succeed for you. He is a specialist in this type of movement. You will need to meet him in person in Kingston and pay him up front to finalize your transaction with him."

"Can he be trusted?"

"Hardly, but he has a reputation to maintain."

The car arrived at the Poti airport. The two men had a return flight to Ankara in one hour's time. Then it would be on to Jamaica and Venezuela.

8

Istanbul, 8:10 a.m.

Mike went down the stairs and repeated his previous sweep of the hotel. He observed the lobby, but saw nothing unusual. Then he watched through the front windows at the street and the café opposite the hotel.

One man caught his attention, if for no other reason than just his size. He could have been a pro football player. He was very dark skinned, and he wore all black. Mike remembered the last time he had fought a man that size. It was Abu Hassim, a hijacker, and he had come very close to killing Mike in two separate fights.

Something else about this man caught Mike's attention. He looked up over his paper from time to time toward the hotel. The move was very casual, and it was probably nothing, but it made a hair or two stand up on the back of Mike's neck.

Mike walked through the lobby toward the stairwell he had just come from. He went down one level to the parking garage and then out to a side street. He took an alley to the left and headed north.

~

Okeke checked his watch. He had been at this café for twenty-five minutes. Long enough. On the job, he never remained still. He paid for his coffee and wandered up the street a short distance, pausing occasionally in front of a store window to observe any movement behind him. He concluded that he was not being watched.

He crossed the street and came back down the same side of the road as the Marriott. He stopped at the café on the corner across the street from where he had just been sitting. He went inside and took a seat in a dimly lit corner, where his back was covered, but he could see out of the window. He watched the street and the café opposite him.

~

Mike turned left again, walked two more blocks, and came out at the café where the dark man had been sitting. Mike was around the corner of the café, behind him.

He entered the café and should have been behind the man who had been observing the Marriott. Mike had intended to follow him, but the man was not there. Mike took a seat at the café bar, and while checking his back in the mirror behind the bar, he ordered coffee and eggs.

~

The Nigerian, watching from across the street, was astonished to see the man in the photo—the target—approach the café where he had just been sitting a few moments earlier. The man was approaching from behind, unexpectedly, stealthily, like a lion.

The Nigerian's heart raced. This was an amazing development. Had the man been watching from the hotel lobby, or a window above? Had he seen him? Or was it just coincidence?

No, he saw me sitting there and suspected something, and he went forth on the hunt to check it out. Magnificent! A man who can smell a predator. A man who actually dares to turn things about and try to track me.

Yes! he thought. *He is a lion! This kill will be most gratifying.* The Nigerian pulled from his pocket the lion's ear that he always carried and rubbed it. *There are now added complications*, he thought. *He has seen me, and he is most likely armed. But, so was the lion when I was ten.*

He considered Sadegh Mohsen's instructions. If the Russians showed up, he was supposed to let them take the target. Well, he had seen no Russians, so as far as he was concerned, this kill was his.

The Nigerian stood and exited the café by a door around the corner, not visible from where Mike sat. He circled the block, ending up at the entrance to the Marriott. He entered. Inside, he peered through the big glass front windows. He concluded that the target had not seen him move, and that this was the spot where he had stood to observe Okeke.

Okeke picked up a newspaper and sat in one of the chairs closest to the elevators. He had good visibility of the hotel's front doors. He decided, almost gleefully, that he would kill the man now, either in the elevator, or the stairwell, whichever direction the man chose to take. If he slipped into the hotel by another way, Okeke knew the man would eventually come back down to this lobby to scan the streets again through the front window, as he did before.

If he returned through the lobby now, when he entered the elevator, Okeke would step in just as the doors were closing. Once locked inside like a cage of death, it would be the two of them. Predator upon predator. They would fight to the death. One would be victorious. If other guests happened to be in the elevator as well, it would be unfortunate for them.

He had not felt this much primal energy in many years.

He held the newspaper where he could carefully watch the entrance, yet his face and upper body were concealed. That's when he noticed two men enter the lobby through the front entrance. They wore long coats, as if it might be raining and cold outside. It was not, and this attire was not normal. He knew they had automatic weapons concealed under those coats.

The men split up and wandered about the lobby as if they were bank robbers casing a heist. As they came together briefly near him, he heard them speak to one another in Russian. They eventually got newspapers, took seats, and continued to scan the lobby.

~

From the café, Mike watched the street for thirty more minutes but did not see the man again. He was letting his imagination get the better of him, he decided. The man was just having coffee before going to work. He hoped.

Mike retreated the way he had come, back through the alleys and into the parking garage of the hotel. He went up the opposite stairwell of the one he had come down before. In his room, he stripped down to his boxers again and sat on the bed. For now, he needed to think. After his breakfast settled, he wanted another workout.

~

The Nigerian continued watching the lobby. Three more men entered the hotel, almost identical in dress and mannerism to the first two. Those two rose and went to the newly arrived men. They conferred briefly, and then one of them left the group and walked away toward the rear of the hotel.

The Nigerian had to assume that these Russians were here for *his* target. That disappointed him, but he could not risk his own safety to find out. This looked like trouble about to happen, and he did not want to be here, not registered as a guest, when Turkish authorities arrived and locked down the building. It would invite too much scrutiny. Besides, it was what Mohsen wanted him to do.

He got up, and folding his paper on the move, walked out of the hotel, turned left, and continued down the street. *If my lion survives, which I will bet that he does, our meeting will take place at some future time and location*, he thought.

He tapped out a message to Mohsen on his phone: *Russians are here, withdrawing.*

~

8:45 a.m.

Mike sat on his bed thinking about the scant clues they had managed to piece together. He sipped on soda water from the room's minibar.

His phone lay on the bed next to him. Only two people knew the number—Max and Striker. At least that's what he was told. The phone disguised its location through some algorithm Mike didn't quite understand when they explained it to him. Messages vanished after reading them. Useful features when operating alone in hostile territory.

Mike turned over in his mind what little they knew, or speculated. The Russian had said that the nukes were being moved through Turkey—unconfirmed. Local Turkish assets and CIA operatives had turned up nothing. The CIA could not be sure who had stolen the suitcase nukes, but many within the agency felt it had to be Vladimir Grigor. He probably had access to the codes in Moscow. Without them, the devices were worthless junk.

Max was busy working the assets the CIA had in place in Turkey. Mike would soon meet with an Israeli agent, and later in the day, hopefully, with a mafia contact. Maybe one of them could provide a tip on Nelson's killer. Otherwise, he would sit tight for a day or two until they shook loose a lead—if they ever did. He was also prepared to hop to another location if something developed elsewhere.

Mike's phone vibrated. He picked it up and scanned the text message: *Attack team, 5 men, in lobby.*

Shit, thought Mike, *off to a great start in Istanbul.*

Mike started the stopwatch on his wristwatch. The seconds began ticking. He knew he probably had no more than two minutes. The watch was silent, but in his mind, he definitely heard: *Tick-Tock, Tick-Tock.*

While taking stock of the situation, he was already up and moving. As he dressed, thoughts flowed through his mind in a rapid, well trained, and orderly manner:

How was my cover blown? Was it the man at the café? What nationality? I need to find out. My weapons were procured and placed by a Turkish asset on the CIA payroll who is supposed to be reliable. So how was I discovered?

Assumption, they know my hotel, so they probably know my room number. My identity is certainly blown. There will be someone covering the rear of the hotel, and there will be a sniper in an adjacent building covering my balcony. Three or four men will be coming up the stairs and/or elevator.

By now, Mike had dressed. He had his passport, phone, and room key—which according to Max, was a master key. He had his weapons.

He checked his watch—a little more than a minute remaining. *Tick-Tock, Tick-Tock.*

Possible courses of action raced through his mind.

He considered engaging the attackers as the elevator doors opened, but he wouldn't know how many men he was facing until the doors actually opened. With a round in the chamber, the Ruger held eight rounds. If one of the men was concealed by the edge of the elevator wall, Mike could end up having to change magazines. One of them might get lucky before he could eliminate them all.

He decided to go down the stairs to a lower floor, hopefully before they could get a man into position in the stairwell on the tenth, where he was now.

He glanced at his watch: *Forty-five seconds.*

Another text arrived: *Three men entering elevator now.*

Mike grabbed the packet of shims, flipped open the blade of his knife and slit the packet open. He jammed a handful of shims into his side leg pocket, keeping six of them in his hand. He opened the door to his room and glanced in both directions. As he slipped into the hall, he hung the DO NOT DISTURB sign on the doorknob. He turned left toward the elevators and the closer stairwell.

His silenced Ruger, secure in a waistband clip holster and concealed by his shirt, pressed against his back. He walked rapidly to the three elevators. He could hear the cables whirring. He jammed a wooden shim into the cracks along the outside edge of each elevator door—six in all.

He felt his phone vibrate again. He checked it while on the move: *Come to 817.*

Mike pulled his pistol as he cautiously entered the stairwell, pausing to listen. He carefully leaned over the railing to peek up and down the stairwell. He heard footsteps four or five floors below. Pistol leading, he quietly bounded downward toward the eighth floor.

Holding his pistol behind his back, he entered the eighth floor hallway and made his way toward 817. As he approached, he could see a petite young Asian woman leaning slightly out of a doorway looking back and forth in both directions of the hall. Her hair was long, black, and shiny, and it swayed slightly as her head changed directions. She gestured for him to hurry.

Mike entered as she backed inside and closed the door. Keeping an eye on her, Mike moved into the room, pistol raised.

He cleared the suite. Satisfied they were alone, he returned to her, pistol by his side.

Mike had to check his emotions. She reminded him of Lynn—slim, pretty, dark eyes. Mike didn't want to go there and quickly shut down all thoughts of Lynn and of this young woman as anything other than an asset to help him get out of this situation and back on the hunt. He also had to suppress his natural instinct to protect the so-called weaker sex. Assuming this woman was the weaker one might prove unwise.

"Who are you?" he asked.

"Mya Ling. I texted you."

"Who do you work for?"

"Istanbul chief of station, but I was assigned to Max for this op."

"How did you know they were here, and who are they?"

"Our man on the hotel staff informed me, and I let you know. As for *who* they are, I don't know," she said with a slight shrug.

"Best guess?"

"Iranians or Russians. Iran has the most to gain in getting the devices. Even if they develop a bomb, it would be fifteen years before they could design and build a man-portable device. Russia wants them back because this is a huge embarrassment for them."

"Could these guys be Turks or Israelis?"

"Anything's possible, but I doubt it."

"Okay, I need to find out who they are."

"You should stay here," she said.

"And if your guy downstairs is playing both sides, which I'm betting he is, the attack team will be here shortly and we'll be trapped."

"He's not."

"How else would they know I'm here? I'm not taking any chances. We're changing rooms. Would he know if I use this key? He placed it in my room safe for me."

"I placed everything in the safe. And no, he wouldn't know. The hotel security software is not that sophisticated. I hacked it and checked."

"Smart girl."

"I like to think so."

"Do you have anything in the room?"

"One bag," she said, hurrying toward the bed. She scooped up a small backpack, slipped it on, and came back to Mike. He was already peeking out the door.

"Let's go."

They moved down the hall, past several rooms. Mike picked a room at random. He inserted the key and opened the door slightly, peeking inside. It seemed empty. He called out and got no response. They slipped in and locked the door. Mike cleared the room and then peeked cautiously out the edge of the curtain.

A tiny glint of light sparkled from the corner of a curtained window in the opposite building—a reflection from the lens of a scope. *There's my sniper*, he thought. He made a mental note of the floor and how many windows over to the location, in case he needed to go there.

Without disturbing the curtain, he checked the glass door; it was not screwed shut.

"The glass door in my room was screwed closed. The room was set up to be a trap."

Mya raised her eyebrows in surprise.

"They are here to capture me. They want info. And they certainly know my room number. How would they have gotten that, and how would the glass door have gotten screwed shut, except for your man in the hotel?"

"Why would he set you up and then warn us?"

"They paid him. Now he would also like to stay on the CIA payroll," said Mike. "Stay here. I'm going to find out who they are."

"I don't think so," replied Mya, tilting her head and looking at Mike. "If you are right, then we need to get out of here. We only know about the five men in the lobby. There are likely more. There will certainly be one man in the back of the hotel, probably one or more covering each stairwell, and one in the lobby. Two to three men will be coming up in the elevator to the tenth floor going to your room. When you're not there, they will move to seal off every exit."

Mike looked at her with a raised eyebrow, impressed with her tactical deductions. "There was someone coming up the stairwell below when I came down to the eighth. Let's hope they go on up to the tenth."

"Right," Mya said, "we need to go down the west stairwell and out the rear of the hotel, taking out the one securing the back, and like you said, hope that they went up to the tenth. Our weapons are silenced. Theirs may or may not be, and gunfire in the stairwell will attract a lot of attention."

"All right," Mike agreed.

Mya reached under her jacket behind her back and extracted a silenced, 9mm Kel-Tec PF-9 automatic.

"Okay then," said Mike with a nod, "we stay together and go down the west stairwell. We'll try to avoid engaging them until we can be sure we're going after only one of them. But we need to know what nationality they are. I assume you speak Turkish."

"Yes."

"Farsi?"

"Some."

"We find out what we can. If we have to kill one or more of them, we will."

She nodded again, her smooth face devoid of expression.

"Do you have a master key?" asked Mike.

"I do."

"Once we hit the stairwell we're heading down, carefully. One or more of them will be just two floors above us. We have to get out of the hotel before the police seal off the building. We'll go out the back, and as you said, there will be at least one man, maybe more, to deal with somewhere in the rear of the hotel, probably out of sight. If we are forced to duck into a room, we'll improvise."

Mya touched his shoulder and Mike looked back.

"Once we clear the hotel," she said, "follow my lead. I know the city. I have a safe house we can go to."

Mike nodded, turned to the door, and opened it. He observed the hallway in both directions, and then slipped out and turned right. Mya followed close behind. Mike covered the hallway ahead, and Mya oriented her pistol to the rear. They moved quickly.

Mike opened the stairwell door and they stepped in carefully, silently closing the door. They listened for several seconds. Mike heard a slight noise from above and pointed upward. Mya nodded.

They started down, moving quickly but quietly and keeping close to the wall. They had nowhere else to go but down.

Somewhere along these stairs, on one of the next few floors, might be more armed, well-trained, hostile foreign agents bent on capturing Mike, and probably Mya as well.

They reached the first floor without encountering anyone else on the stairs. They put away their weapons and walked at a normal pace through the maze of conference rooms, storage areas, maintenance rooms, and kitchens, toward the rear of the hotel.

As they passed a rolling cart full of folded waiter's uniforms, Mike grabbed a waiter's jacket and slipped it on. Mya did the same. They moved on toward the rear of the hotel. On the move, Mike picked up a large, round metal serving tray and continued.

As they left the kitchen and entered a storage area, they could see the loading dock. The big roll-up door was open. A truck was backed up to the ramp, and men unloaded boxes of lettuce onto wheeled carts. A large man wearing a trench coat stood to the side watching. He was obviously not a hotel worker.

He watched with interest as Mike and Mya approached. Mike walked past the man, and when he was close enough, he swung the tray and smashed him in the forehead. It sounded like a gong. The man's head bounced off the doorframe. Mike punched him in the solar plexus twice, but the man recovered and came back at him with several punches and a kick. Mike blocked the first two punches and the kick, but then he grazed Mike's chin with an upper cut.

Mya brought her pistol down hard on the back of the man's head. His eyes rolled up, and he collapsed to the floor. Mike pulled him over and quickly checked his pockets. No identification. No labels in his clothes. Mike found a silenced PP-2000 9mm submachine gun slung under the coat and a silenced Makarov pistol tucked into a holster in his waistband.

"Russian GRU."

She nodded agreement.

Mike tucked the man's pistol into his belt. He pulled off his waiter's jacket, wrapped the submachine gun in it, and they exited the hotel. They continued quickly, but calmly, down the access road from the rear of the building, keeping to the side of the road and close to some thick foliage. They wandered through an ancient maze of alleys and side streets; some passages were only a few feet wide between old stone structures or walls. They were particularly careful to watch for a tail.

As they walked, Mike asked her, "Do you suppose there is anybody in Turkey who doesn't know my itinerary?"

"Well, I'm not sure yet how the Russians knew about you, but I suppose you must be right. It had to be our man at the hotel. We thought he was reliable."

"Isn't it nice when you can count on your employees?"

"It's all about money."

Mike nodded.

Mya had a car parked on a small street about eight blocks from the Marriott. They quickly inspected the car underneath, inside, and under the hood. It did not appear to have been tampered with. When Mike was satisfied, they got in the vehicle and drove casually out of the area toward Mya's safe house. They parked several blocks away and walked hand-in-hand toward the house, like a romantic couple out for a stroll.

9

Hamadi Hassan and Yousef Amad returned to Ankara following their meeting with Khorasani in Poti. They now awaited departing flights—Hassan to Kingston, Amad to Caracas.

Hassan pulled Amad aside near one of the large windows, away from any people. They were about to separate, heading to different terminals. They each carried a small backpack and nothing more.

Hassan put his hand on the older man's shoulder and looked him in the eyes. "We will communicate by messaging, but this will be the last face-to-face conversation we have until we are together in the World Trade Center. The tasks we will perform in the next few days will be the culmination of a lifetime of struggle against the infidel west."

Yousef Amad appeared calm. His resolve was strong. He felt nervous but confident.

Hassan continued, "If any single task fails, our entire plan fails. Every single piece must fall into place."

Amad nodded solemnly.

"Yousef, you *must* ensure that you properly contact the cartel member. Then receive the device and the codes from the Saudi. I will hire the Jamaican and send you instructions on how to transfer it to his men for shipment. Then I will also deal with New York— forming a company and leasing space. When we meet again, you will activate the device. You must have the codes from Khorasani with you when you arrive in New York."

Yousef Amad smiled. He actually looked forward to getting his hands on the device and setting it up.

"I will accomplish my tasks. Do not worry. Then I will revel in the moment when I activate the device, my personal gift to

America from the holy warriors of Islam. After, I will be prepared to die in peace."

~

Istanbul, CIA Safe House

Mike and Mya stayed at the safe house overnight, sleeping in separate bedrooms. Mya had made coffee, and they now sat at the kitchen table sipping the strong brew from steaming mugs. Mike's pistol lay on the table in front of him.

Mike noticed that Mya's hand was trembling. "Mya, are you okay? What's wrong?"

She hesitated for a moment, and then said, "Mike, does it get any easier?"

"What do you mean?"

"I've been in the CIA for four years, but this was the first time I've been in a life or death situation. I was afraid."

"You didn't act like it. You handled yourself just fine."

"I don't *feel* just fine. Will I be looking over my shoulder for the rest of my career fretting about when the next deadly encounter will arise?"

"You'd better keep looking over your shoulder, because when you get complacent and you let your guard down, that's when you'll be compromised. And for what it's worth, I was afraid too."

"Somehow I don't really believe that you were."

"Well, call it a healthy dose of respect for the adversary. And as for fear, we all have it sometimes. It's how you handle it that counts. We often rise to the occasion and do things we didn't know were in us. Like you did. You'll be fine."

She smiled slightly. "Thanks, Mike."

"No. Thank you for being there. You did your job, and I'm still around because of it."

Mya's phone buzzed. It was a message from her boss in the embassy instructing her to pick up Max. Mya grabbed her backpack and left.

An hour later, Mike received a message from Mya: *We're here.*

He checked the door, looking through the peephole. Max and Mya stood outside. After greetings, they grabbed coffees and the three of them settled in around the kitchen table.

"Close call," said Max, shaking his head.

"Yeah," replied Mike, "guess it would have been if there had been no warning."

"Well, that's why when we can, especially now, we take precautions. Mya was that precaution."

Mike raised his cup toward her and nodded. "That she was."

Getting up, Mike said, "I have something for you." He went into the bedroom and returned with the weapons he and Mya had taken from the Russian. He laid them on the table.

"Wow," said Max, picking up the submachine gun and checking the chamber. Mike had unloaded and cleared them both. "This is their new model 9mm parabellum," added Max. "Only carried by Spetsnaz and intel operatives. It's sweet." Max put it down and picked up the pistol, obviously admiring it. "Do you know what this is?" he asked.

Mike said, "A Makarov?"

"Not just any Makarov, but a 6P9. This baby was designed and built from the ground up as a silenced pistol for the special operators and agents. These will go into the training arsenal."

"So, Max," began Mike, "you didn't come all this way for coffee."

"No. Mya tells me you believe our man in the hotel sold you out. He probably did. Like you've already figured out, I think he is also on the Russian payroll, but he still wants to keep our money coming as well."

"What are you going to do?"

"Just let him stew for a while. Then we'll see. The Russians probably didn't plan to kill you, at least not right away. They wanted to get you to a secure location where they could identify the broker handling the nukes, and then bargain with him."

"That would have been fun," said Mike, shaking his head.

Max continued. "The embassy is monitoring the situation at the Marriott East. You are checked out of the hotel, and you aren't implicated in any way with the dust up there."

"That's good," said Mike. "You know, Max, even if the hotel concierge tipped them off, I suspect they already knew I was there.

The Russians seem to be getting really good intel lately. They know my schedule before I do. First Beirut, then here. Do you think it was also the Russians who killed our two agents in Tbilisi and Istanbul?"

"It wouldn't be normal protocol to start whacking each other's agents. We weren't doing that, much, even during the cold war. Then again, this is an unusual situation with some of their most sensitive weapons missing. That aside, information *is* getting out from somewhere, and headquarters doesn't know where."

"Great," muttered Mike.

Max continued, "Striker's pretty worried about it. They're looking for the leak in headquarters. Anyway, back to you, the Russians will definitely be looking for Steve Holt. They want those nukes badly."

"Yeah, figured so," Mike said, taking a sip of his coffee.

"I've got a new identity for you." Max reached into a jacket pocket, pulled out a new passport, and handed it to Mike. "You're now James Finch." A folded piece of paper was tucked into the passport. "The details of your identity are there. Once you're comfortable with it, burn the paper. The passport has an entry stamp into Turkey. You'll need it to fly out."

Mike pulled out his old passport under the name of Steve Holt and handed it to Max.

"Okay," said Max, "we don't have a lot, but a few things are shaking loose both from communications intercepts and from the two Russians you snatched in Beirut. Baskov lied about Turkey. He doesn't really know. But the second Russian you guys picked up in Beirut, says the destination is Poti. Also from communications intercepts, the word out of Russia pretty much confirms what we already believed; Colonel Grigor planned and executed the heist."

Mike and Mya listened intently as Max continued the rundown.

"He's somewhere hiding from Russian intelligence and hoping to spend some of the money he made, but we don't know where that might be. He's probably already unloaded the devices to an international arms dealer, and of course if we could find Grigor, he could tell us which one that is. But, we do know that Genadi Meskhi in Poti could handle a transaction this big, and that matches what the Russian is telling us. So that's your next destination. Just remember, Meskhi is dangerous. We don't know for sure if it was him, but before this nuke affair even began we sent in a Georgian asset to see what he could dig up on the guy, and we never heard from him again. Then Ingrid was murdered in Tbilisi. So, watch yourselves."

Mike and Mya both nodded.

Max took a sip of coffee and continued. "The biggest danger is if the broker splits them up and sells them to multiple parties. All the more reason to find them before that can happen. Go check out Poti and the arms broker there. Both of you. It'll give you better cover to be a couple. A briefing packet on Meskhi has been sent to your phones. It also has info on a Georgian asset who will provide you with weapons and other assistance. Once you open the file, you'll have thirty minutes before it erases. And remember, a U.S. agent and a Georgian asset that we sent there are no longer with us."

Mike nodded.

Max reached into another pocket, pulled out an airline folder, and handed it to Mike. "You don't want to fly directly into Poti. Meskhi, basically a mafia don, owns the town and would probably know it. Fly to Batumi on the Black Sea, rent a car, and drive up the coast to Poti. You have reservations at the Villa Reta Hotel and Spa on the Black Sea, just a couple of miles north of Poti. Your reservations were made by a Manhattan travel agency."

Mike asked, "Is someone going to continue to look for Ronald Nelson's killer here?"

"Yeah," Max said, "we'll bring in a replacement. I know I'm repeating myself, but you two watch your backs. I've got a feeling it's going to get worse before it gets better."

~

Prague, Czech Republic

Vladimir Grigor sat reclined on a thick, padded examination chair. Bright lights illuminated his face. His surgeon, magnifying glasses over his eyes, leaned in close and scrutinized Grigor's face. Standing up straight and removing the glasses, he said with a broad smile, "I am *very* pleased with your progress. You are almost ready."

Grigor himself was amazed at how fast he had healed, given what he looked like when they first removed the bandages on the second day after the surgery. Every two hours since, around the clock, a nurse had applied various medicated lotions to the ever-fading scalpel lines. Now, six days after the procedure, only faint traces remained.

As if on cue, a young man entered the exam room. The doctor said to Grigor, "If you will be so kind as to accompany my assistant, he will take your photograph. There are still some tiny signs of the surgery visible, but he will eliminate them from the photo. We will have your new documents by tomorrow morning. And rest assured, once your identification documents are produced, any information concerning you will be purged from our system. It will be as if you were never here.

"Once he has taken your photo, our hair stylist will escort you to her studio to change your hair color. Then I would like to resume the treatment on your face for another twenty-four hours, and you will be ready to depart."

Grigor nodded his approval.

The following morning, Grigor sat in his room, dressed and waiting. The doctor entered and once again checked Grigor's face. He was satisfied.

A few moments later, a young man entered and handed the doctor a passport and a driver's license. He donned his magnifying glasses and spent a full five minutes carefully inspecting the two documents.

He nodded to the assistant. "Excellent work, as usual. Thank you."

The assistant departed.

"This, Mr. Reimer, is your Thai driver's license," he said, handing Grigor the colorful plastic card. "And here is your German passport. It has a permanent residency stamp for Thailand."

Grigor took the two IDs and studied them. His new name was Hans Reimer. "Are these real?" he asked.

"Absolutely. Both are quite genuine. You are now German. Even the German government thinks so. And the driver's license was issued by Thailand. It is in their database along with your driving record. And you have an excellent driving record by the way," he said, amused by the brilliance of his own system.

He pulled an envelope from the pocket of his white medical jacket and handed it to Grigor. "Here are the flight tickets you requested. First class to Bangkok, departing in four hours. Our driver is waiting outside the door for you when you are ready."

Grigor departed, leaving behind the weapon he had arrived with. He was now simply a wealthy, German expat living in Thailand.

~

Approaching Batumi, Georgia

Mike and Mya caught the morning flight from Istanbul to Batumi on Turkish Airlines. The Embraer E190 made its approach over the Black Sea. From the passenger cabin, it appeared as if the jet was landing on the water. Then an instant before touchdown, the runway suddenly appeared beneath the plane.

Mike and Mya processed through Georgian customs—just a happy tourist couple on a holiday to the beautiful Black Sea coast. They rented a car and drove the coastal road north toward Poti. The views of the expansive Black Sea were actually quite stunning.

The trip to Poti was quick. Mike and Mya skirted around the Poti port complex. Busy cranes, huge ships, and massive warehouses filled the horizon.

They headed north. Beyond the port, the shoreline became more touristic in nature. The Black Sea coast around Poti could be mistaken for 1950's Miami Beach—the coastline, with its wide beaches, was beautiful, but the hotels and apartments were dated.

The Villa Reta Hotel and Spa, where they had reservations, was a short distance farther up the coast outside of Poti. It was a fabulous resort right on the Black Sea, but Mike didn't intend to stay there.

He drove past the hotel entrance and parked in a spot concealed by some short palm fronds and hedges. He instructed Mya to conduct counter surveillance while he walked to and entered the hotel to check-in. She did as he asked.

Carefully observing his surroundings, Mike went into the hotel, sat down, and watched the lobby for a few minutes. Everything appeared normal. He checked in. The receptionist inquired about luggage. Mike said that they would bring it in later. They were heading to the beach for now.

He returned to the car via a circuitous route. Mya stood, concealed, a few yards from the car. She spotted him approaching.

"See anything?" he asked her.

"Nothing unusual."

"Let's go," he said, getting into the car.

She got in. "Where?"

"To another hotel."

"Mike, you think we're going to be targeted here, don't you?"

Starting the car and pulling out of the lot, Mike replied, "I have a feeling that someone will be looking for me here by tomorrow. I intend to find out for sure."

Scanning around them, he said, "For the moment, let's just make certain we're not followed from here. Next, we need to meet the Georgian asset and get ourselves armed, sooner rather than later."

Mya tapped out an encrypted message to their asset in Georgia: *Meet at previously designated coordinates, 1 hour.*

~

Kingston, Jamaica

Hamadi Hassan looked at the Jamaican, barely concealing the disgust he felt for this man. He and his kind were sadistic criminals. Hassan was not above brutality, but his use of violence was for a higher purpose. The Jamaicans, though, were unavoidable. He needed them to complete his mission.

"When can it be delivered?" Hassan asked the Jamaican.

The tall black man toyed with one of his waist length dreadlocks. The braided, knotted hair was only washed by seawater. Hassan's sensitive nose could smell it, and the man, from across the small crate that served as a table.

The scene appeared tranquil, even beautiful, as the two men sat in this makeshift seaside café. A tropical breeze blew through the little hut; white sand shimmered, and the fronds of tall coconut trees wafted in the wind. Children scampered around them. But this was far from a placid scene. Hassan knew he was surrounded here in the heart of M3 territory, a ruthless gang of cutthroats, pimps, pushers, and thieves. Murder was their daily business. Their preferred method was machete—done slowly. They had enough firepower to rival the police and the army combined, particularly in their little corner of Jamaica.

The Jamaican responded finally. "There be risk," he said softly.

"Of course there is risk. Otherwise there would not be an equally great reward," said Hassan.

"Of course," replied the Jamaican.

Hassan continued, "There is also the absolute necessity that no mistakes be allowed. This transfer cannot be compromised. Too much is at stake."

"You know, mon, I don't really care what is at stake. I do job, you pay me. Dat's all I care, mon," hissed the Jamaican. "What will be in the container?" he asked.

"I thought you did not care," said the Arab.

"I don't."

"Then it does not matter."

"How true," the Jamaican muttered under his breath. "We can move it from Venezuela to New York, no problem."

"You can do it? You are sure?" asked the Arab.

"Of course we can," replied the Jamaican. "It is best to use caution and finalize plans at the very last minute. There be less chance for talk dat way."

"Of course."

"It be well taken care of. Once it arrives in New York, we deliver to da' address you provide, and then it be up to you what to do with it. Dat be not my concern," said the Jamaican.

"I understand," said Hassan.

"And the balance of payment be due *now*."

"That will not be a problem. It will be done exactly as the first payment," said Hassan.

"Good, mon."

~

McLean, Virginia

Gerald Billings sat at the kitchen table in his modest apartment. It wasn't much, but it was close to work. Almost midnight and he still couldn't sleep. He heard a noise and jumped. The refrigerator motor had started. He had been chewing his nails again, in fact, so far down that his fingers throbbed.

His personal cell phone on the table before him buzzed, and he jumped again. He worried that he might have a heart attack. Picking up the phone, he wondered who could be sending him a text message at this hour. He wasn't close to family and had no friends.

He read the message: *Where is he now?*

Gerald did a double take to be sure what he was reading. His pulse surged, and he realized that he was shaking violently. He dropped the phone to the table as if he had just picked up a hot pan and burned himself.

He knew what the message meant and who had sent it. He had exchanged encrypted texts with the Arab man to coordinate their meetings. This was the first time, though, that he had demanded information by phone, other than telling Gerald to message him if he learned something new. He could feel the noose tightening.

Gerald took several deep breaths and tried to calm himself, but he couldn't stop the shaking. He just wanted out. *How could I have gotten myself into such a mess?* he wondered. *What if he knows where I live? He probably does. He mentioned his hit man standing beside my bed.*

He could hear the Arab's words in his head: … *the fellow I use to take care of things for me, is a very bad and very efficient man….*

Gerald knew from another meeting in Director Berg's office, that Mike Elliot was attacked in Istanbul. He also knew that Striker and Berg were sending Elliot to Poti, Georgia, but he had been determined not to give up that information. He did not want to respond to the message. He already had two dead agents on his conscience, and he didn't want another. He was probably responsible for the attack in Beirut as well, he just didn't know for sure.

But he feared for his life, and he needed time—time to finalize his plan. He knew he would have to run, but he needed to take care of a few things first.

He picked up the phone cautiously, as if it might burn him again, and he slowly typed a message: *Poti. Villa Reta.*

He hit send, dropped the phone on the table, and began to sob.

~

Caracas, Venezuela

A bored Venezuelan customs agent stamped Yousef Amad's British passport and ushered him along. Amad caught a cab to a modest Caracas hotel where he had made a reservation.

His first order of business was to contact the cartel man. He sent an encrypted message according to Khorasani's instructions. Within a few minutes, he received a response: *Package en route, arvs 5 hours time, will msg w/ pick up time at hotel.*

Amad smiled. He took a towel from the bathroom and spread it on the floor. He knelt on the towel facing Mecca, as best he could reckon. This was not the traditional time for prayer, but he had not prayed in many hours. He had his Imam's blessing not to pray when operationally necessary, and he never prayed in public while traveling. It would draw attention. Today, Amad added a special prayer, asking for success in his mission.

~

Over the Atlantic

Behdin Khorasani departed Poti on Meskhi's Lear the day after he had met with the two Al-Qaeda men. He was now en route to Venezuela to deliver their one device and collect the balance of his money. In the cargo bay, was one RA-115 nuclear bomb. In his briefcase, he carried the PDA containing the code needed to activate it.

Meskhi's plane was an impressive piece of hardware. The crew was notable as well, especially the two female flight attendants—one a shapely blonde Swede, the other a brunette Thai. Meskhi knew how to live.

Khorasani doubted he would be able to afford this much airplane, even with fifty million in wealth. The jet was a long-range version packed with lots of extras. Even so, it couldn't fly non-stop from Poti to Venezuela. They had refueled in the Cape Verde islands off the horn of Africa, also known as Cabo Verde. Now they were on a five-hour leg to Venezuela. Khorasani had notified the Venezuelan cartel contact of his impending arrival as soon as they landed on Cape Verde.

The Swedish girl brought Khorasani another glass of French champagne. She wore a stylish, pale blue uniform skirt that was short and tight. She rubbed against his arm. Khorasani took the champagne glass and set it on the tray table. Then he ran his hand up and down her leg.

Soon, the Thai girl joined them and stood beside him, smiling demurely. The two of them gently tugged on him until he stood. Then they led him to the back of the plane and into the private bedroom and the large circular bed.

~

Poti, Georgia

Mike and Mya drove to a park on the north side of Poti. Mya checked her messages.

"He'll be in a yellow taxi, by the fountain," she said.

"We'll park at a distance," Mike replied. "I'll approach him. I want you to do a moving counter surveillance about a hundred yards behind me. Hold your position and scan the area while I talk to him. If he checks out, I'll get the package, and maybe we'll use him tomorrow for a recon."

Mya nodded.

They parked and got out. Mike gradually approached the Georgian asset's taxi with Mya some distance back, looking over the area for anyone who might be watching Mike or the Georgian.

Eventually, he approached the cab and asked the man in English if he had the time. The driver responded that it was midnight, even though it was broad daylight.

The Georgian got out of the car and stood with Mike.

"What have you heard," asked Mike, "about anyone moving any kind of special hardware, like large bombs for example?"

"Nothing. Not a word. Not that I've exactly been asking around. Just listening. I have to warn you, it's not wise to ask too many questions around here."

"Meskhi?"

"Yeah. People disappear."

"Do you have something for me?" asked Mike.

The Georgian reached into the car through the open window and pulled out a white paper bag with the logo of a local fast-food restaurant on it. He handed it to Mike. It was solid and heavy.

"Everything your people asked me to get. None of it traceable. There's a Colt and a Beretta."

"What are you hearing about Meskhi?" Mike asked.

"The usual stuff—the arms business is booming. The locals talk about him and his businesses. But they do it very quietly. He does a lot of work for Iran. He delivers Iranian hardware, explosives, and munitions to Hezbollah and to a half-dozen other Iranian clients.

"He sells Russian military hardware all over the world. He's like a Mafia Don, and he's got a huge organization with lots of guns. Most of the police and public officials around here are bought and paid for. But nobody has mentioned a word about any bombs."

Mike said, "We want to do the tourist thing. See the sights, and while doing it, have a quick look at Meskhi's operations."

"We can do it in my cab. I take tourists around all the time. I'm a familiar sight making the rounds. Meskhi has two main locations—a warehouse at the port and his personal compound on the outskirts of town. When?"

"Tomorrow morning. There will be one person. Female. She will message you the pickup location and time."

"Got it. No problem."

Mike asked, "Why do you do this?"

The man replied with a smile, "Because I like the money, and I like America. I hope to live there someday."

"Tomorrow," Mike said. "Be available.

10

Caracas, Venezuela

Yousef Amad waited in his hotel room. He was impatient. It had been four hours since his communication with the cartel. He checked his phone constantly. He paced. His engineer's mind imagined, repeatedly, the procedures for arming the bomb. He had also received instructions from Hamadi Hassan to take the package directly to the Jamaican's warehouse in Caracas, and he had sent that information with the address on to the cartel. But he had heard nothing back, and he was worried.

Finally, his phone buzzed. He jumped for it and read the message: *Out front, 5 mins, silver land rover.*

Amad stuffed his phone in his pocket, scooped up his backpack, and headed for the stairs. He dropped his key at the front desk and went out to the street. Within a minute, a late model silver Land Rover pulled to a stop on the small street in front of the hotel.

Amad walked up to the vehicle. A man in the front passenger seat asked, "What is your name?"

"Y.A.," responded Yousef Amad.

"Get in," he replied, nodding to the back seat.

Amad opened the back door, threw his backpack onto the seat, and climbed in.

The Land Rover sped off through the tiny, congested streets of Caracas. After thirty minutes of winding through town, they finally reached the outskirts of the city.

After another half-hour of driving through the countryside, the driver turned onto a small side road, drove a hundred yards, and pulled up to a gate. A gray SUV was parked inside the gate to one side. Four men, carrying automatic weapons, pistols stuck in their waistbands, stood guard behind the gate. One of the men slung his weapon over his shoulder and opened the gate.

The Land Rover drove through. Both men in the front seat casually waved at the other men as they drove past. They continued down a narrow, winding, dirt road full of ruts and holes. Jungle encroached on both sides. At times, the little road seemed nothing more than a wide path. After twenty bumpy minutes, they came out on a clearing.

There was a shack of sorts, a fuel tank, and some fuel pumping equipment. A rusting, faded-yellow road grader sat near the edge of the jungle. A hard-packed dirt runway stretched off in the distance. A small, enclosed delivery truck was parked there as well, with two men waiting.

The Land Rover came to a stop near a fuel tank where a couple of men wearing grease-stained coveralls stood smoking and chatting. The proximity of the jet fuel didn't seem to concern them.

The two Venezuelan cartel men got out of the vehicle and Yousef Amad followed.

"This is where your package will be delivered," said one of them. "The plane is due any time now. As you requested, we will transport the package to the warehouse you gave us where you will transfer it to your shipper. Our boss says that for what your people are paying us, we are to take very good care of you. So that's what we intend to do."

Yousef Amad nodded and said, "Thank you."

Amad walked away from the men and checked his phone. He had a weak signal. He had not considered the possibility of not being able to communicate from the transfer site, but gratefully, he could still do so. He messaged Al-Qaeda's finance chief and instructed him to be prepared to wire the balance of payment to the seller's account soon.

~

Thirty minutes earlier, Khorasani's plane had flown into Venezuelan airspace several hundred miles east of Caracas at barely two hundred feet altitude. Once over dry land, it veered southwest and made a wide circle around the capitol city.

Meskhi's plane carried three pilots for long-range trips such as this one. All three were former Russian Air Force jet fighter pilots, and Meskhi paid them well. They were accustomed to flying into places where the mob boss didn't want to be seen, or bothered by formalities—mostly into third world countries.

The jet was equipped with practically every electronic gadget that fighter pilots employed, except for the armaments. One such tool was radar-evading technology, which they were putting to good use on this trip.

The plane neared the cartel airstrip still flying low at two hundred knots. They did a flyby to have a look before lining up for an approach. The Lear jet roared past overhead. Landing a jet on a short jungle airstrip would be a daunting task for most pilots, but not for these men. This was routine business.

Moments later, the Lear touched down smoothly onto the dirt strip. A cloud of fine white dust trailed the plane down the runway. The jet came to a stop next to the fuel tank. The cabin door opened, folding downward from the top. It had steps on the inside of the door.

A crewmember bounded down and went directly to the two fuel men. His only concern was to ready the jet for immediate takeoff. One of the pilots exited the plane and began an inspection of the exterior of the aircraft.

Behdin Khorasani came down the aircraft steps. Another member of the crew came out and went under the plane to open the cargo hatch. Khorasani waved for him to wait. The man stopped what he was doing and stood by the plane.

Yousef Amad walked over to Khorasani. They simultaneously nodded to one another. Khorasani gestured toward the plane's ladder and entry door. Amad climbed the steps and went in. Khorasani followed.

They took seats in easy chairs at a small conference table mid aircraft. Khorasani had his laptop computer in front of him. The computer had a satellite communications receiver plugged into one of the ports.

Amad asked, "You have the device?"

"I do," replied Khorasani, "but I warn you if there is any trickery, the codes you require to use it will be inaccessible without a randomly generated PIN that will be sent to me only after the money is deposited into my account. I don't even know what that PIN will be."

"We have the money. There will be no tricks. May I see the device?"

"It is in the cargo hold. Transfer the money. I would like to conclude our business and depart."

Amad tapped the word *Now* into his phone and hit send.

Khorasani watched his computer. Tense moments ticked past. Then Khorasani smiled and closed the laptop.

"Let's unload your device," he said.

"What about the codes?"

Khorasani pulled a small PDA from his side leg cargo pocket, powered it up, and opened an app. He typed in a six-digit PIN. He swiped to a second screen and handed the PDA to Yousef Amad.

"You may enter your new PIN. Six numbers."

Amad took the PDA, tapped in six numbers, and hit enter.

"Don't forget that PIN," said Khorasani, "or you will never get it open again if you do. Three wrong tries and everything on it will be erased."

"You didn't have a PIN sent to you."

"No. That was just a security precaution."

"What is on this PDA?"

"When we get to your nuclear device, you will notice that the serial number imprinted on the PDA's case matches the serial number of your bomb. Contained on the PDA, are the device's activation and deactivation codes, as well as detailed instructions to set up and activate the weapon. It's in Russian, but that couldn't be helped. The code numbers are written as numerals. So once the PDA is opened, anyone can read them."

"I can read Russian well enough."

"Well then, you are all set."

"How many times can one open and close the PDA using the PIN."

"Unlimited, as far as I know. Now would you like to have your nuclear weapon?"

"Yes."

In the cargo hold, Amad verified the serial numbers, and then he and Khorasani wrapped the SADM device and heavily taped it before reclosing the wooden crate. Yousef Amad was well accustomed to warm climates, but he found himself sweating profusely at the overwhelming magnitude of this moment.

~

The Jamaican's warehouse in the suburbs of Caracas was located in a rundown industrial park dotted with rusting metal buildings.

Yousef Amad rode in the back seat of the Land Rover. A cartel man with an MP5 submachine gun resting on his lap rode in the back seat next to him. The two men who had picked up Amad were in the front of the vehicle.

The delivery truck, carrying one small wooden crate, trailed the Land Rover. A black SUV with four armed cartel men followed the truck.

The three vehicles came to a halt about forty yards from Number 31, *Calle Ricardo Alvarez*. Yousef Amad, and the cartel man sitting next to him, got out and walked toward the warehouse and the three men standing near the building.

As he approached the three men, Amad surmised, correctly, that two of them were Venezuelan, or Latin American from some other South American country. The third man was Jamaican. He was a black man with short-cropped hair.

The cartel man with Amad stopped about fifteen yards out, his MP5 cradled in his arms. Amad continued forward. The Jamaican walked toward him. As they arrived face-to-face, Yousef Amad asked in English, "Is it warm and sunny in Jamaica?"

With a heavy Caribbean accent, the man replied, "No, it is snowing."

Amad smiled, and the two walked together toward the warehouse. Amad signaled the truck forward, and all three vehicles drove into the building through the big open doors.

The cartel men all got out, automatic weapons ready, scanning the area for any sign of trouble. No one else was present. One of the men opened the truck's cargo door, and several of them slid the wooden crate out and carefully set it on a roller cart.

Amad intended to ensure that the Jamaican and his men would not open the wrapping on the nuclear device. They could never see what they were sending to America. It would almost certainly cause problems.

Amad and the Jamaican man walked away from the group.

Amad asked the man, "Is everything set?"

"Yes it is. We will carefully remove your item from the crate...."

Amad interrupted him, "Without unwrapping it."

"Yes, of course. What you are shipping is not our concern. As I was saying, we will only remove the package from the crate. Then we will very professionally repack it inside a brand-new mainframe computer. Then we will ship the computer by UPS to the address that you will provide to us."

"I will have the address very soon. But I am concerned. How can you possibly do this? The Americans have so much security."

"Isn't that what you are paying us for? If it was easy to do, you wouldn't need us, now would you?"

"You are correct. When will it go?"

"As soon as you furnish the address in New York, it can be there in one day. UPS is very efficient."

"Excellent," said Amad, turning and walking to the Land Rover.

The three cartel vehicles drove away, the truck and the SUV going one direction, the Land Rover heading toward the airport.

Yousef Amad, the PDA in his pocket close to his heart, would fly to New York and go to a small hotel just across the river from Manhattan. He would wait there, studying the PDA's instructions, until Hamadi Hassan sent for him.

~

Manhattan, New York

Hamadi Hassan had arrived in New York from Jamaica the night before and checked into a Manhattan hotel. He was now on his way to meet with an attorney who would lease space for him. A militant group that Al-Qaeda sometimes dealt with in Iraq recommended this particular attorney. He had moved money for the Iraqis on several occasions. Hassan had been told that the attorney could make things happen, without asking too many questions.

He crossed West Broadway on Leonard Street and caught glimpses of the new World Trade Center, soaring skyward, between Manhattan's many skyscrapers. He felt a surge of emotion at just how close he was to success. He had received a message from Yousef Amad in Venezuela telling him that the Jamaicans had the device and needed a delivery address. Amad had the activation code in his possession.

Hassan's people had already paid the attorney a three hundred thousand dollar retainer through a British bank. Hassan was expected.

He entered an office building on the corner of Church and Leonard. He found the attorney listed on the lobby directory and climbed the stairs to the third floor. He entered the office and announced himself. A young secretary, wearing a very short tan skirt, ushered him immediately into the attorney's office.

The attorney showed him to a chair in front of his large oak desk and then went around behind the desk and took a seat.

"I received your retainer. Thank you. I understand that you wish to incorporate a business and lease some office space. Is there any particular space you have in mind?"

"Yes. One World Trade Center."

"Oh? You know that there is a new city ordinance that requires a background check?"

"No. I did not."

"Are you in a hurry to do this?"

"Yes, as soon as possible."

"Well, I *am* known for getting difficult things done quickly. My retainer is generous. I'm quite happy with it, so don't get me wrong, but if you want to get all this done right away, and without too much probing by the authorities, I will need to make a few payments, to grease the way, so to speak.

"But I do know for a fact that the WTC is actively leasing. They have a lot of space to fill. For an additional seventy-five thousand, I can have your incorporation papers completed and stamped, and have a lease at the WTC ready for you to sign, let's say, in a day. Will you be an officer of the corporation?"

"Yes, I will."

"And the name of the business?"

"British Industrial Engineers."

"Excellent."

Hassan was using his real name. He needed his British passport to travel freely and to conduct this business. He also knew that when this was over, the American government would eventually track him down and kill him. But he didn't care.

"And will you be authorized to sign the lease?"

"Yes. I will sign the lease. How soon can you have a physical address for me?"

"Probably by this afternoon."

"Okay, text me with the information as soon as possible." Hassan would message the Jamaican the moment he received the delivery address from the attorney.

"Okay, I certainly will. Now, I will need a copy of your driver's license, or passport, or something official."

Hassan pulled his British passport from his shirt pocket and handed it to the attorney. The attorney made a copy of it and handed the passport back.

Hassan took the passport knowing that his fate was sealed, but rejoicing nonetheless. He would dispose of the passport and join the Sheikh in hiding, or he would die a martyr. Either way, he would complete this mission.

11

Poti, Georgia

The morning following their arrival in Poti, Mike went down to the lobby of their new hotel. A little later, Mya would meet the Georgian asset and look at Meskhi's operation.

The previous day, both Mike and Mya had thoroughly checked out the hotel, including the stairwells, parking garage, conference facilities, and lobby. Mike got a coffee and a newspaper and sat down. He watched the lobby for a while. Then he took a walk around the outside of the hotel. He didn't find anything unusual.

He went back inside to the concierge desk and arranged for a second rental car. Within a few minutes, one of the hotel's parking attendants pulled up in front with a small, white sedan.

Mike headed north, generally toward the Villa Reta Hotel. He made several detours checking for surveillance but detected none. He gradually made his way up the coast and found a spot to park, well off the road, about three hundred yards before arriving at the Villa Reta.

His car was concealed, but he had a good view of the coast road leading to the hotel. This was the only route to the hotel from Poti without making a lengthy loop through the countryside and then coming back down the coast from the north.

Mike had started growing a beard at the safe house in Istanbul. He now had a couple of day's stubble, a hat, and sunglasses. Not much of a disguise, but better than nothing. Checking his surroundings every few seconds, he settled in for the long haul. It would probably be a long day.

~

Shortly after Mike left, Mya messaged the Georgian asset and instructed him to pick her up in his taxi at a nearby beachside café. While she waited for him to arrive, she took a few selfies on the beach with her phone camera. She wanted some typical tourist photos on her camera roll.

Mya returned to the café just as he drove up. She went out and hopped in the front seat.

"Where to first?" he asked her.

"You said there were two known locations."

"Yeah, he has a warehouse at the port. That's where his import business is. He has a large personal gated compound where he lives. Well, actually, there *is* a third location. He has a hangar at the airport where he keeps his jet."

"What kind of jet?"

"Some kind of Lear jet. I hear it is very expensive, top of the line. Four or five Russians work for him, flying and taking care of the plane. They keep pretty much to themselves."

"Okay," she said, "let's have a look at everything. Start with town, so I can snap a few tourist photos. Then to the warehouse."

"Okay," he said, "we'll go by the cathedral." He eased the yellow car forward.

"I assume you know how to be discreet?" asked Mya.

"I do. I have no desire to end up being Mr. Meskhi's guest."

Ten minutes later, he parked the cab in a taxi zone across the street from the cathedral in downtown Poti. The huge stone building resembled a series of large columns, like grain silos, jammed together into a bundle. Three rows of tall, narrow windows decorated each column. A golden metal dome with a cross on top capped the center column.

"This is the Soboro Cathedral," said the asset, with obvious pride. "It's Georgian orthodox and was completed in 1907."

Mya thought it looked a bit awkward but didn't say so.

She got out, snapped a few photos of the cathedral and a nearby statue, and hopped back in.

"Okay, the warehouse," she said.

The Georgian drove the short distance to the industrial port area and cruised around telling her about the various industries located there.

Then he said, "Okay, coming up on our left is Meskhi's business. He has one of the biggest warehouses here. Supposed to have offices inside as well. At least, so I'm told. Never been in there and don't ever want to visit."

Mya snapped a photo with embedded GPS coordinates, emailed it to Max, and then deleted it from her phone.

The Georgian continued past the warehouse. "We can't linger here," he said. "Not safe. Meskhi has eyes everywhere."

"Okay, drive by the airport. Then we'll go to the compound."

~

Mike alternated between sitting in the car and stretching. It had been three hours, and he had seen nothing but the usual traffic. He continued to check his surroundings and watch the road.

A gray sedan, driven by a man with a dark complexion, drove slowly past headed north toward the Villa Reta. Mike couldn't tell if this was the man he was looking for. The black population in Georgia was small, but it could be a local or a tourist. Mike had no choice but to find out. The car had a rental sticker on the bumper, so it probably wasn't a local.

Mike started the car, pulled out from his spot, and followed the gray sedan at a careful distance. He had no idea if this might just be a wild goose chase. It might even cause him to miss his actual target.

If this *was* the assassin, then Mike figured the man would find a location where he could park and observe the hotel. He would watch the Villa Reta trying to pick up Mike's trail. At least Mike hoped so. If he did, Mike would try to approach from an unexpected direction. He would likely be in a spot not readily visible by passing traffic. Mike would kill or capture him. If he could capture him, the CIA might be able to find out who hired him.

But the gray sedan did not stop near the hotel. It drove past and continued north on the coast road. Mike couldn't risk getting close enough to verify that this was the man he saw in Istanbul, but he also didn't want to lose him now that he had potentially acquired him. Mike had no choice but to follow.

The gray sedan turned right onto a smaller, rural road, leading into the countryside. Mike slowed to increase their distance, then turned right and followed.

The small road went through rolling hills, past fields, forests, and a few farmhouses. Mike was feeling edgy. This was not going according to plan. Mike toyed with the idea of just breaking off and falling back.

In the end, he knew he couldn't. He had to follow through. Even though his gut told him that if this was the man who was killing CIA agents, and who was tailing Mike in Istanbul, he was setting Mike up. He also knew that if it didn't end here, the next time he turned around the dark man would be behind him.

Mike realized that the man had not come to the hotel to observe it. He came there to show himself. He knew that Mike would be watching. He was just trolling. *What choice do I have*, he wondered, *but to take the bait and see where it leads*.

~

The asset drove Mya along the outside of the airport fence past Meskhi's hangar. There was nothing to see except a hangar large enough for a 747. The bay doors were closed, and it appeared to be locked up tight with no one in sight.

He next drove Mya along a scenic highway on the southern outskirts of Poti. They drove a pastoral route through gently rolling hills.

They arrived at a scenic overlook, and he pulled in and parked. The view was pleasant, spreading across a lush green valley. One also had a distant view, from slightly above, of Meskhi's expansive walled compound and home. Mya snapped a zoom photo, emailed it to Max, and then deleted it.

She took a couple of selfies with the beautiful valley in the background, but not Meskhi's compound.

~

Mike drove around a bend in the road. To the right was a pull off with several picnic tables under some tall pine trees. A thick forest surrounded the area just outside the small park. The gray sedan was parked by one of the tables, but the driver was nowhere in sight.

Mike drove past and continued along the road for about a hundred yards, until he was out of sight from the park. He pulled off on the right and parked.

He got out and walked straight into the woods about fifty yards. Then he started to circle right, back toward the woods behind the gray sedan. He intended to circle around, flank the black man, and approach from behind. Mike knew, however, that a flanking maneuver was such a basic technique, that the man would anticipate it.

Memories of a thousand such walks, over too many years to count, through forest, jungle, or urban terrain, where a brutal enemy was nearby, flowed through Mike's mind like so much unwanted clutter.

Vines and dense underbrush filled the thick, silent woods. Nothing moved. No birds. No animals. Not even a breeze. The only smells Mike could detect were the green foliage around him and the rotting vegetation under foot.

He knew that this man was no ordinary adversary. Every sense told him that this was a trap. Still, he took another quiet step forward. The bushes ahead were thick. Visibility low.

He heard a swooshing sound break the still air and reacted instantly. He twisted his body, bending backward as he did so. With a loud *thwack*, a long dagger hit a small tree where he had just been standing. It missed him by inches. The dagger hit with such force that the tip of the blade buried itself three inches into the wood.

Mike had obviously found his man. He jerked out the silenced 9mm Colt Commander he had gotten from the Georgian asset and crouched behind the tree, listening and looking for the assassin's next move.

~

Mya and the Georgian were about to leave the scenic overlook, when a car with two men in it drove up and parked. The asset started pointing out a distant farmhouse and telling Mya about it.

As he pointed, he said to her, "Police detectives, but they are Meskhi's men."

The two men got out of their car and walked toward Mya and the asset. They looked like husky, washed-out prizefighters with thick features and flattened noses. But Mya took his word for it that they were cops.

The men approached, and the asset continued, "…That farmhouse was built in 1792, and is still owned by the same family. They grow vegetables and sell them in Poti."

As the two detectives stopped next to them. The asset said in Georgian Kartuli, "Good morning, gentlemen."

One of the men spoke to Mya in Kartuli. "Your passport, miss."

Mya just shook her head.

The asset said in English, "He wants to see your passport."

She had a small bag slung over her shoulder. She fished out her passport and handed it to him.

"Where are you from?" the cop asked in English.

"Michigan," replied Mya.

"What do you do?"

"School teacher. I teach geography, and I travel to learn about different regions of the world."

"Your phone," he said, gesturing with his fingers to hand it over.

She gave it to him, and he looked through the contacts and photos. "Our cathedral is very beautiful, no?"

"Yes, gorgeous," replied Mya.

He handed the phone and passport back and said, "Enjoy your stay in Georgia, miss."

The two men walked back to their car and drove away.

The asset had sweat on his brow. He said, "One wrong photo on that phone, and we would be on a one-way trip to Meskhi's warehouse right now."

"Good thing there wasn't then," she said. "Let's go. You can take me back to the café."

~

The vegetation around Mike was so thick he still could not see his attacker, even after the man had managed to throw a dagger at him. Underbrush laced with vines made movement difficult.

He was accustomed to operations on difficult terrain, and he was good at it, but he had a sinking feeling this man had chosen this specific site for a definite tactical reason—he was totally at home in it.

Mike strained to hear—anything. Movement. Breathing. A cough. But it was silent. He knew a deadly and efficient assassin was almost near enough to reach out and touch, yet he could not see or hear him.

Then he heard a noise to his left, but he didn't react to it. He focused his senses ahead, where the dagger had come from. An enormous man, skin like midnight, suddenly crashed through the bushes to his right front and lunged. Mike jumped back. The man held an identical second dagger, thrust forward, aiming for Mike's gut.

Mike tried to get his pistol into position, but the Nigerian slapped the pistol with the big dagger sending it flying into the brush. Mike continued backing up as the big man closed on him.

As they came together, Mike grabbed the man's wrists. He rolled onto his back and kicked upward at the same time. He used the attacker's forward momentum and flipped the man over him. Okeke did a complete flip in the air and landed hard on his back.

Mike jumped up and tried to land a kick to the man's head, but he rolled to the side. Mike's kick missed and he almost fell. He was down on one hand and one knee. The attacker was already back on his feet, crouched, facing him. Mike rolled away and sprang to his feet.

Okeke thrust the dagger at him repeatedly, but he couldn't find a clear opening. Mike managed to parry the attacks while trying to maneuver in the snarl of vines and brush. He worked desperately not to trip. It would be fatal.

He felt himself tiring. The fight alone required enormous energy, but this tangle-foot terrain was completely draining. Other than sweating, Mike's adversary didn't seem at all bothered by the exertion.

Okeke suddenly lunged straight at him, dagger thrust out. Mike tried to back pedal. A vine caught his heel, and he tripped and fell backward. The attacker dove toward him and came crashing down hard on top of Mike, knocking the wind from Mike's lungs.

Struggling to breathe, Mike managed to grab the big man's wrists again. Okeke gripped the dagger in both hands, the hilt pulled tight against his chest. He used his full weight on top of Mike, trying to drive the blade home.

The attacker's wrists were sweaty and slippery. Mike fought to maintain a grip. If his hands slipped, the blade would plunge into Mike's chest.

Okeke completely covered Mike's body. His full weight pushed downward. The blade tip inched toward Mike's chest. The Nigerian's determined face hovered just over Mike's. The man's dark eyes were fierce. His tribal scars glistened with sweat and bulged with strain.

Beads of stinging sweat dripped into Mike's eyes. He tried to roll to one side, but the big man spread his feet and legs to stabilize himself and stay on top. Mike couldn't roll, he was pinned, but the Nigerian's move created a vulnerability.

Mike brought his right knee up hard and slammed it into Okeke's groin. The man uttered a moan and his eyes rolled up in pain. He repeated the knee slam and Okeke went limp. With great difficulty, Mike shoved the man off, slipped around behind him, and was now on top. Okeke was face down on the ground. He snaked his arm around the attacker's neck and cinched down on a rear naked chokehold.

Before Mike could choke him out, Okeke started blindly slashing and stabbing behind him with the dagger. He cut a large gash in Mike's left leg. He had to get away quickly or risk a deep puncture wound. He let go and rolled away, his leg bleeding badly.

Mike jumped to his feet, the pain in his leg intense. He pulled his tactical knife from his right front pocket and flipped open the blade. Okeke was already on his feet, facing him. He moved the dagger back and forth between his two hands, staring intently at Mike. He almost seemed to have a grin on his lips.

Mike had a knife with a four-inch blade. He faced a larger man with several inches more reach and a much longer blade.

They began circling a spot on the ground, each man carefully looking for an opening to attack the other. Mike limped, his left leg bleeding freely. He knew he didn't have long. The man seemed to be enjoying this struggle to the death. Mike was not.

"Who sent you?"

The Nigerian smiled and said, "The Lion."

"Who are you?"

"The Lion Slayer." Then he lunged at Mike, the dagger pressed forward in his right hand.

Mike stepped back with his right leg into a back stance. He blocked Okeke's jab with a left forearm block. Then he pushed forward off his back leg and spun to the right, his arm out straight, spinning in toward his attacker. He held his knife in his right hand, blade pointed back.

Mike's hand and knife came around in a spinning blur, and he rammed the full blade into the Nigerian's neck. Okeke dropped the dagger and slowly sank to his knees. Mike jerked the knife out and blood spurted a good three feet. The man gasped for breath as he fell onto his back.

Okeke lay on the ground mortally wounded, trying to get a last breath. Mike knelt beside him and leaned in close to the dying man.

"Who sent you?" he asked the dark man again.

Okeke raised a trembling hand and slowly pulled Mike down to him. The Nigerian whispered, "The Lion," and his hand dropped. He lay still.

Mike sat back. He looked at his own leg. It was bleeding profusely. He felt weak, both from the fight and from the loss of blood. He cut into the dead man's pants leg at thigh level all the way around the leg. Then he ran the knife blade the length of the pants leg and slit it open. He pulled it off Okeke's leg.

Mike folded the cloth lengthwise and then wrapped the long strip tightly around his wound and tied it off. He folded his still bloody knife and clipped it back in his pocket. He crawled around on his hands and knees, painfully, feeling in the brush until he located his pistol. He returned it to its holster behind his back.

He searched the dead man's body and found nothing but some sort of animal ear in the man's pocket. Mike studied it but wasn't sure what animal it was from, except that it was from something large. He tossed it aside.

He stood and limped straight out to the road to Okeke's car. He searched the vehicle, but again found nothing, not even the rental company paperwork.

He quickly made his way up the road to his own car. He knew he needed to get out of the area before someone saw him. He grabbed the keys from the console where he had left them, started the car, and made a U-turn. He headed back toward the coast road.

He arrived back at the hotel, parked in the underground garage, and made his way shakily to the elevator. He hoped that he wouldn't run into any guests on the way to the room. He was a filthy, bloody mess, who looked like he had just fought a man to the death.

He had no idea where his room key might be. He got to their room, praying Mya was already back. She was. She looked through the peephole and then jerked open the door. She gasped as Mike stumbled in. He pulled out his gun, put it on the desk, and then collapsed on the bed on his back. His left pants leg was completely soaked in blood from waist to cuff.

Mya ran to her backpack and pulled out a small, soft-pack, first-aid kit. She unfolded the kit and spread it out on the bed next to him. She untied the makeshift bandage Mike had put on his leg and removed it. She pulled off his shoes. Then she quickly unbuckled his belt and pants and pulled them down over his legs, tossing them aside. Blood oozed from the wound, and Mike moaned in pain.

She ripped open a gauze pack and pressed it hard against the gash on Mike's leg with her left hand. It was bad, and he was in serious pain. With her right hand, she grabbed a syringe pre-filled with morphine. She pulled off the safety cap with her teeth, squeezed a tiny amount out of the needle, and then jabbed it into Mike's arm, injecting the full contents.

Then she pulled out a second syringe of local anesthetic. She injected small amounts in multiple places around his wound. She got out a small paper packet and ripped it open with her teeth, all the while keeping direct pressure on the wound with her left hand. The packet held a stitching needle, with surgical fibril pre-threaded.

She tossed the bloody wad of gauze aside, pulled out a small bottle of antiseptic, and poured it over the wound. Then she pinched the severed flesh together with the thumb and forefinger of her right hand and began rapidly applying stitches with her left, so cleanly, and so neatly, that any observing doctor would have certainly applauded.

It took twelve, double stitches, twenty-four in all, to close the deep wound. She applied antiseptic cream and bandaged it. Finally, she gave him a shot of antibiotics. Then she cleaned up the mess, removed the rest of Mike's clothes, got a washcloth, and cleaned him up too. He was out, and she knew it would be a few hours, at least, before he would be coherent again.

12

Gerald Billings sat in his office at work with the door closed. It was early morning and he had been at work for about a half hour, all of that time sitting here pondering his dim fate. He knew he should run, but he was paralyzed with fear. He would have to adopt a new identity, leave the country, hide, and endeavor to remain alive.

Fortunately, he had already laid the groundwork for most of this—not because he had ever considered fleeing the country and hiding from the CIA, murderous foreign agents, and skilled assassins. Even *his* imagination had not included that scenario.

He shivered and swallowed the bile burning his throat. He couldn't imagine being on the run, one of the most wanted men on the planet.

The Arab had paid him another hundred thousand, as promised. Gerald now had two hundred thousand in the Grand Caymans under his false name. His own savings, here at home, totaled around two hundred and fifty thousand, though he knew he couldn't get it out of the country. It was all in bearer bonds.

He wasn't sure why he had put his life's savings into bonds that he physically held, other than the fact that he liked to touch them occasionally. But it turned out to be a blessing. He would not have been able to withdraw two hundred and fifty thousand in cash from any U.S. financial institution without the government knowing.

With paper bonds in a safety deposit box, though, he had put them in a bag, walked out of the bank, and no one was the wiser—particularly the U.S. government. He had then opened several new boxes at different banks using his fake identity, and hoped that if he did have to run, that someday he would have the opportunity to retrieve them.

Maybe when all this blew over.

He had a fake American passport in the name of Joseph Felts. Once the Arab man had convinced him to pass on information for money, he had begun developing a fake identity. He needed it to hide the money he was paid from snooping eyes.

He located a contact on the dark web two years earlier, who for a thousand in bitcoin had put him in touch with a forger in D.C. For an additional four thousand in cash, the forger had added Gerald's photo to a stolen U.S. passport.

Plus, Gerald thought it would be fun to have an alter ego. It somewhat fulfilled his old dream of being a spy. Though in reality, he knew it was just a stupid fantasy game he played using his fake identity. Now, however, he realized it may save his life—*if* he actually had the courage to run and hide.

He had even used the passport for travel *within* the United States but had never tried it on international travel. He had no idea if it would be adequate for entering a third world country, such as Chile. He prayed that it would. But he also knew that if he left the country he could never try to use the fake passport to reenter the U.S. It almost certainly would not stand up to the scrutiny of U.S. Customs and Border Protection. When they scanned it, the identity would show up on the State Department's list of lost or stolen passports.

He had never even considered that his *own* life might actually depend on this fake passport. He just knew that spies kept cash and fake documents stashed about the world for emergencies. Now he understood why.

He had also read several books on *disappearing oneself.* Again, not because he thought he would ever *have* to vanish, but because the subject fascinated him. As a fugitive, he knew that he would have to live completely off the grid. Still, despite the techniques these authors recommended, he knew that the CIA, and probably the Arab too, had extraordinary capabilities to locate and track anyone, anywhere in the world.

He shivered. Maybe he could just ride this out and things would eventually settle down.

His train of thought was interrupted when one of the secretaries knocked and opened the door. "Something's going on," she said. "Our office has to get polygraphs right away—all of us, even the DO. Yours is at nine this morning."

Gerald just stared at her blankly, seemingly in shock.

"Gerald, did you hear me?"

He tried to nod but barely succeeded.

"Gerald, are you okay?" she asked.

He managed a weak yes, and she stepped out and closed the door. Gerald looked at the clock. It was almost eight. He stood robotically and walked out to the outer office.

"I'm going downstairs to get some breakfast," he told the two women.

"Don't forget, nine o'clock."

"I won't," he muttered under his breath.

~

JFK International Airport

The UPS driver sat in his brown delivery truck, waiting. He was in line with twenty other UPS trucks and drivers. He waited for his turn to pull forward, swing his truck around on the tarmac, and back up to the huge UPS 747 jumbo jet parked a hundred yards in front of him.

It had arrived from Caracas, and U.S. Customs and Border Protection officers were clearing the shipment. The CBP officers moved in and out of the cargo hold—some had dogs, others had clipboards with manifests. He didn't know if the dogs were looking for drugs or bombs, but he figured it was probably drugs since the plane was coming from Venezuela.

He glanced around the sprawling tarmac of the UPS cargo hub adjacent to JFK. It was busy, as usual. Dozens of jets dotted the sprawling air cargo terminal, and hundreds of trucks waited to haul away the thousands of packages the jets brought in daily.

As he waited, he read over his manifest and checked his UPS PDA for his planned delivery route. He had sixty-two packages, all headed to lower Manhattan, his regular route for the past twelve years. Sixteen of his deliveries were going to One World Trade Center, including his largest, a mainframe computer.

According to the manifest, the server was in a wooden crate, five feet square, one hundred and seventy-two pounds. The Venezuelan manufacturer was a subsidiary of Benson Computers located in California. The Venezuelan company shipped thousands of items into the U.S. each year and most likely had a sterling record with U.S. Customs. He was familiar with the company. He had delivered their products many times in the past.

This would be the only delivery today that would pose any problem, but only because of the weight. He would have to wrestle it onto a wheeled cart, and then off again at the delivery point on the sixtieth floor.

The line of trucks began to snake forward. As he inched his truck up in line, a jet took off on a nearby runway with an ear-shattering blast. Thirty minutes later, he had his load and departed JFK. Once off the tarmac, he headed out onto I-678. He had his ear buds in, listening to his favorite music—cool jazz. He tapped his fingers on the steering wheel in time with the drumbeat.

He soon crossed the Brooklyn Bridge, drove straight across lower Manhattan to Vesey Street, and arrived at the WTC.

He pulled up to a vehicular security checkpoint for service vehicles and deliveries. He was in yet another line of trucks—deliveries, electricians, computer technicians, and the like. When he made it to the front of the line, a uniformed guard directed him to pull off to the side. He knew the procedure. He was a regular here, and the guards all knew him as well. Nevertheless, this was protocol.

He got out, clipboard and manifest in hand, and opened the huge sliding door on the back of his truck. One of the guards looked over the manifest and spent some time rummaging around among the parcels.

The guard asked about the crate. The driver showed him the item number on the bill of lading. "Just came in through customs," he told the guard. "You want to open it?"

The guard thought for a minute and said, "Nah, go on." He handed the clipboard back to the driver.

"No dog today?" asked the driver. They usually ran an explosives detection K-9 through his truck.

"Got called to check out a suspicious package in the lobby."

"Want me to wait?"

"Naw, you can go on."

He closed the door and hopped back into the cab, started up, and eased forward onto a service entrance leading to the lower levels under the WTC. He pulled into an area designated for service and delivery vehicles and backed up to a loading ramp.

He wrestled the large crate onto a cart and headed to the service elevators. On the sixtieth floor, he soon found suite 60-163. The door had no company name on it, but was unlocked. He pushed it open and yelled out, "UPS." The huge room was empty except for piles of construction materials everywhere. The floor was bare concrete.

A man suddenly appeared, startling the driver.

"Oh, hi," said the driver. "British Industrial Engineers?"

The man in the suite seemed to be Indian, or maybe Arabian, but he had a lanyard around his neck with a WTC tenant's card on it, and when he answered, he spoke with a British accent. "Yes, I was expecting you. The tracking number showed that our package had departed JFK."

"Yeah, just about an hour ago."

Looking at the crate he asked, "Is this our computer?"

"That's what my manifest says."

"And it came from Caracas?"

"Yes," he responded, pulling the cart in through the door. "Where do you want it?"

"Over here," he replied, walking toward the center of the large suite.

The driver and Hamadi Hassan unloaded the crate, and Hassan signed the UPS receipt.

The driver gave him a copy of the receipt and left, thinking he was glad to have the heavy one done. The rest would be a breeze.

~

Poti, Georgia

Khorasani had arrived back on Meskhi's Lear jet the night before. He returned to the hotel room in Poti that he had not checked out of from his previous stay, before going to Venezuela. He was now on his way to meet with Meskhi to finalize the deal.

He was soon sitting in front of Meskhi's big desk.

Khorasani said, "My superiors have authorized a second payment of fifty million to be made now."

Meskhi nodded and opened his laptop. He logged into his account and nodded at Khorasani.

"Please do so then."

Khorasani hit send on a message in Farsi he had already prepared. Less than a moment later, he received a reply: *On the way*.

Khorasani put down his phone. He smiled and gestured at Meskhi's computer.

Meskhi stared at the numbers in his account. After a few seconds, the balance changed. Fifty million dollars transferred into Meskhi's account from an Australian business named Sydney Industries.

Meskhi smiled and closed his computer. "Doing business in Australia now?"

"Wherever we can. You know how it is these days."

"So, Mr. Khorasani, what is your plan to close out this deal?"

"I have a truck and an escort team en route now. They will be here tonight, probably very early tomorrow morning. We have a larger military force waiting just over the border in Iran.

"We have now paid you one hundred million with a balance due of one hundred and fifty million. We will be able to pay another fifty million upon transfer of the devices to our men. The final one hundred million will be transferred when our convoy is safely out of Poti and has encountered no problems."

Meskhi's face had already turned red. He jerked the cigar out of his mouth and shouted, "That was not our deal!" Meskhi jumped up and slammed his fist on the desk.

One of Meskhi's men bounded in through the door, weapon drawn. Meskhi held up his hand, and the guard slowly backed out and closed the door.

"Genadi, relax. I thought I would be allowed to make full payment upon transfer. Now I am under new orders. My superiors are just being cautious. The money will be paid, unless our convoy is hijacked before clearing your territory. We know you own this town. My superiors don't know you like I do. They are just being careful."

Meskhi sat back down and considered this for a moment.

"I don't like it. We had a deal."

"I know. We still do. You know my country will pay you."

"How do I know?"

"We have always paid our debts to you. Have we not? We value our relationship and wish for it to continue."

Meskhi leaned back in his chair and stuck his cigar back in his mouth.

"How much firepower do you have in your escort?" asked Meskhi.

"Ten special operators in three vehicles, heavily armed."

"Then I will send two additional vehicles with eight shooters to ensure that it is safe. I need to protect my investment until the final payment is made. No more changes."

"No, that is sufficient. Do not worry, you will not be betrayed. We value our relationship and wish it to continue. The convoy will come directly to your storage building. I will return here. Do you have the codes?"

"Yes, I do."

"Early this morning, when we transfer, I would like only the PDA device that has the codes for all five devices. I would like the other four individual code PDAs to be destroyed. It will be easier to manage."

"Okay, I will take care of the four PDAs, as you wish, and I will keep only the one with all codes on it."

"Excellent. I will message you as our convoy nears Poti, and I will return here before it arrives."

~

Jersey City, New Jersey

Yousef Amad rested on his hotel bed, still mulling over the steps he would take to set up the nuclear device. He had them memorized. He was anxious to begin, and to be done.

When his phone buzzed, he jerked it up from the bed and read the message from Hamadi Hassan: Come now. You are listed as a company officer for British Industrial Engineers, and you are on the access roster for WTC. Come to Suite 60-163.

Amad jumped up. He was already dressed and had his small backpack ready. He rushed into the bathroom and washed his face. He stared into the mirror. He was about to seal the fate of hundreds of thousands of people. He looked into his own bleak eyes and saw only death.

He threw the towel on the floor, grabbed his bag, and left the room. He caught a cab into Manhattan and went directly to One World Trade Center. He crossed the promenade and entered the lobby. At the security checkpoint, he walked through a magnetometer and his bag was x-rayed.

The security guards compared his passport to the tenant's access roster and asked him to sign in. They gave him a badge on a lanyard and waved him through. He took the elevator to the sixtieth floor and found Suite 163 on the north side of the building.

Yousef Amad opened the office door and walked in. Hamadi Hassan came over and hugged him in greeting. Then he locked the door.

"Any problems?" he asked.

"None."

"Here it is," said Hassan, walking to the center of the room and removing a painter's drop cloth covering the crate. "I didn't open it. I wanted to leave all of this part for your expertise."

Hassan had placed a crowbar on top of the crate.

"It will be inside a mainframe computer."

"Yes, I know," said Amad, "I will have to disassemble the computer to get it out. Did you get the tools I requested?"

Next to the crate were three containers. Two resembled large, sturdy briefcases. One was a medium sized toolbox.

"These are the tool kits you requested. How long will it require?"

"I am not sure. At least several hours. I must take my time and be precise."

"Of course."

"You have the code? And you think you can do it?"

"Yes to both. I have carefully studied the information on the PDA. I can do it. I will activate the bomb with its anti-handling function activated. I will set it to detonate in thirty hours time."

"Very good. When you have completed your work, we will conceal it, lock this place, and leave. We have flights to London tonight."

"Very well. I must begin work now."

~

Poti, Georgia

Hours later, Mya finally finished cleaning Mike and the room. She had stuffed all the bloody and dirty clothes, bandages, and linen into a laundry bag and disposed of them in a dumpster near the parking garage entrance.

She called Max. After several rings, he answered. He knew it was Mya calling.

"Yes, Mya, Max here."

"I've got a report for you."

"Mike there?"

"No, he hasn't come back yet."

"Okay, Striker wants to hear from you. Let me conference him in."

He called Striker and joined him to the conversation with Mya.

"Striker here. How are you doing, Mya?"

"Fine. No problems, except that we've not had a breakthrough."

"Is Mike there?"

"He's still out. I expect him back soon."

"What have you learned?"

"I saw Genadi Meskhi's warehouse in the port, where his import-export business is located. I also got a look at his personal compound where he lives. Also his hangar at the airport. Nothing to see there. Locked up tight. I sent Max photos."

"No leads?" asked Striker.

"No, sir. Nothing yet, but I feel like Meskhi is our man. It's just a hunch though. I'm going to watch the warehouse and see where it leads."

Striker said, "I agree. Our analysts are leaning toward Meskhi. They've picked up on an association between him and Vladimir Grigor. I'm betting this arms dealer is our man."

"Okay," said Mya. "Still no idea where this colonel is?"

"He seems to have vanished, so we need to focus on Meskhi. He does a lot of work for Iran, so he has a ready-made customer. And if those devices get to Iranian soil, we've lost them for good. We need to know where the bombs are now, before they can be moved."

"Yes, sir," replied Mya.

Striker continued, "Now that we're focusing on Meskhi and Poti, I'm concerned that Incirlik Air Base is not a good location for our strike force. It's much too far away. Even if you were to find the devices, they might be long gone before Delta Force could get there.

"Mya, contact Mike, I want him on a plane back to Turkey within the hour. Have him fly to Istanbul. We'll send a plane to get him from Istanbul to Incirlik. I want my own man on the ground with Delta when this goes down. Tell Mike to coordinate with Barrington and move the assault force to somewhere in eastern Turkey. Somewhere near the Georgian border.

"Once in position there, they will be within a few minutes striking distance of Poti or the Iranian border. We'll send Barrington the pictures you took and the satellite images as well. See what you can find for us, Mya. We need a location."

"Okay, will do."

"And Mya, we've had a new development that we think is related to our three dead agents."

"Yes, sir?"

"Gerald Billings, Alan Berg's executive assistant, has gone missing. We can't find a trace of him. Berg confirms that Billings knew the cover identities of all three murdered agents as well as Mike's alias. I've removed Berg, and there will be a new DO before the day is out. We think either someone kidnapped Billings or he's gone underground. CBP says he didn't leave the country, at least not as Gerald Billings.

"But we'll worry about him later. With no further access, he should no longer be a threat. You can be sure, however, that we will get back to him in due time."

Striker paused, "Do you have everything you need to continue on there, Mya?"

"Yes, sir."

"Good. I'm counting on you Mya. Keep me posted if you find anything."

"Will do." She disconnected.

Mya went over to Mike and shook him several times. He was still out from the morphine. She went down to the hotel lobby to the small gift shop. She bought a bottle of 5-Hour Energy, marveling at what you could find even in the most remote parts of the world. She also picked up a couple of cokes and a handful of protein bars.

She returned to the room, grabbed the ice bucket, and went to the icemaker in the hall. Back in the room, she shook Mike again. He started coming around. Groggy, but waking. Mya helped him sit up.

She put some ice in a cup, poured in the bottle of 5-Hour Energy, and filled the cup with cola. She handed it to Mike.

"Drink this," she said, "it will either kill you or get you going."

Mike took a sip and realized just how thirsty he was. He chugged it down and pushed the cup out to Mya.

"More," he said.

Mya poured more coke, ripped open a protein bar, and gave both to him. He ate the bar in three bites. She gave him another and he gulped it down too. He drank the three cokes she had bought and then laid his head back and took a few deep breaths.

"Did you see anything?"

"First things first. How do you feel?"

"My leg hurts like hell."

"Good. Probably not too much nerve damage."

Mya sat on the edge of the bed next to him.

"Mike, you're not telling me everything. What's going on? Who did you kill, and why?"

"What makes you think I killed someone?"

"You made it back here. I'm assuming he didn't. I want to know what the fallout might be for the mission here."

"Mya, an assassin was tracking me. He was in Istanbul when the Russians came. At first, I thought he was scouting for the

Russians, but then I realized he wasn't working for them at all. Their attack probably threw him off. So he came here to Poti to finish the job."

She nodded.

"Mya, I think this guy killed our agents. And I was on his list. Maybe you were too for all I know."

"And you killed him?"

"Yes, but I don't know if there might be a replacement here tomorrow."

"He obviously didn't go easily."

"No."

"Mike, what did he cut you with? That was a nasty wound."

"Some sort of wicked-ass, ceremonial dagger."

"Well, I double stitched it. It won't come open, but it's going to be sore as hell."

"The guy I fought was African, I think. He had three rows of tribal scars under each eye."

"Dark skin?" she asked.

"Very."

"Mike, that sounds like the Nigerian. Some say he's just a legend. Somewhat mythical in his skills. You're lucky to be alive."

"It was close."

"Anyway, I just talked to Striker and Max. Striker says that Gerald Billings is missing and they think he had something to do with the compromised agents. He said that Billings shouldn't pose any additional threat now and they would take care of him later. Striker wants you to get to Istanbul ASAP. They'll have a plane to take you to Incirlik from there. Then he wants you to move the assault force to eastern Turkey, within striking distance of Poti."

"Did you tell them I was injured?"

"No. I said you hadn't returned yet."

"What did you find out about Meskhi?"

Mya recounted the details of her recon tour with the Georgian asset.

"Not much to work with. We're going to have to get inside his operation somehow."

"Not *we*," said Mya, "*you* need to hit the road. I'm staying here."

"I'm not leaving you here."

"Mike, despite our earlier conversation, I *am* a big girl. I can take care of myself."

"I'm staying," Mike repeated.

"No, even if we found the nukes, we wouldn't have the means to deal with it. Meskhi has too much firepower. We need to have a team nearby. Incirlik is over six hundred miles away. You have to do what Striker says. Get Barrington and his men positioned closer to Poti."

Mya frowned. "Mike, without a strike force nearby, we could lose track of the devices even if we found them. I know the lay of the land here. I'll be fine."

"What do you have in mind?"

"I'm going to conduct surveillance and see what turns up."

"Mya, don't go out there and try to prove something."

"Don't worry. I'll be careful, but I *will* maintain a healthy dose of respect for my adversary," she said grinning. "We have orders and a new mission. Now get moving."

13

Ronald Reagan Washington National Airport (DCA), 12:05 p.m.

Gerald walked down the concourse toward his gate. He was nervous, as usual, and sweated, even though the temperature in the terminal was almost chilly.

He knew they would be looking for him. When he failed to show for his appointment in the security office for the polygraph earlier in the morning, he had basically announced that he was the traitor they were seeking.

He knew they had probably already visited his home and now had it staked out. They would also be looking for him at the airport, but hopefully not at DCA. He had gone through TSA screening as Joseph Felts using his fake passport without problem. The flight he was about to take was also in the name of Joseph Felts, and he had purchased the ticket with a prepaid charge card that could not be traced to Gerald Billings. He had purchased a round-trip ticket to Santiago, Chile, changing planes in Miami. A one-way ticket was significantly cheaper, but he wanted to avoid the additional government scrutiny a one-way ticket might bring.

Earlier in the day, he had also bought a one-way ticket online to Toronto under his real name using his personal credit card. It departed Dulles later that evening. The CIA would quickly discover the ticket for Canada and, he hoped, would be focused on Dulles and not DCA. Agents would already have Dulles staked out in an effort to intercept him there, but by the time that flight departed Dulles, he would already be in South America.

Gerald approached his gate. His flight was already boarding. Once aboard, he found his seat and settled in. He was as scared as he had ever been in his life, but he was also feeling quite proud of himself as well. He might just beat the CIA at their own game.

~

Igdir, Turkey, 7:10 p.m.

The three-vehicle Iranian convoy headed northwest toward the Black Sea. At the coast, they would cross into Georgia and on to Poti, an eight-hour drive from their current location. At considerable expense to the Iranians, the convoy had pre-approved border-crossing papers for their agricultural business to pass from Turkey into Georgia and return.

The small convoy appeared to be from an agricultural produce company, but the men were actually an elite Iranian Quds Force special operations unit. They drove two modified pickup trucks, and a box-type cargo truck.

The cargo truck was a late-model Mercedes. *Produce Co.* was written on both doors of the red cab in the Georgian language Kartuli. The cargo compartment was bright green with *Produce Co.* written in large letters on both sides. It had an image of large red tomatoes under the company name. The truck carried two men.

Two Toyota Tundra quad-cab pickups provided escort. The trucks were dull gray, slightly scratched, and strategically dented. *Produce Co.* was also displayed on the front two cab doors. They appeared to be well-used farm trucks. Both pickups had boxes stacked in the beds marked Produce. The trucks carried four men each.

The ten men were heavily armed special operators. They were dressed as farm workers, but beneath their shirts, they carried silenced pistols and grenades. On their laps rested 9mm submachine guns. These men were Iran's transfer team.

The Iranian Quds Force had begun immediately to prepare this team and these vehicles for a very special mission the moment the Supreme Leader had approved Khorasani's proposal to acquire the nuclear weapons.

The convoy anticipated a 4:00 a.m. arrival and link up with Meskhi's men at the warehouse. Khorasani would be with Meskhi at the arms dealer's compound.

~

Washington, D.C.

Sadegh Mohsen sat at a sidewalk café sipping his second espresso. He tapped his fingers impatiently on the table. He was expecting two separate communications, neither of which had arrived.

He knew that Iran was very close to succeeding in securing the nuclear bombs. He wanted to ensure that *nothing* interfered with that success, but he was feeling stymied. He had instructed the Nigerian to intercept and kill the American agent Mike Elliot at the Villa Reta Hotel in Poti, and to report the completion of his assignment.

The assassin was extremely efficient about taking care of his assigned targets. He was quick, quiet, and discreet. But Mohsen had not heard back from Okeke. It was not like the man not to follow his orders to the letter. So Mohsen had to assume that Okeke had failed in his mission.

Mohsen had also messaged Gerald Billings, but he too had not responded.

He reluctantly picked up his phone and tapped out an encrypted message to his superiors in Iran: *American agent believed to be in Poti, Georgia. My man was unable to intercept.*

~

Poti, Georgia, 8:00 p.m.

Mya dressed in black. Then she methodically placed her weapons and equipment—including the 9mm Beretta provided by the asset, a knife, a small LED flashlight, and binoculars. Her CIA phone, on mute, went into a side leg pocket. The Colt Mike had left behind would go into her rental car's glove box as a backup.

She pulled on a bright yellow cotton blouse over her black T-shirt and left it unbuttoned. The yellow shirt was for one purpose only—to walk out of the hotel dressed like a tourist rather than a spy. She would take it off once in the car.

Mya headed to Meskhi's warehouse. During her visit there with the Georgian asset, she had identified the spot where she would park. She intended to stake out the warehouse, keep it under surveillance, and see where it led.

If nothing worthwhile turned up, then before daylight, she would check out the inside of the huge building. If Meskhi had the nukes, they were either in this warehouse, or in a nearby building like it, she surmised.

~

Incirlik Air Base, Turkey, 8:15 p.m.

Mike had caught the first flight out of Poti to Istanbul. After clearing Turkish customs, he went out front of the terminal to a waiting CIA driver and car. They drove a half hour to a small Turkish military airfield just outside the city, where Mike hopped on a CIA Lear jet. His plane had just now landed at Incirlik air base in southern Turkey.

Barrington's team had set up in the spec ops compound in a small hangar on the flight line.

Mike's plane taxied to a ramp parking area and shut down. A crewmember opened the cabin door, and Mike exited the jet. A small sedan, with a U.S. Air Force driver, was waiting on the ramp nearby. They drove to the outer gate of the U.S. compound. The driver showed his military ID to the U.S. Air Force security police, and Mike handed over his passport in the name of James Finch. Mike's alias was listed on the access roster for the compound. The officer waved them through.

They drove to Delta's hangar. Mike got out, and the driver left with the sedan. A detachment of U.S. Army Rangers provided local security. Four Blackhawk and three Chinook helicopters were parked on the flight line. The crews were busy prepping their birds. It was dusk, and they would soon be using the portable light stands located near the helicopters to continue their work.

A sergeant approached Mike.

"Mike Elliot. Sergeant Major Barrington is expecting me."

"Yes, sir. We were told to be on the lookout for you. This way, sir," he said, as he started walking toward the hangar. Mike limped slightly and grimaced in pain with each step.

Inside the hangar, Delta had set up a command post and a logistics hub. The sergeant took Mike over to Barrington. He and his operators were huddled around a large table with a map of the region spread out before them.

The Ranger sergeant took Mike up to Barrington and then left. Barrington noticed Mike and stopped what they were doing. He shook Mike's hand, pulled him in for a quick hug, and introduced him to the Delta operators standing around the table. Palmer was there and grabbed Mike in a bear hug.

"This man can shoot," Palmer said. "You guys are good to go with him by your side."

"I second that," Barrington said.

That was all the Delta operators needed to hear. Mike was unofficially one of the team.

Barrington said to Mike, "Let me give you a quick rundown of what we've got ready to launch. We have the four Blackhawks you saw on the ramp. They're from the 160th Special Operations Aviation Regiment. We've got two MH-60Ms to carry the assaulters, and two MH-60Ls, Direct Action Penetrators, each equipped with M134 mini-gun pods on stub wings to provide air cover."

Mike was very familiar with mini-guns. They had saved his bacon on more than one occasion when he was about to be overrun by a superior force. The six-barreled, 7.62 mm chain gun had a rotating barrel. This was an awe-inspiring weapon capable of laying down a devastating two to six thousand rounds per minute. Someone could do a lot of damage quickly with just one of these guns. Between the two MH-60L Blackhawks, they carried *four* mini-guns.

Barrington said, "I've got thirteen assaulters, plus you and me. We have a detachment of Rangers for local security. We've also got a detachment of three CH-47D Chinooks."

The Chinook was a twin-engine, tandem-rotor, heavy-lift helicopter. What it couldn't carry in its large cargo bay, it could sling load beneath its belly.

Barrington continued, "I've got medics, of course, and a couple of top-tier bomb techs, as well. A captain from our staff is running logistics for us. We're all set."

"Sounds good," Mike said. He nodded toward a corner, "Can we talk a minute?"

"Sure."

They walked to the corner of the hangar.

"Scott, did you get the photos and satellite telemetry on Poti?"

"Yeah, we've been studying it. Anything solid?"

"Not solid, but CIA *thinks* it's Genadi Meskhi in Poti, Georgia. He's basically a mafia-style arms dealer with *lots* of muscle. We have someone on the ground trying to get a fix on a location."

Mike's leg had been bleeding again. A bright-red splotch at thigh level had spread across the left leg of his khaki pants.

Barrington noticed. "Have a little problem in Poti, Mike?"

"Yeah, I had a run in with a bad-ass African who didn't like the way I looked."

Barrington whistled loudly and the large room fell silent. "Medic over here," he shouted.

Barrington grabbed a chair, pulled it over, and Mike sat down. The Delta medic, carrying a backpack medical kit, hustled over.

"Drop your pants, sir, and let me have a look at that."

Mike did so and sat back down in his boxers.

The medic removed the wet bandage. Mike and Barrington continued their conversation.

"Anyway," Mike said, "if we do get a location in or near Poti, we need to be able to act on it immediately. We also think that Iran might be the customer. If they get to Iran with those things it's bad news. We can't let that happen. Scott, we need to set up a forward operating base in eastern Turkey where we can quickly strike either toward Poti, or the Iranian border."

The medic had removed Mike's bandage and cleaned up the blood. "Wow," he said. "Nice work."

"What?"

"The stitches. You obviously had a top-notch surgeon fix this. This is nice work. It's just oozing a little blood. That's normal. No problem."

"Actually," Mike replied, "It wasn't a surgeon. A female CIA operative did the stitching in a hotel room near the Black Sea."

The medic just shook his head in wonder. He applied some cream and prepared a new bandage for the wound.

"Before you do that," Mike said, "give me some local anesthesia shots. I need to be able to move."

"You got it, sir. Did she give you antibiotics?"

"I don't know," replied Mike.

"I'll give you a shot just to be on the safe side."

Barrington said, "I don't see a problem with moving the team. Soon as you're done with that we'll get everyone together and discuss the logistics."

Mike got his shots and a new bandage.

Barrington called over a Turkish Major.

"Mike, I'd like you to meet Major Adem Dal. He's from Turkish Army special operations. He's our liaison."

Mike and Major Dal shook hands. Major Dal was tall and slim, but muscular. At first glance, Mike surmised that he was probably a very capable special operator. He had that look that Mike could easily recognize after all these years in the business.

"Major," said Barrington to Dal, "we need to stage our team in eastern Turkey near the Georgian border. Is that possible, and if so, where?"

Grinning broadly, the Major replied, "Anywhere you like, as long as I am with you."

Barrington smiled and said, "My pleasure, but we may be violating some borders, and the shit is probably going to get really nasty before it's all over."

The major replied, "I am authorized to go anywhere you go. This mission is critical to my country as well. If one of our neighbors, like Syria or Iran for example, got their hands on these devices, we would be at great risk."

"Let's get the team together and look at the map," said Barrington.

Barrington whistled again and waved his hand over his head in a circle. "Log chief, operators, chief pilots, Ranger leader, around the map table please."

Everyone quickly gathered. A young army captain on Delta's staff was in charge of logistics in support of Barrington's team. The senior pilot for the four Blackhawk crews, a chief warrant officer five from the 160th, stood by the table, as well as the chief pilot for the Chinook detachment, a chief warrant officer four. A sergeant first class was in charge of the Ranger detachment. Then there was Major Dal, Mike, Barrington, and thirteen Delta operators.

Barrington opened, "Okay, folks, here's the situation. We need to move to eastern Turkey near the Georgian border. CIA thinks they might have a lead in that area. We'll be on standby for a quick launch from there."

Gesturing toward the Turkish Major, Barrington said, "Major Dal from Turkish Special Forces is joining us, as well as Mike Elliot from CIA. Both of them will be on the assault element on my bird."

Turning to Major Dal, Barrington asked, "Where would you recommend, Major?"

The major leaned over the big map table and without hesitation dropped his large index finger on the map. "Here, in the Posof Forest, on the border with Georgia. I have hunted there, and we have conducted numerous exercises there. It is basically wilderness, sparsely populated, and has plenty of open spaces in the interior. It's a twenty-minute flight to Poti from there."

Barrington turned to the two chief pilots. "Can we fly there without refueling?"

The chief pilot from the 160th responded, "Yes, it looks like about a four-hour flight, but we would need to refuel once there for whatever follows."

The chief Chinook pilot added, "We can haul the fuel."

Barrington looked at the Captain, "Sir, what's your take on logistics?"

The captain stepped closer to the table. "We can do it. How long will we be there?"

Barrington answered, "Don't know. Maybe a few days, maybe longer. Let's prep for a week."

"No problem, Sergeant Major. We'll carry the Rangers and my staff on the three Chinooks. We'll sling load six fuel pods with the Chinooks and land them on the site, spread out so all the helos can land close to a fuel pod. I'll ensure we have rations for a week. We'll set up a med station and build a field latrine. It'll be just like home, Sergeant Major."

Barrington nodded.

The 160th chief pilot said, "We'll work out flight and landing plans so we'll know in advance exactly where the fuel pods will be placed and where everyone will land. Just give us about a half football field's size space."

Barrington said, "Major Dal and I will pick the spot. The chief pilots will give a yea or nay."

The pilots nodded their approval with Barrington's plan.

"How soon can we move?" Barrington asked the group.

The captain said, "Logistics, one hour."

The pilots replied, "We're ready. It'll be dark, so we'll all be operating on night vision, but no problem with that."

"Ok, folks," said Barrington. "One hour. It's twenty-thirty-five hours now. We liftoff at twenty-one-forty, with a four hour flight time."

Major Dal interrupted, "It's a one hour time difference between here and the eastern border."

"All right, we lose one hour en route. That puts us on site at approximately oh-two-forty. Give or take a half hour to scout a site, set down, and set up shop. That puts us on the ground and ready at oh-three-hundred hours. Any questions?"

There were none.

"Let's get cracking, folks."

~

Poti, Georgia, 11:05 p.m.

Mya drove to Poti's industrial area at the port facility. She made several detours en route to ensure that she was not followed. The port area and the warehouses were well lit, so she had chosen a spot to park that she knew would be dark.

She was at least a hundred yards from the warehouse, but she would have a good field of view with her compact binoculars. Bushes lined her parking spot, and she got out and stood in between some hedges. She didn't want to be trapped in the car if someone suddenly appeared. If someone did drive up, discover her car, and decide to investigate, she had a concealed escape route behind her that she could take on foot.

She focused in on the warehouse with her binoculars. Even in the middle of the night, the massive building buzzed with activity. Tractor-trailers came and went; huge forklifts moved about carrying pallets and crates. Workers in coveralls with *Meskhi's Import-Export* printed on them busily attended to various tasks.

Then there were the men in civilian clothes standing off to the side of the building—watching, pacing, smoking, talking on cell phones, and occasionally chatting with each other. Those men were not workers. They were soldiers in Meskhi's organized crime syndicate.

Mya wasn't sure what might turn up. After all, any one of the trucks coming or going could be carrying the nukes. But she doubted it. The truck carrying something so valuable would have heavy security. She would just have to look for something out of the ordinary.

Bottom line, she knew that she might have to go in there to find out what that was.

~

Near Bangkok, Thailand

Hans Reimer, formerly Colonel Vladimir Grigor, stood by the pool at his villa. He sipped Dom Perignon from a crystal flute, savoring each unique flavor in the exquisite elixir. As he did so, he admired the expansive view of the Gulf of Thailand spread out before him in the distance.

He was feeling quite satisfied with himself. He wore only a bathing suit. His body was lean and tan. His blond hair was fuller now. He wore a short, neat blond beard and of course no longer had a scar on his cheek or a patch covering his eye.

He also admired the view by the pool. An attractive young Thai woman half his age lay by the water in a lounge chair reading a fashion magazine. Her string bikini left little to the imagination. He smiled. His plan had come together nicely. He was no longer a prisoner of the Russian establishment, or of the Russian winter. He was free and wealthy.

His property had fourteen lush, tropical acres surrounding his home, which was perched on the top of a hill at seven hundred feet elevation. His villa held the high ground, and Grigor of all people appreciated that tactical advantage. The property was less than an hour's drive southeast of Bangkok in a rural area off coastal Route 3.

Through paid intermediaries, he had carefully planned and acquired this property over a year ago as his final refuge. It was owned by a corporation he controlled. Yet nothing about the legal entity or the property could be traced to his former identity.

There was only one road up the mountainside to his estate. A steel gate blocked its entrance. A sturdy fence laced with high-tech security cameras and motion sensors encircled the entire property. Anyone touching the fence would immediately draw the attention of a camera, and the system would silently alert Grigor. He controlled it all from his phone.

He had cell service, but only because he needed it to monitor his security system and to check on his bank account through an encrypted app on the phone. He didn't make telephone calls on it, however, for security reasons. Besides, there was no one he needed or wanted to call. If the need arose, he would use a prepaid burner phone. For additional security, an app on the phone spoofed the cell towers, disguising his location so that he couldn't be tracked via cell signal.

Despite using a smart phone to control his environs, he was otherwise enjoying life off the grid. He remained disconnected from the electronic treadmill of world media that engulfed and smothered modern man. It had been a longtime goal. He was grateful to have the opportunity now to tune out all the media hype, that constant mind numbing flow of electronic gibberish that filled others lives. He had a library full of *real* books that he could touch, see, and smell. It was intellectually refreshing.

Still, since he controlled everything with it, he always had the phone nearby, and he *always* had a pistol within arm's reach.

He wasn't really paranoid. He was just taking the reasonable precautions that any wealthy man should take. He was comfortable visiting Bangkok and the surrounding areas for dining, entertainment, and women. He bore no resemblance to his former self. He was confident that no one could identify him as Colonel Vladimir Grigor.

He was also taking financial precautions by avoiding electronic transactions. He simply used cash, at least for the time being. Every few weeks, he returned to his bank in Bangkok and withdrew fifteen to twenty thousand in cash for spending money— and he was very much enjoying spending it.

Through his arms dealing over the years, he had acquired significant wealth. He had consolidated those holdings in a secret, numbered account in Bangkok. Meskhi made the final two payments for the nukes to that same account, so his holdings were substantial.

He thought of Meskhi and grinned. He had known that the little mob boss would sell the bombs to the Iranians. In fact, that's exactly what Grigor had wanted him to do. The Iranians would study the devices and use them to develop their own nuclear program. But they would never dare to actually deploy and detonate one of them. So in essence, the devices would never again see the light of day. They would simply vanish into a black hole. When things settled down, no one would care about him, and he didn't have to worry about accidentally being in the wrong city at the wrong time when some lunatic terrorist destroyed it.

Yes, it had worked out just fine. He set his glass on a table next to the book he was reading, picked up the phone and gun, and walked past the young woman, signaling for her to follow. She slid off the chaise-lounge with a practiced grace and cozied up next to him, slipping her arm around his waist as they walked. For what he was paying her, she was more than happy to accommodate his wildest desires.

~

Manhattan, 4:05 p.m.

The World Trade Center architectural team was making a top-to-bottom review of all finished space and cataloguing all areas still requiring build-out.

The team included the architect and his assistant, the building owner's representative, the building manager and his assistant, the leasing agent, the WTC director of security, a city building inspector, a WTC assistant fire marshal, and a secretary taking notes.

They had been at this task for weeks, and were now working through the 60th floor. They all had clipboards or binders and were making their own notes for follow-up. They arrived at the entrance to suite 163. Referring to a page in his binder, the leasing agent briefed the group on the new tenants.

"We just completed a lease for 163. The tenant is a corporation called British Industrial Engineers. Not sure exactly what type of engineering they do, but they executed a lease on fifteen thousand square feet on a ten-year renewable. They will still have to build-out."

The building manager's assistant unlocked the door with his master key and they all filed in. The room was a large open space with a bare concrete floor. Metal framing beams and sheetrock panels were stacked in piles about the room.

The group glanced around. Nothing out of the ordinary. Some of them made notes. The assistant fire marshal headed across the room while the others conferred.

"Who is doing the build-out? Us or them?" asked the building manager.

"They are," replied the leasing agent. They all continued working through their checklists.

The WTC had a safety department whose job it was to conduct fire safety inspections throughout the property. As the others talked, the assistant fire marshal checked the large space over, looking in boxes and under tarps. He couldn't count the number of times he had discovered safety hazards left by contractors and tenants alike. The work crews were especially notorious for leaving hazardous materials unsecured, or oily rags piled in a corner, or any of a dozen other hazards.

The group was slowly making its way to the door, still discussing minor details and making notes for themselves. The fire inspector was completing his inspection, making notations on a checklist on his clipboard. He headed toward the door. Near the center of the space, he passed a pile of something covered by a painter's drop cloth. Next to that, there was a partially disassembled mainframe computer.

He lifted the cover and peeked under. He did a double take but still couldn't figure out what he was looking at. An electronic display had numbers on it, and they were ticking down. At first, he thought it was some kind of fancy new portable generator or compressor.

He called the building manager's assistant to come over. When he saw the object he was alarmed, and he called over the director of security. Everyone else came over with him to see what the fuss was about.

When the director of security saw it, he nearly had a heart attack.

"Don't touch it," he ordered, "and turn off your cell phones, now!"

He walked over to the fire alarm and pulled it. "We're evacuating the building."

He went into the hall to a black security box on the wall. He inserted a key into the slot, turned it, opened the box, and picked up a handset. A security guard answered in the control room.

"Connect me to the police commissioner and the mayor, ASAP."

The World Trade Center director of security had immediate access to both of those public officials in a crisis. The two men were quickly on the line.

The security director said, "We have a large bomb on the 60th floor. We're evacuating now."

"Was this a bomb threat?" asked the commissioner.

"No, I'm on the 60th, and I saw it with my own eyes."

"We're on our way," replied the commissioner.

14

McLean, Virginia, 4:47 p.m.

The NYPD bomb squad had taken one look at the device and informed the New York Joint Terrorism Task Force (JTTF) that they needed a nuclear weapons expert ASAP. The JTTF notified the command centers for the FBI and the CIA. The White House was informed. At that point, the entire U.S. government was energized for this crisis.

Max was now in the back seat of a CIA sedan, a federal agent at the wheel, blue lights flashing and siren blaring. They were headed to DCA where the FBI had a Lear jet waiting.

A similar federal law enforcement vehicle raced across Washington, D.C. from the Department of Energy, carrying Dr. Edward Mackey, a renowned DOD nuclear weapons designer assigned to Los Alamos, and in town for meetings. He would meet Max at DCA.

~

Ronald Reagan Washington National Airport, 5:10 p.m.

Max's sedan raced through an open gate at DCA, where more federal agents stood by the gate waving the car through. He arrived planeside at the same time as Dr. Mackey.

An FBI agent greeted the two men and quickly ushered them onto the plane. The jet's engines were already turning. The agent pulled the door closed, and the jet immediately began rolling forward.

The plane had absolute priority. The FAA had ordered a complete ground stop at DCA. They would do the same at JFK in a few short moments.

The jet raced through the taxiways and straight onto the runway. The pilot gunned it and with a few seconds, they were airborne and en route to JFK in New York. The agent informed Max that a DHS Blackhawk would be waiting on the ramp at JFK.

~

John F. Kennedy International Airport, 5:50 p.m.

The FBI Lear jet touched down. It pulled quickly onto the first adjoining taxiway and braked to a stop next to a Blackhawk helicopter. The helicopter's engines were running and the rotors turning. Nothing else moved at the sprawling airport.

Max and Dr. Mackey ran to the Blackhawk. Its passenger door was open. They climbed in, took a seat, and buckled in. The crew chief slammed the door closed, and the pilots immediately increased throttle.

Within a few seconds, the big helicopter lifted up and soared away toward Manhattan and a seven-minute flight to the World Trade Center. Nothing else was flying over New York City. The FAA had halted all overflight of the city except for law enforcement and military aircraft.

~

Manhattan, 6:04 p.m.

NYPD had secured a landing site on the World Trade Center plaza near the skyscraper. The DHS Blackhawk touched down with a slight bounce, and a DHS agent on the ground stood by as the crew chief opened the sliding side door.

Max and Dr. Mackey jumped out and followed the agent. An FBI bomb tech met them in the lobby and ushered them directly into the elevator.

~

One World Trade Center, 6:09 p.m.

The elevator door opened on the 60th floor. The small group of men hurried into the hallway. An agent led them into suite 163. Several top bomb techs from the FBI and ATF were looking at the device.

Dr. Mackey approached the bomb, and the other men backed away slightly to make room. He walked slowly up to the device, his mouth agape.

"Oh my God," he stammered under his breath.

"Is this what I think it is?" asked the senior FBI bomb tech.

"Yes, it's our worst nightmare, and it has finally arrived."

"Doctor?" asked one of the other men.

"I'm sorry." He paused, looked around at the group, and said slowly, "It's a Russian RA-115 SADM, a Special Atomic Demolitions Munition. It's a two kiloton tactical nuclear weapon, a so-called suitcase nuke, and the timer shows four hours and twenty-one minutes until detonation."

He carefully pointed at the electronic control panel. "You see that flashing red light?" he asked the group.

They nodded yes.

"It indicates that the anti-handling function has been enabled. If we so much as bump it, it will go off."

The mayor and police chief walked into the room. An agent quickly briefed them on what Dr. Mackey had just said.

The mayor asked, "Can you disarm it, Doctor?"

"Not without the deactivation code."

"Four hours and twenty-one minutes," said the mayor, shaking his head.

The commissioner asked in a shaky voice, "Can we evacuate the city and surrounding areas in four hours? It will be total chaos."

"I don't know, but we have to try," said the mayor. To Dr. Mackey he asked, "Doctor, how far will the blast be?"

Mackey thought for a moment and said, "They were pretty clever, or diabolical, if you will, to put it on the sixtieth floor. It will essentially be an air blast—meaning above the surface of the earth. This is where it will do maximum damage. This high up, the immediate destruction area will probably be a four-mile radius.

Burns and subsequent radiation poisoning in an eight-mile radius. Then who knows how much farther the radiation might drift."

"Oh my God," stammered the mayor.

Max said, "Mayor, I'm from the CIA. We're pulling out all stops looking for the codes to deactivate the device, but there's no guarantee we'll find them in time."

The mayor said, "Commissioner, I'll make an announcement out front in ten minutes. Get the press together. After that, I'm remaining here."

"Mr. Mayor," he replied, "maybe we shouldn't disclose that it is a nuclear bomb. That really would create panic and chaos."

"What can we say?"

"We can just say that we have a bomb threat. So we're evacuating the surrounding area as a precaution."

"You're right. Okay, that's what we'll say."

15

Mya had been watching Meskhi's warehouse continuously for three and a half hours, but had not detected anything other than normal business operations. The men in civilian clothes had changed shifts at midnight. Trucks were still coming in and out; forklifts moved things about.

A black sedan had visited the warehouse twice, arriving on the main road from Poti. Then it had returned toward Poti, the way it had come. She lowered the binoculars. They hung on a strap around her neck. She rubbed her eyes, not so much from lack of sleep, but simply strain from staring at the warehouse for so long.

The black sedan returned to the warehouse and pulled to a stop by several of the men standing by a pedestrian entrance at the corner of the building. The driver got out and talked with the other men for several minutes.

Then he got back in his car, turned around, and drove out of the driveway to the road. This time, however, he turned left instead of right. This was different. Mya jumped into her car, started up, and pulled out. She followed the car at a safe distance without turning on her headlights.

The black sedan only drove a few blocks and then turned left down a small alley between two large warehouses. Mya continued straight ahead, but as she passed the alley, she caught a glimpse of a smaller building at the end of the alley. Lights on the front of the building glowed brightly. A group of men stood in the building's small parking lot where the black sedan had stopped.

She drove around the corner of a darkened warehouse and parked. She made her way on foot down the side of the long metal building. Weeds grew through cracks in the pavement. Broken glass crunched underfoot. She moved cautiously.

Mya carefully worked her way around the back of the old warehouse to a spot where she could see the lighted building and the group of men in the parking lot in front of it. She scanned the men with her binoculars. More of Meskhi's soldiers, she was sure.

She scanned around her position. It seemed secure. She watched the men. They were talking, smoking, walking back and forth. They were guarding something. Maybe something special. But she had to know for sure before calling in Delta. They would have one shot at conducting an assault. She had to be certain.

~

Eastern Turkey, 2:45 a.m.

After a four-hour flight, Barrington and his team had reached the Posof Forest. Part of the flight and landing plan was for Blackhawk One, Barrington's bird, to scout out and select the site for Forward Operating Base Posof. The remaining helicopters formed up in a holding pattern at two thousand feet.

The team operated on Night Vision Goggles or NVG. The view of the ground was generally clear, except for a few shadow areas, but the image appeared in stark black and white with a high contrast tone.

Blackhawk One identified two possible sites. They lowered down into the second site and hovered at about one hundred feet. The grassy field was on a gently rolling hill encircled by thick forest. The manner in which the grass swayed from the rotor wash indicated that it was not very tall. Major Dal and Barrington nodded their agreement.

"Chief, you good?" Barrington asked the Blackhawk pilot.

"Looks good. I'll put her down. Let's do the ground survey."

"Roger," replied Barrington.

The pilot lowered the big helicopter down and carefully made a soft touchdown on the grassy field.

Barrington, Dal, Mike, and the other operators on board sprang from the helicopter and spread out in all directions for at least a hundred yards. The grass was knee high, but the terrain was generally smooth. One of the men found a large, flat boulder. He left a red chem light resting on it. Another man found a stump and did the same. Looking through NVG, the small chem lights seemed like bright beacons.

Based on the landing plan devised by the pilot's, the men on the ground marked six locations on the field with yellow chem lights taped to short sticks stuck in the ground.

When the men had reassembled at Blackhawk One, the pilot radioed the Chinooks. The twin-rotor, heavy-lift Chinooks came down to a hover one at a time and placed the two fuel bladders they had slung beneath their choppers.

Once a Chinook had placed its fuel and dropped its slings, it moved over to a predetermined landing position. One of the operators on the ground held two chem lights overhead, one in each hand, and guided the big helicopter into its spot. They repeated the process until all the fuel bladders were in place and all seven birds were safely on the ground. The plan placed every helicopter near enough to a fuel bladder to refuel.

The Ranger unit was on the first Chinook to land. They had immediately exited by the rear ramp, hurried into the edge of the woods, and spread out around the perimeter to establish local security.

The entire process was completed, all birds on the ground, and security established in less than six minutes. The landing plan went like clockwork.

Within minutes, the logistics officer and his senior NCO were directing their team. The fuel technicians and helicopter crew chiefs quickly had the fuel pumps assembled and attached to the fuel bladders, generators running, refueling begun. Supply techs unloaded rations, supplies, and ammo. Soon the odor of aviation fuel was in the air.

Barrington called over the radio for the Blackhawk pilots and Delta operators to assemble on Blackhawk One. Mike stood by the bird waiting as the men grouped. He wore the same uniform as the Delta operators—solid black jungle fatigues with no insignia except a small American flag attached to the left shoulder with Velcro. He had on a tactical vest and his weapons, an M4A1, 5.56 carbine and a .45 caliber Colt commander pistol.

The men quickly gathered and Barrington said, "Okay, we're going to get refueled and ready. Check your weapons and equipment. Check everything we have on the birds—fast ropes, ammo supplies, med packs.

"We don't know what our target will look like. It could be a convoy. It could be a building. It could even be a ship or a fast boat. Just be flexible. Once we know what and where we're assaulting, I'll call a play.

"We also have no idea when this might go down. It could be ten minutes, three days, or never. When word *does* come, I want to be in the air in ten. Any questions? Concerns?"

The men all shook their heads.

"Get some chow. Need to take a nap, do it on the bird, gear on. That's all for now."

Mike had checked in with Striker upon arrival at Posof and learned about the World Trade Center. He and Barrington discussed possible options, but without specific intel, anything they did at this point would be a blind stab in the dark. Mike prayed that Mya would come through. She was their only hope.

~

Poti, Georgia, 3:25 a.m.

Through her binoculars, Mya continued watching the building, and the men guarding it. Five men stood in front. They paced, smoked, and talked. She had not seen the black sedan again. Apparently, it had left while she was maneuvering into position. She watched the men, but she carefully checked around her position frequently.

Why would this building, here in the middle of nowhere, be so heavily guarded? She wondered. Another hour passed, and still no other activity. She grew impatient. She checked her watch—4:27. The first light of dawn would break shortly after 5:00 a.m., and she would no longer have the cover of darkness. She would have no choice but to break off her surveillance.

Then she heard a cell phone ring, and one of the men answered. She could barely hear his voice, but he spoke Georgian Kartuli. The other men were checking their watches, and their guns, as if they might be expecting trouble.

The black sedan suddenly drove back up to the building. The driver got out and had a brief conversation with the men.

More vehicles came down the drive. Two Toyota pickup trucks and a box-type delivery truck arrived at the building. The larger truck turned around and backed up toward the small warehouse. The cargo section of the truck was silver, and it had large images of tomatoes on the side. The cab was red. *Produce Co.* was printed in Kartuli on all three vehicles. She could hear the men from the trucks speaking Farsi to each other, but they spoke English to the Georgians. The new arrivals were Iranian.

A second black Mercedes sedan arrived with three more men. They were Georgians, certainly Meskhi's men. One of the Georgians unlocked and opened the building door, and several of the Georgians went inside. One of the Iranians opened the big sliding cargo door on the box truck.

Within a minute, the men began moving crates out of the building on wheeled carts. The Iranians hoisted each crate up into the truck as it came out, four in all. The Georgians rolled the carts back inside. One of them closed and locked the building door.

The Iranians took a few extra minutes inside the truck. Probably verifying their cargo and strapping down the crates, Mya surmised. Then they jumped down, pulled the door closed, and locked it. The Iranians loaded back up in their three vehicles and drove off. All the Georgians got into the two black sedans and followed the three Iranian vehicles.

This is it, thought Mya.

She looked around to check her surroundings. The place seemed deserted now. She was alone. She crouched down against the warehouse, pulled out her cell phone, and dialed Striker at the CIA command center. It took a full, torturous minute to route the call through the cell system and establish a secure encrypted connection.

The director answered, "Striker, here."

She whispered, "It's Mya. I found the nukes. Iranians have them. They just drove off from the Poti industrial park."

She quickly described the Iranian vehicles and the two Georgian cars.

"They will be heading for Iran," she said, "either via Tbilisi or Batumi. It will be the only box truck on the road escorted by two Toyota Tundras, and possibly two black Mercedes sedans as well."

Striker started to respond but heard the sounds of a scuffle. Then as Mya's phone hit the pavement and skidded, a loud screeching noise filled Striker's earpiece. Then there was silence.

"Mya?" he said several times.

There was no answer.

~

Meskhi's Compound, 4:33 a.m.

Behdin Khorasani sat across the desk from Genadi Meskhi. Both men held crystal goblets filled with Louis XIII de Remy Martin cognac. At $2400 a bottle, Meskhi was in a generous mood. He was feeling satisfied with his investment in the Russian devices.

The Iranians had just paid him another fifty million prior to the transfer. The bombs were on their way out of town and he now had a clear one hundred million in profit in his account. He did not intend to let his guard down, however. The Iranians still owed him another one hundred million when the convoy was safely out of Poti.

He also knew that if he wasn't paid before they reached the border, then they were trying to stiff him, and he would be well within his rights to kill the Iranians and take back his goods. That's why he had sent his men along, and he believed that they had the firepower to take down anybody.

Meskhi's bodyguard stood by the door, his arms folded, watching the two men sip the expensive cognac. Meskhi had given him a glass of the good stuff once. He didn't even like it, but he didn't tell the boss that. He just drank it.

Khorasani asked, "Did you destroy the four remaining single-code PDAs as I requested?"

"I did as you asked, my friend." He opened his desk drawer and pulled out one PDA. "This is the only one left, and it has the codes for all five nuclear devices."

"And may I have it?" asked the Iranian.

Meskhi dropped it back into the drawer and pushed it shut. "Of course, the moment full payment is made."

"Of course."

Khorasani's phone vibrated. He knew it would be from his commander. He opened and read the encrypted message: *American agent believed to be in Poti whereabouts unknown.* He said to Meskhi, "This message tells me that there is an American agent in Poti somewhere."

Meskhi smiled. "I wouldn't worry too much about it. I was just informed that we have the agent. Now down to business. They will be well clear of Poti shortly, are your people prepared to make the final payment?"

"They are. Once our lead man with the convoy calls me that they are on the highway and there are no problems, I will signal for the payment. Then have your men return to Poti."

Meskhi raised his glass in a toast, "To our mutual profit."

"Yes," replied Khorasani, taking a sip, and considering where he might like to retire.

~

CIA Operations Center, 8:35 p.m. (Poti, Georgia, 4:35 a.m.)

Within minutes of Mya's call, Striker's staff had set up a conference call. On the bridge were Max, Mike, the commander of Delta Force, DOD, and the commanding general of the U.S. Air Force drone command center in Colorado. The president and his senior advisors were on the line in the White House situation room.

Striker began, "This is acting DCI Striker. We have located the remaining four nuclear devices. They are being moved by truck now from Poti, Georgia under the control of an Iranian team and a Georgian escort."

He went on, "Mike, are you there?"

"Yes, sir."

"Mike, you know that if you don't find the deactivation code for the nuke in the WTC, we lose New York City. Max is there at the WTC. I will keep him on the bridge with my ops center. If—when—you find the code, you can call me. I will have him on the line."

"Yes, sir," answered Mike.

Striker provided the description of the truck and the armed escorts.

"The convoy is probably headed to Iran, and will be moving out of Poti *either* east on E60 toward Tbilisi, or south on the coast road on E70 toward Batumi. We think it will be Batumi, but we need to watch both. The truck will be the only one on the road with at least two, and maybe a four-vehicle escort."

The Air Force general in Colorado spoke, "Mr. Striker, we've got two predator drones on station near Poti, as requested."

"Okay, general," replied Striker. "We need to find them, not destroy them. We *have* to find those codes."

The general replied, "We will find them, and then continue to transmit the moving coordinates to Delta's pilots."

"Good," replied Striker.

The president spoke up, "This is the president, gentlemen, for God's sake, please find those codes. The future of our nation may depend on it."

"Yes, sir," answered Striker. "Mike, get the team airborne, direction Poti. Exact coordinates to follow. And Mike, you know what your first priority is, the nukes and codes, but something happened to Mya just as she was reporting to me."

"Yes, sir."

16

Forward Operating Base Posof, 4:39 a.m.

Mike terminated the call with Striker. He whistled loudly and waved his arm over his head. "Mount up," he yelled. "We have a target!"

The men exploded into action. Pilots scrambled into their cockpits. Delta's men not already on a chopper, bounded for their birds. Blades immediately began turning on the four Blackhawk helicopters.

The chief pilot said over the radio, "Combat start, get 'em off the ground." The lengthy start-up checklist would be completed by the copilot in flight.

Mike jumped onto Blackhawk One, tapped the pilot on the shoulder, and yelled, "Poti!"

The pilot nodded.

Barrington climbed on. Major Dal was already there. The remaining Delta operators were loaded. Crew chiefs, fire extinguishers in hand, ran around their helicopters scanning for sparks or fire, and then quickly piled on.

The first Blackhawk lifted to a hover forty-seven seconds after Mike first called out. Ten more seconds and the four Blackhawks were flying at a hundred feet, below radar, on a heading of three-two-zero degrees, toward Poti.

Mike slipped on a communications headset and briefed Barrington, the pilots, and the operators on all four helos over the radio. "The target is a convoy of Iranians—a box truck and two Toyota pickups. Should be eight to ten Iranians. Probably Quds special operators and certainly heavily armed. They *may* also have an escort of Georgians in two Mercedes sedans."

The four Blackhawks were now flying just above treetop level at one hundred and fifty knots, a little over one hundred and seventy mph.

The chief pilot came on the radio, "Seventeen minutes to Poti."

Black splotches of forest streamed by just beneath the birds in a dark blur. The wind and noise were fierce. The four helicopters had linked up in a diamond formation—the two MH-60M medium assault Blackhawks flew side by side; the two MH-60L gunships flew lead and trail.

Mike continued his briefing, "We've got two predator drones overhead looking for the convoy. As soon as they pick it up, they will transmit the coordinates directly to the pilot's nav computers."

Mike paused, and then said, "Guys, listen carefully. You know already that one of the nukes is in the World Trade Center in New York and it is active. It has less than two hours until detonation. It can only be shut down with its deactivation code.

"We want the remaining four nukes, but we *have* to find that code. Like I briefed you already, it's probably on some kind of PDA, but it could just as well be written down on something—a card, a scrap of paper, a matchbook.

"We have to search every vehicle and every man. No one gets away. It could be the one man with the code."

Mike nodded at Barrington and said, "Sergeant Major."

"Okay, listen up," said Barrington over the radio, "We'll come in from the flank, perpendicular to the road. Gunships in first for a twenty-second prep of the target. Don't destroy the vehicles, just disable them. Take out as many shooters as you can without making mush out of them. We have to be able to search them.

"After the prep, gunships crab left and right and cover the road in both directions in case reinforcements or police show up. The instant the gunship prep ceases, I want both assault birds on the ground before the survivors can get their shit together. Bird One on the left, forty-five degrees off target, bird two on the right also at forty-five. I want to be as close to them as possible without the rotor blades hitting the truck. Pilots, when you hit the ground, get your ballistic shields up. It's going to be hot.

"If there are obstacles and we can't land, we will fast rope right on top of them. Search everyone and every vehicle. Find the codes. Get the four nukes loaded, two on each bird."

Four minutes had passed since the launch.

Barrington asked the chief pilot, "Chief, you got the coordinates?"

"Nothing yet."

"All right," Barrington said, "they're coming. Okay, guys, let's get ready to kick some ass."

~

Colorado, 6:45 p.m. (Poti, 4:45 a.m.)

In a command and control pod located in a classified Air Force facility, two Air Force drone pilots, both civilian technicians wearing civilian clothes and tennis shoes, sat in front of their consoles. A central console of electronic controls separated them.

Each pilot had two monitors side by side built into the console directly in front of him. Two large monitors were stacked vertically above those, straight ahead. Two more monitors were slightly left of the left-side pilot, and two to the right of the right-side pilot.

They wore communications sets, and each pilot cradled their drone's power control loosely with his left hand, and the maneuvering pistol grip, or joystick, in their right hand. Their feet rested on the rudder pedals. They each controlled a drone on the other side of the world flying at twenty thousand feet over the Black Sea near Poti, Georgia.

The drones' cameras were set to high magnification and thermal imaging. Warmer objects glowed bright red and stood out in contrast to their surroundings.

The commanding general stood behind the pilots, also wearing a headset. Next to him was a senior CIA officer, wearing a comset.

The general described the convoy to the two pilots over the communications system and then issued their mission orders. "Bravo-two-two proceed from the Poti port facility eastbound over highway echo-six-zero, toward Tbilisi. Break. Bravo-two-three, same start point, proceed south on the coast road highway echo-seven-zero, direction Batumi."

One of each of the pilot's monitors displayed the drone's location over the ground overlaid on a map of the area. It currently showed the Black Sea with Poti off to the east. Both drones rapidly veered east toward Poti.

The general continued, "When you identify the target convoy, Mr. Smith and I will concur or non-concur," he said, referring to the CIA officer standing next to him. "When we concur that we have the right target, you will mark the coordinates and transmit them directly to Blackhawk One's nav computer. Weapons are hold. How copy?"

"Bravo-two-two, roger, copy weapons are hold."

"Bravo-two-three, roger, weapons hold."

A moment later, "Bravo-two-two, highway echo-six-zero acquired, following on an azimuth of eight-eight degrees."

"Roger," replied the general.

"Bravo-two-three, I'm on the coast road echo-seven-zero, course one-eight-seven degrees. No vehicular traffic to speak of."

"Roger."

A few seconds later, "Bravo-two-three, contact, one-seven miles south of Poti, highway echo-seven-zero.

The image on the screen was clearly a box truck. It had one large pickup truck in front of it driving in the lead. A similar pickup trailed the cargo truck. Two identical sedans trailed the second pickup truck.

The CIA officer and the general looked at each other and nodded simultaneously.

"We concur," said the general.

"Roger, bravo-two-three marking coordinates, now. Transmitting coordinates."

"Keep it in sight and update the coordinates every thirty seconds. Begin video transmission to the White House situation room."

The pilot typed several commands on the keyboard in front of him on his console. "Streaming video," he said over the intercom.

~

Southeast of Poti, 4:59 a.m.

The Blackhawks had been in the air for fourteen minutes and had covered forty miles toward Poti. The navigation computer in Blackhawk One beeped a signal in the pilot's helmet communications set, and a yellow light flashed on the nav computer. The copilot punched a button on the console and silenced the alarm.

As he veered slightly left, the chief pilot said, "We've got coordinates. Ten miles to the coast. Three and a half minutes to target."

"Roger," said Barrington. "Everybody copy?" asked Barrington over the radio.

"Blackhawk Two, roger, good copy."

On both troop Blackhawks, men held up three fingers to each other indicating three minutes to target, making sure everyone knew.

Blackhawk One and Two reduced airspeed slightly, and the trail gunship moved ahead to a position side by side with its sister gunship.

The men had attached the fast ropes to an anchor point overhead. They were ready. If the helicopters could not land, the birds would come to a hover and the men would shove the kit bags holding the coiled ropes out each side door and fast rope down.

Delta would have the element of surprise. Barrington was counting on that, *and* the softening up by the gunships. Quds Force special operators were not men to underestimate.

"One minute to target," the pilot said over the radio and intercom.

Every commando held up an index finger and tapped the buddy next to him.

The gunships were three hundred yards ahead. They popped up over the treetops and had the convoy in sight. All four mini-guns came to life, spitting out short bursts. Even with controlled fire, thousands of 7.62 rounds headed downrange toward the convoy. Tracers, every 20th round, streaked toward the target like laser beams.

"Blackhawk One, you have an LZ," said the lead gunship pilot over the radio.

Barrington's pilot said on the radio, "We're landing, we're landing, twenty seconds."

Barrington repeated it several times, and the men shoved the fast rope kit bags back toward the inside of the bird, out of the way.

The vehicles in the convoy were immediately crippled, and many occupants killed or wounded. The vehicles careened in different directions. The cargo truck hit the guardrail and came slowly to a halt. Smoke poured from the engine compartment. Other vehicles veered onto the beach and quickly became bogged down in the sand.

One of the Mercedes flipped over and skidded along, upside down on the guardrail, until it hit the pickup truck in front of it and abruptly came to a stop.

The remaining men in the convoy not injured, wounded, or killed—about a quarter of the men—climbed out of their vehicles trying to find their weapons and orient themselves. Meskhi's men were in disarray, but a couple of them managed to return fire.

The remaining four Iranian Quds operators quickly found covered positions and fired on the gunships. The gunships laid down one more burst of fire, suppressing the Iranians hunkered down behind the guardrail, and peeled away left and right.

"Blackhawk One, you've got active shooters," said the lead gunship pilot.

Just as the two gunships turned away, the two MH-60M Blackhawks carrying the assault element landed with a hard bounce. They came to a quick stop with the rotor blades still spinning not five feet from the guardrail.

Delta's men were firing as they hit the ground, spreading out. Each time a Quds fighter, or one of Meskhi's men, tried to shoot, Delta's commandos laid down quick suppressive fire. It was all too fast for the men in the convoy—Delta was already on top of them.

Pairs of commandos moved in rapidly toward the vehicles, using fire and maneuver techniques perfected through years of live-fire training and combat. The action was sharp and quick, and the Iranians fought bravely, but they were overwhelmed in a matter of seconds.

The teams closed in, engaging the Georgians and Iranians, taking them down in short order. Delta quickly secured the objective. All the men in the convoy were dead but one Iranian and one Georgian. These two were severely wounded and losing blood fast. Medically trained commandos struggled to keep them alive. Delta suffered no serious injuries.

Barrington spoke over the radio, "Search everyone and every vehicle." He jogged toward the center of the convoy. Mike followed, the acrid tang of gunpowder filling his nostrils.

One of the commandos was already removing the padlock from the cargo door of the truck and sliding it open. Mike sent Major Dal to interrogate the remaining Georgian. Mike worked on the Iranian. He spoke English to the man, but the Iranian wouldn't respond. Then he died. Mike and the medic searched him but found nothing.

~

Poti, 5:04 a.m.

Moments before Delta hit the Iranian convoy, the Iranian team leader had called Khorasani and informed him that they were on the coast road and well out of Poti. Khorasani informed Meskhi and then sent an encrypted message to Teheran requesting the transfer of the last installment—one hundred million.

Meskhi smiled and took another sip of cognac. *What a lovely elixir*, he mused. He even wondered if he should retire after this deal. He could set up his long-time lieutenant to take over the business—who would continue to pay Meskhi a portion of the profits for the privilege—and he would just retire and relax. Maybe cruise his yacht around the Med or the Caribbean for a while with a bevy of young women to pass the time. He would have to consider it, he determined.

Meskhi opened his laptop computer, logged in to his account, and watched the numbers. Nothing changed.

"Is there a problem?" he asked Khorasani.

"I'm sure there is not. It will be along any moment."

~

South of Poti, 5:07 a.m.

Barrington and his men pulled the wooden crates from the truck, prying each one open as it came off. They verified that the four crates held the RA-115 SADMs, and then searched each crate for the codes, including carefully checking the crates themselves for a number scribbled somewhere on them, to no avail. They replaced the crate tops and hoisted them over the guardrail to other men who loaded the boxes, two on each Blackhawk. Crew chiefs and commandos strapped the crates to the helicopter's deck.

Reports were coming in over the radio to Barrington and Mike on the progress of the search—they had found nothing in writing, or any type of electronic device except for two cell phones. A Delta operator handed the two phones to Mike. He searched through them. The phones had no apps, notes, contacts, or documents. Not even a log of phone numbers. Even the message stream had been erased. Nothing.

Barrington came to Mike. "No codes, Mike. We have to pull out. There will be some kind of response from the Georgians soon."

The commandos piled back onto the two Blackhawks, finding space where they could. Most of the men sat on the crates, gripping straps on the ceiling.

Barrington tapped the pilot on the shoulder, and he gave a thumbs up.

The Blackhawks lifted to a hover at 5:19 a.m., pivoted one-hundred-eighty degrees, and headed off over the trees, back toward Posof.

"Eighteen minutes to Posof," said the pilot over the radio.

~

Poti, 5:20 a.m.

Meskhi and Khorasani awaited the transfer of money to Meskhi's account. Meskhi wasn't completely alarmed yet, but he was definitely annoyed, and when he got annoyed, someone usually died. He raised an eyebrow at the Iranian and said, "Where is my money, Khorasani?"

The guard by the door tensed at the tone of Meskhi's voice.

"It's coming, I'm sure. We have been faithful in paying. The payment will be made."

"Yes, you were faithful before you had control of the devices." He stood and leaned over his desk menacingly.

Khorasani replied, "You know they are worthless without the codes, and we do *not* have control of the codes."

Meskhi thought for a moment and then sat back down.

"You are right," said Meskhi in a softer tone.

"If it doesn't come soon, I will inquire," said Khorasani.

~

Southeast of Poti, 5:22 a.m.

As soon as his helicopter lifted off from the coast road, Mike slipped off one earmuff of his communications headset and called Striker via his sat phone. The noise made it difficult to talk.

"We've got the four nukes under our control," yelled Mike into the phone, "but there were no codes with the convoy."

"Not surprising. Whoever is controlling this operation would be controlling the codes as well."

"How long do we have?" asked Mike.

Max answered, "One hour, eight minutes, Mike."

"How long?" yelled Mike, straining to hear over the noise.

"One hour, eight minutes."

Mike said, "The codes have to be at Meskhi's compound, or with the buyer. Let's just pray he's still there. It's another sixteen or seventeen minutes to Posof in Turkey. Three minutes to unload these nukes, then twenty back to Meskhi's compound. Transmit the coordinates to Blackhawk One."

"Will do," answered Striker, "and Mike, hurry for God's sake."

Mike terminated the call and tucked the sat phone securely back into a pouch on his tactical vest. He would need that phone the moment they located the codes.

He slipped the earmuff back over his ear and tapped Barrington, "We've got an hour to find the deactivation code," he said over the intercom. "The next place we have to look is in Meskhi's residential compound."

"Once we drop off these nukes," replied Barrington, "then that's where we're going."

"Striker's sending the coordinates."

As the helicopters raced past just over the dark forest at breathtaking speed, Barrington flipped the switch on his comset to both intercom and radio. "Heads up, all hands, Barrington here, standby for new orders."

Palmer on Blackhawk Two answered, "Roger, Palmer here, we're on."

The chief pilot responded, "Pilots on."

"Okay," said Barrington, "we've got to make sure these four devices get safely to Posof. Rangers will secure them until we get back. We're going back into Georgia to Meskhi's residential compound. You've all studied the satellite imagery. You know the layout.

"I'll brief the tactical plan once we're back in the air en route. Once we get the crates off-loaded, reposition the fast-rope kits. We'll be going in hot on top of the target," briefed Barrington.

"Gunships, do you need to reload?"

"Negative."

"Roger, fuel?"

The chief pilot answered, "Negative."

"Okay, when we get to Posof, gunships stay in the air while we off-load the SADMs. Get these crates on the ground ASAP. I want to be back in the air in ninety seconds."

To the pilot he said, "CIA is sending the coordinates, chief."

"We have them."

"Roger."

The chief pilot came back on the air, "Two minutes to Posof."

Barrington and his men slipped off their comsets, coiled the cords, and hung them on hooks on the airframe out of the way. A moment later the two assault Blackhawks came in fast over the treetops and landed in Forward Operating Base Posof.

The men sprang into action unloading the crates. Barrington issued one general order to the Ranger platoon sergeant securing the base—"Do not let anything happen to these nukes."

Barrington and his men quickly loaded back up, and the two Blackhawks were back in the air sixty-three seconds after touchdown. It was now 5:42 a.m., and the early-morning glow of sunrise formed pink and purple streaks just above the horizon.

"Nineteen minutes to target," said the chief pilot over the radio.

The men were busy positioning the fast-rope kits and double-checking the anchor connections. They passed around boxes of pre-loaded M4 5.56mm and .45 ACP pistol magazines. The men swapped out magazines from their weapons that had been fired and restocked the ammo pouches on their tactical vests.

Barrington called over the radio and intercom for all hands.

Everyone responded.

"Okay, this is mission brief. Gunships you have twenty seconds to do your thing. Then cover the road for reinforcements. Blackhawk One will come in over the white stone terrace on the second level of the mansion. The mansion appeared in the sat images and photo to be three stories total. We're going onto the second level so your hover needs to be about forty feet over the terrace, Chief.

"Blackhawk One will fast rope onto the stone terrace. Team Alpha ropes while Bravo keeps suppressive fire on any visible targets from the chopper doors. You know the drill, when Alpha hits the ground, you cover while Bravo ropes in. First two men on the ground will cover the terrace while the rest of us go straight into the house by the glass doors. Spread out through the house, clearing as you go.

"Palmer, there should be enough room for you to land in the yard. You make the call. If not, rope in. I want your team to have boots hitting the lawn when our first man touches the terrace. Spread out around the perimeter in both directions and then clear in toward the house. Secure the outside unless one of us calls for you to enter the house."

"Palmer here, got it."

"Pilot Blackhawk One, got it."

"Pilot Blackhawk Two, roger."

"That's it," said Barrington, "except that the sole reason we are here is to find the deactivation code for the nuke in New York.

Many lives depend on what we do in the next few minutes. God bless you all."

The pilot said over the radio, "Three minutes to target."

17

Meskhi's Compound, 5:59 a.m.

Genadi Meskhi anxiously watched his account on his computer. He was trying to decide if the Iranians had double-crossed him.

Then suddenly, the numbers changed. Meskhi blinked several times to be sure what he was seeing. A new one-hundred-million dollar deposit had just arrived in his account. Meskhi smiled and closed his laptop. He had made two hundred million in profit from this deal. Khorasani was smiling too. Meskhi opened his desk drawer and pulled out the PDA containing the codes. He also had a card with the PIN written on it.

"You are a man of your word, Behdin. Here are your codes. Iran is now a nuclear power. The PIN will unlock the PDA. Tap the only icon on the device and it will display all of the codes. They are numbered one through five and labeled *Activation* or *Deactivation*—in Russian of course.

Handing the PDA and card to Khorasani he said, "The devices your men have are numbers one through four. You already have number five at your lab in Venezuela. Enter the code number into the nuclear device, and then set the timer. Simple enough, right?"

Khorasani nodded and put the PDA and card in his shirt pocket and buttoned the pocket. He reached out to shake Meskhi's outstretched hand and said, "I will be leaving now."

As they shook, Khorasani reflected on the fact that he knew Meskhi's bank routing and account numbers—Meskhi had given it to him for the transfers. Through casual observation watching Meskhi log in to his account, he had also memorized Meskhi's password. It was going to be a real pleasure siphoning off that money.

Before Khorasani had even let go of Meskhi's hand, the mansion and grounds exploded in a hailstorm of bullets. The heavy buzz of mini-guns firing from just above the treetops shook the building and rattled the windows. Bullets chewed up patio stones, bricks, plaster, windows, and men in a shotgun blast of projectiles raining relentlessly down. Rounds pummeled one of the guards on the terrace causing his already dead body to jerk spasmodically in a sort of macabre dance. The soldiers called it the mini-gun shuffle.

Khorasani released Meskhi's hand and turned toward the bodyguard standing by the door. In a blur, the Iranian pulled a razor-sharp throwing knife and launched it backhand. The blade sank into the guard's throat up to the hilt.

He walked over to the dying man as he clutched at his throat and made bizarre gurgling sounds. Khorasani jerked the man's pistol from his shoulder holster, turned, aimed, and shot Meskhi between the eyes.

He stuck the pistol into his own belt and pulled the knife from the man's neck. As the guard slowly inched down the wall leaving behind a bloody streak, Khorasani wiped the blade on the man's jacket and slid it back into the sheath on his leg. Several rounds zinged overhead and hit the wall.

He dashed from the room, sprinted through the house into the kitchen, and bounded down the stairs to the garage.

~

The gunships ceased firing and veered away left and right as Blackhawk One came to a hover over the white stone terrace. The men shoved the kit bags out the doors deploying the ropes. The first two men hit the braided fast-ropes out the port and starboard doors.

Two seconds later, they were on the terrace, M4'ss up and ready. More commandos slid down the ropes. The men on the ground immediately engaged several of Meskhi's guards running up the steps to the terrace.

Blackhawk Two touched down on the large lawn near the perimeter wall, and Palmer's team poured from both sides of the helicopter heading in opposite directions along the wall.

Mike exited the portside door of Blackhawk One, swinging out onto the fast-rope. The last commando in the bird hit the starboard rope. Suddenly, the helicopter came under fire from somewhere on the ground below. Bullets zipped past Mike's ears as he descended. The man on the opposite side from Mike was hit the instant he swung out onto the rope. He fell forty feet to the stone terrace below.

Mike came down the rope fast and hit the terrace hard. He rolled to the side behind a large concrete flowerpot as several of Meskhi's men began firing from the rooftop. Blackhawk One pulled straight up and peeled away.

Bullets ricocheted off the terrace, concrete railing, and walls. Mike got his M4 into position and fired at a man who had just made the top step, his pistol aimed at Mike. Mike hit him twice and the man collapsed. He returned fire toward the rooftop, and the shooters pulled back from the edge.

~

Khorasani hit the last step and burst through a door into Meskhi's massive garage. It held half a dozen vehicles with spaces for more.

He spotted a silver Land Rover parked just inside one of the closed garage doors. On the wall to his right was a wooden plaque. Keysets hung in rows on metal hooks. Each hook had a label under it. He grabbed the keys for the Land Rover.

Khorasani jumped into the SUV, slammed the door, jammed the key in the ignition, and started the engine. Two remotes were clipped to the visor. He punched the left one and the garage door in front of the vehicle started up. He knew the second remote was for the main gate. He had seen Meskhi's drivers use a remote to open the gates from the inside many times before.

He rammed the center console gearshift into drive and jammed on the accelerator, squealing the tires on the garage floor as the car bolted out the door. He punched the second remote, and the big black iron gates began to open.

~

On the terrace, Mike ran over to the Delta operator who had fallen from the helicopter. He was dead. Gunfire seemed to come from all directions at once. Mike ducked behind the terrace's concrete railing. He shot two guards with one burst of his M4 as they ran along the wall below the railing.

He could see Palmer's men spreading out along the perimeter, methodically taking down targets as they moved. Two Delta men on the terrace near the glass doors fired at the shooters on the rooftop.

Then Mike saw the silver Land Rover speed down the long driveway, race through the open gates, and disappear from sight. He ran down the marble steps to the drive, shooting another guard as he popped around the corner of the building.

Before Mike could turn again, someone grabbed him from behind. He twisted loose and spun right. He drew his knife as he turned and swiped the blade across the man's throat. The guard dropped to the ground. He sheathed his knife and scanned around him.

He saw two sedans and a Ducati 1200 motorcycle parked in the drive forty feet away. He knew that if the codes were in the house, Barrington would find them. But if they had just left in the Land Rover, the mission was doomed unless Mike could catch him.

He rushed toward the motorcycle. Some of Palmer's men were running past him now toward the mansion. Mike tossed his M4 aside, jumped on the Ducati, and hefted the heavy bike up off its kickstand.

He turned the key and hit the start button. The bike roared to life, and he hit the gearshift with his foot. The rear tire spun as he let out the clutch and gunned it. He raced off down the driveway accelerating as he passed through the gate. At the end of the drive, he skidded as he turned onto a small access road leading to the main highway into town. The Land Rover had a lead on Mike, and he couldn't see it anywhere ahead.

He reached the highway, slowed, and hesitated—left or right? It was a toss of the coin. He let out the clutch and spun out turning right, toward Poti. He quickly accelerated to seventy-five on the four-lane highway, weaving from lane to lane, zooming past cars, trucks, and busses. He pushed it up to ninety.

He spotted the Land Rover ahead.

Khorasani saw the motorcycle in the rearview mirror coming up fast. He swerved right onto an exit ramp. Mike squeezed the handgrip front-wheel brake and pushed hard on the rear-wheel brake pedal with his foot. The Ducati's tires smoked as he decelerated from ninety to forty. He almost lost control of the bike and only barely made a wobbly, skidding turn onto the exit ramp.

~

One World Trade Center, 10:17 p.m. (Poti, 6:17 a.m.)

A small group of men on the sixtieth floor stood by the nuclear bomb, starring at the timer. It now displayed *13 MINS 20 SECS* and continued its countdown—*19, 18, 17....*

Dr. Mackey had found a chair somewhere. He sat in front of the device staring intently at it as if willing the bomb to reveal the proper code. He had considered trying to dismantle the control box, but he knew it would be useless. It would go off, as it was designed to do. That was exactly what he had designed into his own bombs.

A second scientist, from MIT, had arrived and stood next to Mackey. He fidgeted anxiously, wondering to himself why he had come here. A couple of bomb techs looked on helplessly.

Max and the mayor stood by a tall glass window staring down on the chaos below. Many had simply ignored the order to evacuate, assuming the bomb threat was a hoax, but enough had heeded it to result in chaos. Within minutes of announcing the evacuation, the bridges leading out of Manhattan were quickly jammed with vehicles and people.

Only a trickle of pedestrians had managed to get over the bridges. The streets of Manhattan were at a standstill as well. The ferries were running at capacity, but it was a mere drop in the bucket.

~

Poti, Georgia

The exit Khorasani had taken from the highway led to a small, winding, two-lane road heavy with local traffic. He raced down the road passing a semi hauling a fifty-foot trailer. He ran an oncoming car off the road.

Mike twisted the throttle and the 1200cc Ducati responded. He passed the truck and swerved back into the right lane inches beyond the semi, barely avoiding a head-on collision with an oncoming truck.

The Iranian drove like a madman. He passed the next car on the shoulder to the right. Mike tried to get around the car but could find no gap in oncoming traffic, and the shoulder was loose gravel. He didn't dare try to pass on the right.

Khorasani was increasing his lead. Mike saw a short gap between oncoming vehicles. He kicked up one gear and opened up full throttle—the bike shot around the car with inches to spare.

He accelerated and was gaining on the Land Rover, but Khorasani passed the car in front of him, running an oncoming truck into the ditch. The truck flipped several times as it careened down the hill. Mike was stuck behind the car.

He had a small gap and he punched it, quickly passing the car. He came up almost behind the Land Rover. Khorasani slammed on the brakes and swiped the guardrail, almost losing control, trying to wreck Mike closing in behind him.

Mike braked hard and backed off. Then they both accelerated rapidly. Mike was soon only a few hundred feet behind Khorasani. They raced down a steep hill. Without warning, a delivery van pulled onto the road in front of the Land Rover.

Khorasani slammed on the brakes and skidded sideways, tires smoking. He crashed into the van. Mike had only an instant to react. He laid the bike down and let it go. Both Mike and the Ducati slid down the road toward the Land Rover. He could feel the burn of the pavement as he slid and tumbled, but he clutched both gloved hands over the satellite phone in his vest pouch. The strap on his holster burned through against the rough pavement and his pistol was knocked from the holster. The .45 skidded off the side of the road and over the embankment.

Mike finally came to a stop in the road. He was bruised and had lost some skin on his behind and right leg, but he was able to move everything. He slowly got up and spotted the driver of the Land Rover running off the right side of the road and down a hill behind a concrete structure of some sort. He disappeared from view.

Mike followed, limping at first, but he forced the pain from his mind. As he ran, he felt for his pistol. It was not there. He thought he had glimpsed it sliding away on the pavement. He still had his combat knife.

He climbed over the guardrail and started down a steep, well-worn, rocky path. He followed it around an old and crumbling concrete structure. As he turned the corner, Khorasani stepped out from behind a tree and fired. Mike dodged, spun, and rolled to the right, landing hard on his shoulder. He looked up and saw the man turn and dart down the steep path. It led down into a deep, wooded gully.

Khorasani tripped on a root and went sprawling, face-first, down the steep hill. He hit hard and tumbled downward. He struggled to break his fall with both hands and lost his grip on the pistol. As Khorasani slid down the hill, his gun bounced several times to the side and then disappeared into the brush.

Mike jumped up and bounded down the path trying to close the distance before the man could recover and find his gun. Khorasani scrambled farther down. Mike lost sight of him again as the trail zigzagged through trees and foliage.

The thought flashed through Mike's mind that he was fighting this guy to the death, and he didn't even know if the man had the codes. Maybe he was just trying to escape Delta's attack. Mike pushed on. He couldn't take the chance that the codes he so desperately needed might be right here within arm's reach.

The path was steep, rocky, and filled with large tree roots sticking out of the surface of the ground. He tried to pick his way over the obstacles as he ran ever faster down the hill. Mike stumbled and nearly fell—Khorasani was waiting in ambush behind a tree.

The Iranian slashed at Mike with his knife. Mike's tactical vest and body armor offered protection from a direct stab to the torso, but it also slowed his movement and provided no protection to the extremities.

He raised his left arm to block the Iranian's attack, and the knife cut a gash on his forearm. He parried and tried to grab the man's arm, but the Iranian countered his move. He thrust the knife straight in toward Mike's stomach, and he barely managed to block it.

Mike parried another swipe of the attacker's knife, and despite the pain in his leg, he managed to throw a left roundhouse kick to the man's ribs. It landed solid, with a loud and gratifying *thwump*. A surge of air burst from the Iranian's lungs.

He staggered back holding his ribs and trying to catch his breath. Mike tried to close on him, but the man turned and dashed down the trail. Mike followed. The light grew dimmer the farther down into the gully they descended.

~

One World Trade Center

The police commissioner returned to the sixtieth floor of the WTC. He would gallantly stand by his mayor and his city. Besides, who would want to live after most of the people you had sworn to protect were incinerated?

He walked up to the mayor and hugged him. "I'm sorry, mayor, that we failed so miserably with the evacuation."

"No, it was an impossible task. We tried. We had to."

"How could we have missed something like this?" asked the commissioner, nodding toward the bomb. He felt like crying for his city.

"I don't know," replied the mayor, "I guess it was just too obvious to see coming."

Max walked up to the two men. He had overheard their conversation. "Don't feel so bad, we're the fucking CIA, and we didn't see this coming."

The scientist from MIT finally lost his nerve, what was left of it, and while dancing back and forth from one foot to the other, he shouted, "I have to go now," as he ran to the door.

Max laughed. "How much time, doc?" he asked Mackey.

"Seven minutes, twenty-nine seconds."

Smiling, Max said, "That's a pretty hopeless gesture. He'll just about be leaving the lobby when Armageddon comes raining down from the sky." Max pulled out a cigarette and lit it. He carried a pack and a lighter, even though he had quit over a year ago.

"I've been wanting one of these all day," he said, exhaling and blowing a thick plume of smoke toward the ceiling.

"Can I have one?" asked the mayor.

Max handed him a cigarette, and then everyone in the room wanted one.

~

Mike saw the Iranian slip around the corner of a crumbling stone wall, part of an old and derelict water drainage system. Instead of following, he ran up on top of the structure.

The man was eight feet directly below now, and Mike didn't hesitate. He dove straight for him, hitting him hard with his full weight. Entangled, the two men tumbled and rolled downhill clutching at each other. Khorasani tried to get his knife into position. Mike held firmly to the Iranian's wrist. They rolled one more time and Khorasani kicked Mike in the gut, shoving him away. Both men came up in a crouch. Mike slipped his combat knife from its sheath on his vest.

The two men faced each other, both crouched, each man an expert with the deadly blade he held. They couldn't circle one another on the steep hillside or one man would be downhill, a disadvantageous position. So they faced each other, both men with one foot down the hill and one up, probing, jabbing, slashing, and blocking.

Khorasani got another strike in and cut Mike's left forearm again. Blood ran down his glove. Khorasani lunged forward with a big thrust, trying to finish it. Mike saw that his attacker was slightly overextended.

With his left hand, he swept downward and to the outside, turning Khorasani's arm away. He lunged forward inside the man's knife hand, and with his right hand, he thrust his own knife at the Iranian. The man tried to block it, but he was an instant too slow, and missed. Mike rammed the blade into Khorasani's Adam's apple.

Blood poured from the Iranian's neck. Eyes wide, he sank slowly to his knees, surprise evident on his ashen face. Mike jerked the knife out and Khorasani fell forward, face down in the dirt.

Mike wiped the knife and sheathed it. He flipped the dead man over, and had to grab him quickly to keep his body from rolling down the hill. He felt down the man's chest, immediately finding something in his shirt pocket. Mike unbuttoned the pocket and pulled out the PDA and card. The card had some blood on it, but he could read the six numbers written on it in blue ink.

He pulled off his gloves and examined the PDA. It had five long numbers etched on the back. He flipped it over, turned it on, and entered the six-digit PIN from the card. The screen opened and displayed a single icon. He tapped it and it opened. It displayed the numbers one through five. Next to each number were the Russian words for *activate* and *deactivate*. Beside each word was a long series of numbers. Ten codes in all. Five activation. Five deactivation.

This is it, thought Mike, shaking his head in awe at finally holding his elusive quest. He glanced at his watch. The crystal was broken. He had no idea how much time had passed. He prayed that it wasn't too late.

He carefully set aside the PDA and pulled out the sat phone, extended the antenna, and powered it up. He moved the phone around, but couldn't pick up a satellite signal in the gully under the thick canopy of trees and foliage.

He placed the PIN card and the PDA in a pouch and closed it. Holding the sat phone in his right hand, he scrambled up the hill, pumping his legs and pulling on saplings, vines, roots, and anything else he could grab with his left hand.

He struggled upward, straining to catch his breath. A knife-like stab of pain shot through his ribs. Every muscle screamed in protest. His leg wound and the cuts on his arm were bleeding badly. He slipped several times, but always protected the sat phone.

Finally, he was clear of the overhead cover. Panting, he turned and plopped down on the trail. He had a signal. He hit a pre-set button, and the phone dialed Striker.

"Striker here, Mike?"

"It's Mike, Max are you there? Max?"

In the World Trade Center, Max heard Mike's voice coming through the speaker on his phone. He had plugged into an outlet to recharge. Max sprinted to the phone.

"It's Max. Mike, is that you?"

"I have it Max. I have the codes, but there are five deactivation codes."

Max glanced at the timer—one minute twenty-three seconds. He spoke to the group, "We have five deactivation codes and we don't know which device this is."

Mike said, "There are five numbers etched on the back of this PDA. Are those serial numbers? Is there some kind of number you can see on the bomb?"

Max looked at Dr. Mackey who was scanning the device.

"Yes," said Mackey. "There's a metal tag, like a dog tag, but I have to touch it and turn the tag to read it."

"You gotta do it, Doc," said Max.

He carefully turned the tag. "Last four on the tag is *one-seven-six-six*.

"Yes," replied Mike, looking at the back of the PDA. "That's the fifth number."

"Give us number five," shouted the Mayor.

"Mike, give me number five," Max repeated into the phone. He held the phone next to Dr. Mackey who hovered over the bomb's electronic control panel.

Mike carefully read off the twelve-digit code as Dr. Mackey meticulously tapped it into the keypad. Mackey looked up at the men around him and the mayor nodded. He pushed enter—the timer stopped on twenty-two seconds.

An instant later, everyone realized that almost to a man, they were all holding their breath. They let out a collective sigh.

Max said into the phone, "Mike that was it. It stopped."

The conference line erupted in noise. Cheers, whistles, and applause broke out in the White House situation room, at the CIA command center, at the Pentagon, and at other locations on the bridge.

Mike had to shout into the phone several times before Striker could hear him.

"Go ahead, Mike."

"Mr. Striker, let Barrington know the bomb is shut down, and tell him I am on my way to Meskhi's warehouse at the port to get Mya."

18

Mike returned the sat phone to its pouch on his vest. He stowed the PDA and PIN card in a pocket.

He pulled up his left sleeve. The two knife wounds were close together and bleeding badly. He took out a field dressing, ripped off the brown paper cover, wrapped the bandage tightly around his arm, and tied off the cotton strips on the ends of the bandage with his right hand and teeth.

He took a big swig of water from his canteen and poured some on his face. He knew he had to keep moving. He stood and looked up the steep hill—it was another grueling fifty yards to the top. He started up, pumping his legs as fast as he could. They felt like mush. He finally reached the road, breathing hard, a searing pain in his side. He pulled himself over the metal guardrail.

A Georgian police officer had arrived at the accident scene and stood nearby, astonished by what had just climbed over the railing and onto the road—a commando, dressed in black, and covered in blood.

There had been a military-style attack on the highway south of Poti earlier that morning, and now calls were coming in about gunfire near Meskhi's compound. The policeman was definitely on edge.

The officer pulled his pistol and walked cautiously toward Mike. He ordered in English, "Turn around and put your hands behind your head."

Mike slowly turned, raised his arms, and put his hands behind his head as ordered. The cop held his pistol in his left hand and reached up with his right to grab Mike's wrist. He started to twist the arm down behind Mike's back to cuff him.

The officer wasn't quite sure what happened next, only that he found himself face down on the pavement, bleeding from the nose and mouth where his face had slammed into the hard surface. Several teeth lay scattered near his face. His hands were cuffed behind his back with his own cuffs.

Mike held the cop's Glock 9mm. He slipped it into his vest holster. He pulled two .45 ACP magazines from pouches on his vest and tossed them over the guardrail. He rolled the officer over, took his two spare 9mm magazines, and stuffed them into the now empty pouches.

"Sorry," he said to the still stunned cop. "I hope I didn't hurt you *too* badly. Didn't want to."

With some serious effort, and grimacing in pain, Mike hoisted the Ducati upright and straddled it. The right mirror hung by an electrical wire. He jerked out his knife, cut the wire, and let the mirror fall to the ground.

He held in the clutch lever and hit the start button. It turned over but wouldn't start. After several more tries and some pumping of the throttle, the big bike finally roared to life. He spun around and headed back toward the main highway. He passed several cars and trucks on the small road. When he reached the highway, he turned right toward Poti and twisted the handgrip throttle. In an instant, the bike was pushing eighty.

Mike could only assume that Mya would be at Meskhi's warehouse. He prayed he was right.

Several miles later, Mike slowed and turned onto the exit for the port industrial park. He had studied a map of the area, the satellite images, and the photos Mya had sent. He knew exactly what he was looking for.

He drove six more blocks and stopped across the street from Meskhi's warehouse. He watched for a moment. Trucks moved in and out of the building. Four or five huge forklifts ran back and forth with crates and stacks of pallets.

He gunned the bike and headed straight toward the big open doors of the warehouse, swerving several times to miss trucks and forklifts. He sped past several men standing outside and raced through the open bay doors into the metal building. He skidded to a crawl fifty yards in, about half the length of the building. He hopped off, landed on his right leg, and let the Ducati roll out from under him.

Within seconds, the three men from out front came running into the warehouse, guns drawn. They spread out. Mike ducked behind a parked forklift as rounds pinged off its metal frame. Then he slipped behind several rows of tall metal shelving filled with dry goods. He circled right and flanked the three men.

He stepped out from behind a shelf, fired, and killed the first man. One of the others returned fire, but his aim was wild. The remaining two men moved toward the sound of Mike's gunfire. He circled back left between the shelves.

He popped out again, now on their other side, and shot them both. One man crumpled to the floor dead. The other, wounded in the thigh, screamed as he collapsed. Mike went to him, picked up the man's gun, and stuck it in his belt. Then he leaned over the man and placed his boot on the wound. The man moaned and squirmed.

Mike leaned in close. "The American woman," he said in a low and steady voice.

The guard just shook his head and started crying.

He pressed harder, and the man screamed.

Mike caught movement out of the corner of his eye. One of Meskhi's men ran toward him. Mike spun left and fired. The man dropped.

He stomped back down on the wound. The man screamed again.

"The American woman," Mike said through gritted teeth, grinding his boot.

~

On highway E60 southbound, about halfway between Meskhi's home and the port, one of Meskhi's black Mercedes sedans raced down the highway doing eighty-five. The sedan passed everything on the road, weaving from lane to lane, in and out of traffic.

Palmer drove. Barrington sat next to him on the passenger seat holding his M4. Two Delta operators rode in the back seat, submachine guns across their laps. Two Blackhawk gunships trailed overhead five hundred feet above the car.

The two assault helicopters carrying the remainder of the team were flying to the extraction point not far from Meskhi's warehouse. They would set up a holding pattern until Barrington arrived with Mike and Mya.

Palmer had to slow for congestion ahead. A vehicle accident blocked the right lane. He saw an opening to the left on the shoulder and gunned it, speeding around the slower traffic.

Three police cars had responded to the accident. The cops tried to wave the car down, but Palmer ignored them. Two of the officers jumped into their cars and took off in chase, lights flashing and sirens blaring.

The two gunships pulled ahead of Barrington and Palmer's car, gradually lowering to about forty feet. They pivoted to face oncoming traffic. The black Mercedes blasted past beneath the helicopters.

As the police sped down the road with lights and sirens, all other traffic pulled over. The two cops approached at high speed but suddenly faced two huge monster machines hovering above the road. It was like nothing they had ever seen.

The cops skidded their cars to a smoking stop. One of them sprang from his car and ran back up the road. The other officer threw his car into reverse and stomped on the accelerator, but he lost control and rammed into the guardrail. Then he jumped out and ran too. The only thing remaining on the road in front of the helicopters were the two empty police vehicles.

The lead pilot said, "Three-second burst, on my mark—now."

The four mini-guns spewed rounds in a thunderclap-like blast. When they stopped, the two cars were flaming, smoking, piles of shredded metal no longer recognizable as automobiles.

The two Blackhawks peeled left and right and flew away.

~

In the warehouse, Mike pressed harder on the wounded man's leg. He was wailing now. He bent down and forced the barrel of his gun into the man's mouth.

"One last time," Mike said, "the American woman."

The man shook his head. Mike stood up and shot the guy in the arm. He screamed and cried even harder.

"The American woman!"

The man raised his other arm and pointed toward a door in the back of the warehouse. Mike left him and ran to the door. It was locked.

He stepped back and was about to shoot the lock when he heard screeching tires behind him. Another car full of Meskhi's men skidded to a halt inside the warehouse, hitting a forklift abandoned by a fleeing worker.

Five of Meskhi's soldiers jumped from the car, two with automatic weapons. They immediately fired on Mike. He turned and dove for cover behind some crates. The men ran toward him, firing as they came. He was trapped. He tried to return fire, but they had him cornered, and they were closing fast.

Then, Palmer drove straight into the warehouse, tires screeching as he braked. The Mercedes slid past the sedan stopped in the middle of the floor, demolishing the open driver's door. Palmer's car came to a bouncing stop.

Meskhi's men turned to face the new threat. The four Delta commandos rolled out both sides of the car and deployed left and right. They opened fire and took down two of Meskhi's men right away. Mike jumped up and shot a third man. The remaining two, threw down their weapons and raised their hands.

Mike turned back to the door, fired twice at the lock, and kicked it open. He could see Mya across the room, unconscious, hanging by chains locked around her wrists. He started toward her, but an enormous bald man wearing a leather apron was pressed against the wall just inside the door. The big man lunged. He had a long knife in each hand.

Mike stumbled back and fell as he fired. He shot the man three times, but the giant kept coming. Desperately trying to scoot away, Mike fired again and hit the brute in the face. He dropped to his knees at Mike's feet, falling slowly forward, the two knives thrust out.

Mike rolled, jumped up, and ran toward Mya. He spotted a metal table covered with tools and cutting instruments. He found a ring of keys there and went to Mya. Barrington ran in, and he and Mike unlocked her chains. Mike carried her out, Barrington covering. Palmer had turned the car around.

Running beside Mike, Barrington yelled, "We've got an extraction point about a mile down the road." For the first time,

Mike was aware of the helicopters above. The two gunships circled overhead.

Mya moaned. She was in and out of consciousness. Mike got her onto the back seat. They loaded up and Palmer gunned the car's big engine. The powerful Mercedes peeled out of the warehouse, tires smoking. Police sirens wailed in the distance.

A Delta operator next to Mya pulled out a small medic's kit bag and started checking her vital signs. He looked at Mike.

"Pulse is strong."

Mike nodded.

Palmer pushed the car hard. He swerved onto the access road leading out of the port and floored it. They were headed to a nearby golf course. A police officer coming in from a side street saw the speeding vehicle, pulled out, and flipped on his lights and siren. A minute later, Palmer turned onto a long drive leading to the golf course. He sped past the clubhouse, down a grassy hill, and out onto the fairway.

The cop was close behind. Barrington rolled down his window and leaned out with his M4. The sedan bumped along violently down the grassy fairway. Barrington fired a short burst and shot out both front tires on the police car. It swerved, spun several times, and hit some trees on the edge of the fairway.

Palmer slid the big car sideways right up to the ninth green. Golfers scattered toward the woods. The doors popped open and the commandos poured out. Mike carefully carried Mya.

He could hear the helicopters overhead. Only one was coming in for a landing. It touched down. Barrington, Palmer, the two operators, and Mike carrying Mya, ran to the Blackhawk. They carefully laid her on the floor of the bird.

They piled on, and the Blackhawk lifted up and soared away. A medic began working on Mya. He started an IV and gave her a shot. One of the operators held the IV bag over her. Seventeen minutes later the four helicopters crossed the border into Turkey. Three minutes after that, they landed at Forward Operating Base Posof.

Medics were waiting with a stretcher. They carried Mya to a tent; it was the mobile medical station. Mike climbed off the helicopter. Even on the black uniform, it was evident that he was bleeding in multiple places. Blood covered his uniform.

Barrington came over and said, "Let's get you over to the med tent."

"We have the nukes, and I have the codes," Mike said, patting his pocket, and then he collapsed.

PART II

THE PIPER MUST BE PAID

19

London, England, Three weeks later…

Mike sat at an outdoor café in the Borough of Newham, just north of the River Thames. The day was warm and overcast. He held a copy of The Times spread open in front of him, but he wasn't really reading it. He kept a casual eye on the subway entrance a half a block down the cobblestone street.

His phone lay on the café table next to him. He had just received a message from Mya: *Thank you, Mike. Looking forward to seeing you.* Striker had visited her in the hospital, presented her with an award for valor, and explained how she was rescued.

Mike knew that she had also received a nice promotion and was now working at CIA headquarters. He didn't think the headquarters gig would last. Mya would end up back in the field where she belonged. She had looked death in the eye and prevailed.

He reflected on the events of the past few weeks, but it was painful since one of those events was the senseless murder of his wife. It was especially difficult, because if he had picked her up after work, she would be alive today.

The harder truth, though, was that if Lynn had not died, he would never have embarked on this quest, and a half million other people might have perished instead. He would not have been there to chase the Iranian and capture the deactivation codes. Mya would also be dead.

So, he thought, Lynn may be gone, but her death has meaning—she would have liked that.

He picked up his phone and opened the photo MI6 had given them. The image was a composite of two photos. It showed the faces of two men of Arabic descent taken separately with a telephoto lens. They were anxious, wary faces, who probably knew their time was short.

He spotted two men coming up the subway stairs to his right. They seemed to be Mike's target, but at this distance, he couldn't be sure. The men in the photos were clean shaven. The men he was looking at now had light beards. They looked around nervously as they came up onto the sidewalk.

He tapped a number on the screen and the phone dialed. "Barrington here." He had it on speaker so everyone in the van could hear.

"Stand by," Mike said.

Sitting next to Barrington, Master Sergeant Palmer started the van's motor. They waited.

Pretending to read his newspaper, Mike said into the phone, "Two males, Arab descent, short beards, wearing jeans, one has a red T-shirt, the other has a gray button shirt with a black baseball cap. Walking north on Olive Road. Crossing to east side of Olive now. Still moving north. It's them. Go, go, go."

Palmer slammed the accelerator to the floor, and the van lurched forward.

The two Arabs entered a small, open plaza just across the street from Mike. A white Citroen panel van that said *SMITH MOVING* on the sides in large letters, came to a halt on the curb.

Three Delta operators sprang from the van's already open sliding side door. Barrington jumped out from the front passenger side.

The operators ran up to the two men, jammed a stun gun against each man's neck, and zapped them with thirty thousand volts. They both crumpled to the ground. Delta's men had them in the van in seconds. Barrington got in the back and closed the sliding door. Mike sat down in the front passenger seat. Palmer hit it, and the van sped away. It had taken twenty-three seconds from start to finish.

In the back of the van, the men secured their prisoner's arms behind their backs with flex cuffs, gagged them, and tied black hoods over their heads.

Once out of the immediate area, Palmer slowed, pulled into a small alley that ran between two buildings, and stopped. Two Delta operators jumped out the side door. One of them slapped a new magnetic license plate over the old one. The other man ripped off the two magnetic signs from the sides of the van that said *SMITH MOVING*. He tossed them into a dumpster.

They jumped back in, and Palmer drove slowly down the alley. He turned left onto a back street heading north. Thirty minutes later, they pulled up to the gate of a small RAF airfield outside of London, a field frequently used by the SAS.

An SAS lieutenant colonel waited for them at the guard shack. He told Palmer to drive in and pull off to the side. Palmer did so. The SAS colonel got into a small British government sedan, and as he drove past the van, he tapped the horn once. Palmer followed.

They drove to a secluded ramp area behind some tall hangars. He led them up to a white, CIA 737. Jim stood by the plane's ladder.

Barrington and his men led the now conscious, hooded prisoners planeside and nudged them up the ladder. Mike walked over and greeted Jim. They watched as the others got the prisoners up the ladder and into the plane.

Climbing the ladder was awkward. The prisoners were hooded, hands bound behind their backs. Barrington and his men shoved them upward. Once they were close to the door of the plane, the CIA men inside grabbed them and pulled them up the last few rungs. They headed the two aft toward the cells where they would be strip searched and shackled.

Mike handed Jim a small card. On it was written: *Hamadi Hassan, Yousef Amad.*

He gave Mike a casual salute and bounded up the ladder.

The team loaded back up and drove away.

Mike said, "You know, payback is a real bitch."

20

Western Pakistan, Four weeks later…

A beat-up, dented, and scratched Land Rover with Pakistani license plates, bounced along a small, winding mountain road spewing a trail of fine dust behind it.

The look of the vehicle was misleading, however. It had a very powerful engine and mil-spec electronics concealed behind a panel—GPS, satellite communications, an electronic scrambler, and a few other useful gadgets.

The hardened, cellular rubber tires, unless shredded, would not go flat. The tires did not provide the best of rides, but could be quite valuable when driving through hostile territory. The vehicle also carried an enormous quantity of fuel.

Palmer drove. Barrington rode shotgun. Mike and three Delta operators rode in the back two rows of seats. All the men wore dark beards and longish hair. Palmer had dyed his red hair and beard black. They were dressed in local garb.

They had been driving for two days from northern Pakistan, passing west of Peshawar. They were headed to the Federally Administered Tribal Area near the border between Pakistan and Afghanistan. They kept to the small, rural back roads and avoided cities and towns.

The terrain west of Peshawar was rugged, mountainous, and rocky with only sparse vegetation. The team depended on finding pockets of forest along the way adequate to conceal their position whenever stopped.

Each man carried credentials that showed he was a member of Pakistani intelligence. It likely wouldn't fool a Pakistani intelligence agent, but probably would fool a rural cop or militiaman who more than likely had never seen such credentials.

Their 9mm Pakistani pistols were concealed under their clothes. They each carried a sound suppressor for the pistol in a pocket. Velcro secured Pakistani Army Steyr 9mm submachine guns to the seats under each man's legs. The suppressed automatic weapons were not visible, but they were readily accessible. Several small kit bags contained pre-wired explosive breaching charges. They each had Night Vision Goggles within arm's reach.

Barrington looked at a handheld GPS that displayed a map with the Land Rover's location. It was connected by Bluetooth to the vehicle's satellite communications system. They drove through a wooded area less than a mile from their objective. They were searching for a place to get off the road, well concealed in the forest.

If no issues arose during reconnaissance, Barrington planned to hit the target that night. He wanted to get in and out as quickly as possible. The longer they remained in Pakistan, the greater the chance for problems.

"There," said Palmer, pointing to a slight opening in the forest. Barrington nodded. Palmer slowed, put the vehicle in four-wheel-drive, and pulled into the opening in the forest. They drove into the woods about fifty yards, skirting around trees, logs, and boulders. Palmer turned the vehicle around so that it was oriented toward the road and shut it down.

Two of the men ran back to the road and concealed the entry point with leaves and brush. Then they worked their way back to the Land Rover, erasing or covering any signs that a vehicle had come through.

The men draped a camouflage net over the vehicle, leaving a small entrance in the back. They carefully scattered leaves and light brush on the net. Someone walking through the forest would practically have to walk right into it to discover the vehicle.

It was late afternoon. They set security watches. Men not on security ate and rested. They already knew the plan. They had devised it, studied it, and then rehearsed it a dozen times before ever arriving in Pakistan.

At 10:00 p.m., Barrington was ready. They would move slowly through the forest, covering the distance to the target in about an hour. Then they would spread out and conduct surveillance for an hour or so before entering the target.

The team did a radio check. Each man wore a throat mic and an earpiece. They wore Night Vision Goggles and carried their silenced submachine guns. A silenced pistol was tucked away in a holster.

They carried breeching charges and grenades as well, but the explosives were for emergency use only. Barrington intended to hit the target and exfiltrate without anyone in the small surrounding community ever knowing that they had been there.

They moved out in a file with Palmer on point thirty yards ahead. In just under one hour, the men took up positions in the edge of the woods near the target. They could see their objective, a large two-story house surrounded by a ten foot, white concrete wall.

Barrington signaled for one of his men to go right and for two others to go left. Barrington, Palmer, and Mike remained in position and watched the target. The other men would scout the perimeter and identify the best location to scale the wall.

Over the next thirty minutes, the men reported to Barrington their locations and observations. One of the men had identified a covered and concealed position on the east side of the compound where they could scale the wall undetected. Barrington ordered the team to converge on that point. In another thirty minutes, all team members had assembled at the location on the east wall.

Barrington signaled three men forward. They moved up to the wall. One man leaned against the wall with both palms. A second man interlaced his gloved fingers and formed a step. The third man stepped up and onto the shoulders of the commando leaning on the wall.

He paused a moment on top and observed the property inside. Detecting no threat, he pulled himself up and over. He hung on the opposite side and dropped quietly to the ground. He pulled up his submachine gun from a position on his back and crouched down facing the house.

One of the men outside the wall pulled a knotted rope out of his partner's backpack, and holding one end, he tossed the coiled rope over. The inside man found the end. It had a loop on it. He attached the loop to a snap link on his belt and then continued to cover the house.

Each commando climbed the knotted rope, slipped over the wall, and dropped down. Once on the ground, each man immediately took up a security position. In less than two minutes, the team was inside. They pulled the rope over, unclipped it, and stowed it back inside the backpack.

From satellite images, they knew that a cottage was located behind the main house. Many of the images showed a woman carrying food trays, laundry baskets, and other items back and forth between the house and cottage. A courier came to the cottage occasionally to visit. They knew the man they wanted lived in the cottage.

The president had authorized enhanced interrogation techniques on Hamadi Hassan and Yousef Amad. Amad was either stronger, or he really did not know the location of the Sheikh. After a few rounds with the interrogators, however, Hassan had been all too willing to give up his leader.

Barrington gave the word to move out. Palmer and the three operators would take the house, kill the courier, take photos and DNA samples, and secure any intelligence they could find. They would search and bind any women or children present who did not show a weapon.

Mike and Barrington headed to the cottage. Their night vision goggles made it seem like daylight, but in black and white. They moved through a flower garden overflowing with blooms. They could see a light on in the cottage.

Both men slung their submachine guns and pulled out their silenced pistols. They flipped up their goggles and moved to the cottage door. Barrington drew back and kicked the door. It burst open and they rushed in, Barrington to the left and Mike to the right.

The Sheikh sat in a low chair in the corner of the room. Next to him was a small table with a lamp. He had a book in his lap. He was stunned to say the least.

Barrington and Mike moved to the bearded man.

Mike said in Arabic, "Your plan wasn't good enough."

He replied, "It would have been spectacular. Now what? You will never succeed in getting me out of Pakistan."

Mike said, "Unlike the capture of Hamadi Hassan and Yousef Amad, who gave you up by the way, this is not a rendition. It is a termination."

The old man's eyes widened.

Barrington started to raise his pistol, but Mike put out his left hand and stopped him. Then Mike raised his pistol and fired one round between the Sheikh's eyes.

Palmer came over the radio, "House secure. One male, one female KIA. No one else here. Samples complete. One notebook, one cell phone only."

"Roger," said Barrington, "Target KIA. Move to the wall, start exfil, we're on our way."

Mike and Barrington took photos, prints, and a DNA sample from the Sheikh. They searched the cottage and found several small diaries in Arabic. Mike stuck them into his side leg pocket.

They moved quickly to the wall. One man waited there beneath the rope. The others had already crossed. Mike, Barrington, and the last commando scaled the wall.

The men made their way back to the Land Rover. They stowed the camouflage net, drove out to the road, and headed north toward a remote part of the Afghan-Pakistan border. They still had a good four hours of darkness remaining.

They reached their next hide location shortly before dawn. Again, they found a spot in a patch of woods and concealed their position. They would wait there through the daylight hours. They could drive no farther. The trail they had followed to this location had ended. They would walk from here.

They rotated security—three on, three off. Mike ate and managed to get a couple of hours rest. He read some of the Sheikh's diary entries. The main thing he saw in the entries was a very twisted mind.

In the early afternoon, a Taliban patrol of about twenty-five men passed by in the woods not more than a stone's throw from the Land Rover. Several very tense moments passed, but the patrol continued on, never knowing that they had almost walked over the Americans.

Before dark, the men rigged the Land Rover with explosives. They set up the primary and back up circuits with timers, each on a six-hour delay.

As darkness fell, they moved out through the forest, and four hours later, the team approached a clearing in the woods. They were approximately ten miles from the Afghan border. They spread out and secured the landing zone or LZ.

Forty-six minutes later, they marked the LZ with chem lights. Two-minutes after that, and precisely on schedule, an MH-60M Blackhawk flew in over the treetops, came to a hover, and dropped smoothly down into the small clearing. Two MH-60L gunships circled overhead just above the treetops.

The team quickly boarded the helicopter and it lifted off. It turned west toward Afghanistan with one gunship in the lead and one trailing. They flew at treetop level, and the cool breeze felt refreshing. Buckled in, Mike sat on the floor, his back to the bulkhead, his knees pulled up close to his chest.

He thought about the traitor Gerald Billings, and wondered if the CIA would ever find him. So far, they had no idea where he might be or even if he was still alive. Mike hoped something would turn up soon. He looked forward to meeting the man in person.

21

Three months later…

Gerald Billings—AKA Joseph Felts—left the tiny *tienda* carrying his tote bag filled with a few vegetables and some meat for his dinner. He had actually lost considerable weight since arriving in Chile and had managed to calm himself somewhat. He was beginning to feel like he just might survive this ordeal after all.

He walked along the dirt road leading away from the village. Puffs of fine, powder-like dust welled up around his sandals with each step. It was a fifteen-minute walk to the small family farm where he had rented a cottage. He had told the owner that he was a writer working on a book. He had bought a used car, but enjoyed the walk.

The local community was a suburb on the south side of Valdivia, a city in southern Chile situated along the Pacific coast on the Cruces and Valdivia Rivers. It was late October, and the weather was beginning to turn warm in the southern hemisphere. Several chickens scurried across the road in front of him, making a racket over something that had disturbed them.

A herder approached. He had a half-dozen bleating, smelly sheep marching obediently along in front of him. A black and white Border Collie scurried about keeping the animals in order. The man walked past Gerald, and they exchanged greetings—the people were friendly, for the most part.

Still, he *had* paid a bribe to a local official who had come by to inquire about him. After some dickering in Spanish, he had paid the man what he wanted. To have someone like him query the U.S. Embassy in Santiago about a strange American man living in Valdivia, would certainly have dire consequences. That was a huge and ever-present risk.

Gerald knew that eventually, he would need to get back to the states, with a new identity, and live off the radar there. The money he had available here wouldn't last forever, especially if he had to keep paying bribes.

A huge rat scurried across the road just in front of him, almost running over the top of Gerald's foot. He jumped back, startled. He felt his heart quicken and took several deep breaths, something he had been doing a lot of these past few months. He continued on, still pondering his future potential moves.

Unseen by Gerald, across the street from the little grocery, a man sat at a makeshift cantina. He had a bronze-like complexion—perhaps of Middle Eastern or Latin descent. He sat on a wooden bench before a rough-hewn wooden table. He had a short black beard and wore a braided straw fedora pulled low over his dark eyes. The newspaper he held before him concealed his face, but past the edge of the paper, he had watched Gerald leave the neighborhood store and walk away up the street.

Gerald arrived home, prepared and ate his modest supper, and then read until about midnight. He fell asleep thinking about the blond girl in the spy novel he was reading.

Hours later, Gerald was having a nightmare about prison when the lamp by his bed came on and woke him. It took several seconds and multiple blinks to realize that someone was standing over him; a man pressed the blade of a long knife against Gerald's throat.

Gerald blinked several times more and then let out a gasp. The man Gerald had always thought of as the Arab, Sadegh Mohsen, stood there calmly looking down on him.

"Hello, Gerald," he said in that oddly familiar, deep voice.

"How…how…," Gerald stammered, his whole body shaking madly.

"How did I find you before even your renowned CIA could?" He laughed heartily, but the knife blade never wavered from Gerald's neck.

"Gerald, for a CIA man you certainly are an amateur. You might as well have sent me your address and a dinner invitation. I knew you had an account in Grand Cayman, remember? The CIA did not. I just followed the money."

"Plea…please. Don't kill me. I…I can still be of use to you."

Gerald could feel the blade pressing ever harder against his skin. A red whelp appeared and a trickle of blood ran down his neck. His mind was in panic. Gerald started crying.

"No, Gerald, you cannot be of further use. You are a liability because you have seen my face, and eventually the CIA will find you. And when they do, I am quite sure you will want to tell them all about me."

Gerald squirmed. "No, no, never!"

"Good bye, Gerald."

"Please! Noooo…."

22

Four months later...

Once again, Mike found himself sitting at an outdoor sidewalk café looking for someone, but this time on the other side of the world. He was in downtown Bangkok on Sukhumvit Road, also known as Route 3. The tropical climate in this Southeast Asian nation was warm and humid.

Upscale bars, clubs, restaurants, and shops, filled this crowded area of the city, which was popular with tourists and expats. A dense mass of people and vehicles churned steadily past along the sidewalks and street, creating a constant thunderous din. Horns blared, people yelled at cell phones, engines roared, and strange music boomed from the bars and vehicles. A heady mix of pungent odors filled the heavy air as well. Steaming coffee and warm bread. Diesel fumes and the sharp tang of human sweat.

The chaotic traffic jamming the avenue slid by incessantly, sometimes at a grind, sometimes insanely fast. Regardless of the pace, daredevil motorcyclists zipped and weaved through seemingly invisible gaps between vehicles.

They didn't always make it.

In Thailand, they drove on the left, and Bangkok was one of the most dangerous cities in the world to drive in. Vehicles of all types weaved crazily from lane to lane, their drivers shouting and honking as they maneuvered for the tiniest advantage. Accidents were frequent. Mike had witnessed at least a dozen while sitting here, several of them fatal. Despite all this, he somehow managed to keep his focus on the target site.

He had a newspaper open on the small table before him, but as usual, he wasn't reading it. He watched the entrance to the Bangkok Bank, the largest bank in Thailand, just across the busy street from his location. The CIA agent sitting in an apartment window three stories above Mike was doing likewise.

Next to the agent, an array of video cameras on tripods scanned and recorded the street and bank entrance below. Numerous black cables stretched across the room's floor to a table crammed with computer monitors and keyboards. A technician carefully watched as the computers scanned every passerby.

As a person walked by below, the monitor displayed his or her image. A computer algorithm highlighted the person's image with a white boundary as it measured the individual's physical characteristics. Hundreds of people passed by every few minutes, so the action on the monitor was frenetic as dozens of white outlines bounced about the screen measuring each person. The computer scanned for facial recognition, but also for height, weight, stride, and even shoe size.

They had screened thousands of people in the two weeks since they had begun this around-the-clock operation. The target would probably visit the bank during regular business hours, but they couldn't ignore the possibility that a special customer, someone with millions of dollars in the bank perhaps, might visit after hours by private appointment.

Barrington and Palmer sat at a table in the next room playing cards. Other agents slept or read in the apartment's living room or in one of the three bedrooms. The two Delta operators were along to provide extra firepower. The target, like them, was a highly trained military special operator. He was dangerous at best. Deadly at worst. He had already killed two experienced agents.

The two Delta men were armed and ready to roll. They had a sedan parked on the curb below. Their tactical gear and additional weaponry were secured in a vehicular gun safe in the car's trunk. If the team acquired the target, it would all go down quickly. They had to be ready to move in an instant.

During the raid on Meskhi's compound, Delta Force commandos had taken Meskhi's personal computers and phones, as well as the mansion's security system computer and hard drive. The data gleaned from those devices had provided a great deal of valuable intelligence. The CIA had identified the Iranian agent Mike had fought and killed. They also confirmed that Iran did in fact pay for the nuclear weapons, which unfortunately for them, they never received.

The CIA learned that Meskhi had recently made a dozen multimillion-dollar transfers to accounts across Europe. The agency had tipped off Russian intelligence, and they were undoubtedly searching for the account holders. The CIA did not inform the Russians about two significantly larger money transfers made to the Bangkok Bank in Thailand.

The transfers alone did not identify to *whom* the money had been sent, since they were made to a numbered account in Bangkok without a name attached to it. With this type of account, the owner would use a key, a fingerprint, or a retinal scan, combined with the account number and PIN, to access the money in person, or just the account number and PIN for electronic transfers. The bank routing number, however, had given the CIA a location. It was also a fair bet that sums that large went to the seller of the nuclear weapons—one Vladimir Grigor.

The hard drive from Meskhi's security system provided actual video of Grigor walking in and out of Meskhi's mansion. Computer analysis identified the patterns in his stride unique to him. It also produced accurate measurements of his other physical attributes. The algorithm could identify him from those features even if his appearance was altered.

Even though the U.S. now already had all five of the stolen RA-115's, and their codes, if they could grab Grigor as well, they could learn much more about the Russian weapons and their tactics. Grigor could tell them how and where they stored the weapons. How they generated and maintained the codes. How they deployed them. He could probably even provide a wartime target list. It could be a treasure trove of information.

The CIA would debrief Grigor in a safe house somewhere, promising him a comfortable life in return for his cooperation. But once the interrogators learned all that they could, he would ultimately be traded back to the Russians in exchange for a U.S. agent they held.

Since Grigor had emerged early on as the prime suspect in the nuke heist, the CIA had further developed the dossier it had on him. He was a former Spetsnaz unit commander well known for his brutal and bloody tactics. Later he moved to nuclear surety and began his moonlighting as an arms supplier. The intelligence analysis was explicit: *Subject will be armed and is an expert in close quarter combat. Do not underestimate subject's capabilities and resourcefulness.* Mike never did.

He checked his watch. It was time to move. He had been in this location for forty-five minutes. He still had another hour of street duty. He rotated street watch with three other agents. If one of the techs upstairs got a match on the target, the street man would pick up the subject on foot. Barrington and Palmer would head for the car and follow the street man's electronic tracker on a smart phone. They would pick up the street man if the subject got into a vehicle.

Mike paid for his coffee and moved up the sidewalk. He had recently learned from Max that Gerald Billings had turned up in Chile with his throat slit. Mike wouldn't get the chance to deal with Billings personally, but he was only mildly disappointed. At least the traitorous scum got what he deserved. Though Mike *would* like to know who killed him. Whoever did it was almost certainly linked to the murders of three American agents. But that was for another day.

For now, the most important loose end left for Mike to tidy up was Vladimir Grigor. He hoped this attempt was not another dead end. He wanted to get this showdown over with, and of course, live to tell about it.

As Mike made his way slowly up the street, a call came over his radio earpiece. "Mike, standby," said the agent sitting in the apartment's window.

"Roger," Mike replied. He turned to face a bookstore window where he could see the bank behind him in the reflection.

The computer tech in the apartment suddenly shouted into his radio mic, "Bingo! Ninety-seven percent probability. Subject just hitting the steps, tan shirt, khaki pants, blond hair and beard, carrying a brown leather satchel."

"I've got him," said Mike. "Watch for him to come out."

"Roger, I'm glued to it. I also recognize that satchel. It's the same worn leather bag Grigor carried in and out of Meskhi's mansion on the video."

"Good copy," answered Mike, "I see it."

Barrington and Palmer scrambled for the door. "Moving to the car," Barrington said over the radio. Four minutes later and they were in the vehicle, Palmer behind the wheel, Barrington shotgun, engine running.

"Car ready," reported Barrington.

"Roger, stand by," said Mike. He stepped into the bookstore, picked up a book, and stood near the front window where he could see the bank entrance.

Twenty tense minutes later, Grigor exited the bank. He stood at the top of the steps for a moment scanning the busy street. Then he bounded down the steps and headed west at a brisk pace on the crowded sidewalk along Sukhumvit.

Mike followed, remaining across the street about sixty feet back. Grigor was cautious, Mike noted. He stopped to window shop, but Mike knew he was checking for surveillance. Maybe he was wary because he was carrying a great deal of cash, or maybe he was looking for an intelligence agent on his tail. Grigor moved on. Mike couldn't tell where it was stashed, but one thing he knew for certain, the man had a weapon somewhere on him that he could draw in a flash.

"Moving west on Sukhumvit," Mike said into his lapel mic. "Better move up a bit, Scott."

"Roger, we've got your plotter. I can see you on the screen," answered Barrington, watching a dot that was Mike slowing crawling over a map on his phone.

"Good, I've got him in sight," said Mike.

Palmer cautiously eased the car into the swirling traffic.

A block farther up the street from Mike, Grigor turned, entered a parking garage, and disappeared from view.

Mike started across the street at a trot trying not to get hit. "Subject just entered a parking garage, north side of Sukhumvit, street number two-zero-eight-three. Are there any other exits from this garage?" he asked the tech in the apartment.

The technician already had the city block pulled up on satellite. "Negative. Only Sukhumvit."

Barrington said, "We're in position, about a hundred feet shy of the garage entrance. Want backup?"

"Negative, stand by," Mike answered.

He entered the garage. "Going in," he said over the radio. Mike debated whether they should attempt to take him down now or just try to follow. If they could somehow get a tracker on his vehicle, they could follow at a safe distance and figure out where he was staying. Then they could nab him when they were ready, making sure the odds were in their favor.

If they ended up having to kill him, all of this would be for nothing. He was of no value to them dead. But neither could Mike afford to lose him. It could be weeks or months before they could reacquire his trail, if ever. At least Mike knew that their theory was correct, and that he *was* in Thailand. He also knew that if Grigor spotted their surveillance, he wouldn't be here for long. He would vanish, and they would be back to square one facing an even more wary adversary.

Mike continued into the garage. At a minimum, he had to get a look at the vehicle so they could attempt to follow it. He spotted Grigor walking down a row of cars on the ground level about fifty yards ahead.

Beyond Grigor, a parked car's lights flashed and the horn honked when he unlocked the doors with a remote. It was too far from Mike, and the light too dim, for him to see the car.

"We're going mobile. Stand by," Mike whispered. He turned back toward the entrance and ducked between two parked cars facing the road. There was a low concrete wall topped with a chain-link fence just in front of the cars.

An instant later, Grigor's SUV backed out of its space. He drove to the entrance, exited the garage, and stopped for traffic.

Mike peered over the low wall in front of him. He snapped a photo of the SUV—it was a high-end, black Land Rover. Grigor crossed over the oncoming lane of traffic, turned right, and drove away.

"Let's go," Mike said over the radio.

On the move, he transmitted the photo to the tech back in the apartment. Palmer stopped in front of the garage and Mike hopped in the back. They pulled out into the mishmash of traffic, almost getting slammed by a delivery truck that suddenly changed lanes. Palmer accelerated and dodged it.

"Black Land Rover," said Mike, thrusting the phone over the seat to Barrington.

With two fingers, Barrington enlarged the image and said, "Plate number is zulu-six-seven-papa-kilo-niner."

Palmer sped up as fast as traffic would allow, but Grigor was nowhere in sight.

"Shit," muttered Mike, drumming his fingers on the seat.

Tense moments later, Barrington pointed ahead and said, "There, five cars up."

"Got it," said Palmer.

"If he parks," said Mike, "I want to get a tracker on the car."

"Roger that," replied Palmer.

They continued along Route 3, which ran south out of Bangkok and skirted the coast around the Gulf of Thailand. Palmer was careful to maintain plenty of distance, but managed to keep the Land Rover in sight. Several minutes later, Grigor pulled into a small, upscale shopping center and parked.

Palmer drove into the lot and parked some distance away facing back toward the highway. Mike twisted around to look out the rear window. He spotted Grigor walking into a ritzy liquor store in the middle of the strip mall.

"Let's do it," said Mike, opening his door and slipping out. Barrington followed. Palmer remained behind the wheel.

They walked to Grigor's car. Barrington stopped several vehicles short and pretended to look at his phone, but his focus was really on the entrance to the store. The last thing they wanted was a gunfight in a public parking lot in Thailand, but if Grigor's alarm went off, or if he spotted Mike near the SUV, Barrington would have no choice but to take him down.

Mike approached the Land Rover. He knew the vehicle would have an enhanced security system that would send an alert to Grigor's phone. How else would he be comfortable leaving his briefcase in the car, which Mike assumed was filled with cash.

He knew that if he touched the vehicle's exterior, jostling it in the slightest, it would alarm. He looked around. No one was nearby. Mike got down on his back, and without touching the car, he scooted underneath. He activated a small, round magnetic tracking device and very carefully set it on the top side of the car's frame.

Palmer was looking at a map of the parking lot and shopping center on his phone. A pulsating dot appeared in the center of it. "Got it," he said over the radio.

Mike eased back out from under the car, stood, and casually walked away toward their sedan. A few seconds later Barrington turned and followed. They got in and Palmer handed Barrington the phone. "We've got the car five-by," he said.

"We've got *him*," added Mike.

Palmer started the car, pulled out of the lot, and continued along Route 3. Now they could trail Grigor at a safe distance.

~

The first crimson rays of dawn peeked through the treetops, highlighting an eerie gray mist that floated over the thick tropical vegetation below. Mike peered through binoculars at the long drive leading up the hillside to Grigor's villa. Concealed in the bush just outside the fence, he had a clear view of the driveway winding up the hill. He switched to the tracker map. Grigor's Land Rover was parked at the house.

They had followed his signal along Route 3, tracing the coast, until he turned into this driveway. Google Earth gave them an instant view of the mansion and pool at the top of the hill. The driveway was one lane and paved. About a hundred yards into the drive from the main road, a steel gate blocked entry to the property. A chain-link fence topped with security sensors encircled the estate.

Their CIA technician was an expert at breaking into places like this and bugging them. That was his specialty, and he could *almost* certainly get through Grigor's security undetected. Considering the adversary in this case, however, that *almost* caveat made going in a risky course of action.

If they set off the alarm and it alerted Grigor silently, he would be forewarned and they wouldn't even know it. It could only end in an ambush and a gunfight. So instead of going to him, they were waiting for him to come to them. When that might occur, was anybody's guess. It could be in the next five minutes, or it could be days before Grigor decided to venture out again.

Across the driveway from Mike, perched on a knoll some thirty yards from the small lane, Barrington and Palmer lay in a camouflaged position. They had a direct line of sight on the driveway just outside the gate.

Barrington spotted with binoculars. Palmer lay behind a sniper rifle. The rifle fired a tranquilizer dart. It was the CIA's high-tech version of the types of rifles used to take down large animals humanely.

They had spread metal spikes on the drive about fifteen feet outside the gate, well concealed with leaves. When the Land Rover rolled over one of the devices, it would flatten the tire.

The CIA team's van, with three agents in it, was parked a mile farther along Route 3. A CIA technician sat in a sedan next to the van with another agent beside him. They monitored the radio net and waited.

~

By midmorning, the sun had risen halfway up into the eastern sky, and the early-morning mist had turned to an uncomfortable, steamy soup.

Mike saw the blip move slightly over the map displayed on his phone.

"Stand by," he said over the radio. Those were the first words spoken by anyone on the team since taking up positions the night before.

The two CIA vehicles located farther up the highway, started their engines, and eased out onto Route 3 in the direction of Grigor's property.

Mike watched the driveway with his binoculars. Grigor's vehicle came into view. "One hundred yards," reported Mike.

The black iron gate began to swing open toward the inside.

"Fifty yards."

Palmer sighted his riflescope on the target area. Barrington covered with his pistol.

"Approaching gate now," said Mike.

The Land Rover drove through the gate, which began closing behind the vehicle. A few more feet, and the front left tire hit a spike and immediately went flat with a loud *swoosh*.

Grigor hit the brakes, slammed the shift into park, and jumped out on the right side of the car, crouched, a pistol already drawn.

He heard only a few, distant chirping birds and a slight rustling of leaves in the treetops. Everything appeared normal. After several moments, Grigor stood and walked around the car, all the while scanning the bush around him for any sign of a threat. He could detect none.

When he turned to look at the Land Rover's tire, Palmer fired. The dart smacked Grigor's left buttock. He spun around, trying to raise his pistol, but he just kept spinning, already going under, winding down to a heap before toppling over.

"Target down," said Barrington over the radio.

Mike was on Grigor in an instant. He kicked the pistol away and slapped flex cuffs on Grigor's wrists behind his back. He jerked the dart out and placed it on the hood of the Land Rover. Then he put flex cuffs on the Russian's ankles. He searched his pockets and found a German passport and a Thai driver's license, both in the name of Hans Reimer. Mike stood over the unconscious Russian and muttered to himself, "You know, my man, payback is such a bitch."

The van, followed by the sedan, screeched to a halt just as Barrington and Palmer popped out of the brush by the road. Agents sprang from the van, scooped Grigor up, and hauled him back in through the van's open door. One of them started an IV. Another slapped an oxygen mask over the unconscious man's mouth and nose. The tranquilizer was a powerful one, and they began pumping antidote into him. When Grigor awoke, he would have a massive headache, which would probably worsen when he realized his hands were bound and his game was up. One of the agents secured the pistol and the dart; Mike handed him the passport and license. Barrington and Palmer scooped up the metal spikes from the drive.

Everyone but Mike and the tech piled into the van. The primary mission was to get Grigor out of the country. The driver backed the van out onto the road and drove away to deliver their captive to an inbound aircraft. Mike and the CIA technician would get the Land Rover off the driveway and check the villa for any information of value.

Mike searched the Land Rover. It had a push-button start, but there was no key fob, nor a remote for the gate. All he found was Grigor's phone. Apparently, he controlled everything with it.

Mike took the phone back to the sedan where the tech sat behind the wheel. His computer was open on his lap. Mike handed him the phone and he connected it to the computer with a thin cable. He tapped the locked phone and an app opened, displaying six blank boxes and a blinking cursor.

"He's using a custom password manager program to secure the phone. The app probably controls everything."

"Can you open it?" Mike asked.

"Let's see."

He started a program on his computer. Incomprehensible code and numbers filled the screen, scrolling upward faster than the eye could process. Mike tapped his fingers on the doorframe as he waited, impatiently. He glanced around to ensure that no one was driving up on them.

A tense four minutes later and the computer screen froze. Six digits were displayed on the screen and the phone opened. The tech tapped an icon, entered the six digits, and handed the phone to Mike, grinning.

"You can change the pass code now."

Mike tapped in a new six-digit code and then repeated it a second time. A message popped up—*Pass Keeper code changed.*

Mike stood and looked at the phone. There were several icons displayed on the screen, each one labeled in English—*Gate, Car, Door, Alarm, Guns, Safe, Bank.*

Mike tapped the icon labeled *Gate*, and the steel gate started to swing open. He tapped *Car*, and the Land Rover started. *How convenient*, thought Mike. It was a nice set up for a high-tech, high-security guy like Grigor, but it was ultimately vulnerable.

"Let's roll," Mike said to the tech as he headed to the running Land Rover. He got in, turned the car around, and started up the drive through the gate. The metal spike still in the tire made a clanking noise each time it hit the pavement, and the car wobbled as it rolled along on a flat tire. The tech followed in his sedan.

They arrived at the house. Mike walked up to a side entrance next to the parking area. He first tapped the icon labeled *Alarm* and saw a small green light come on next to the door. Then he hit the one labeled *Door*. He heard the door lock click, and they walked in.

The tech found Grigor's office and started working on his computer equipment. Mike located the alarm control system, disconnected the hard drive, and placed it by the entrance to take with them. He wanted no record left behind that they were ever in the house.

He went upstairs and found the master bedroom suite. It was lavish. Mike opened Grigor's phone again and pressed the icon labeled *Guns*. He heard a noise, something like an electric motor, coming from the walk-in closet. He went in and saw that the rear wall had slid open.

Arrayed on the wall was a display of just about every kind of elite weapon one could imagine. Mike wasn't surprised that an ex-special operator who trafficked in illegal arms would have a sampling of the best wares.

At the bottom of the hidden compartment, Mike spotted a safe. It was a small, top-of-the-line Mosler. It had no keypad and no dial. Mike tapped the icon on the phone marked *Safe*. The locking mechanism on the safe whirred and clicked, then a green light on its door illuminated. Mike pulled it open.

In the safe, he found stacks of bundled cash. Beneath that, was a gold metal key and a laminated card. He picked them both up and studied the card. The CIA knew the routing and account numbers to Grigor's bank and account. They had found them on Meskhi's computer and used the routing number to track Grigor down. Two of the numbers on this card were those same routing and account numbers. Written next to them was a third set of numbers. Mike knew it was Grigor's PIN. With these three numbers, anyone could access the account and transfer the money. Add the key to it, and you could walk right into the bank and back out with a boatload of hard cash.

Mike tapped the icon on the phone labeled *Bank*. It opened and automatically logged in to Grigor's account at the Bangkok Bank, opening on the balance page. Grigor had $62 million in the account.

Mike slipped the laminated card into his shirt pocket. He put the key and cash back in the safe, reclosed the safe's door, and then closed the wall. He went downstairs to find the tech just finishing his search and the bagging of Grigor's computer hardware.

"Find anything upstairs?" he asked Mike.

"No. Nothing. Let's get out of here."

Epilogue

The president of the Washington, D.C. University Medical Center sat behind his massive oak desk in his spacious, wood-paneled office. He had just signed the paperwork authorizing the placement of a small, brass, memorial plaque for Dr. Lynn Elliot. It would be affixed to a fountain on the campus promenade.

His next task was to find a source of funding to upgrade the parking garage lighting to fix the security shortcomings that had contributed to her death. He knew that it should have been done years ago, and the signing of Dr. Elliot's memorial authorization had driven that point home to him in a very personal and painful way.

As a state-owned institution, he had tried for years to get the state legislature to fund the infrastructure upgrade project, and to authorize additional campus police. In the current budget environment, though, he had been unsuccessful.

He had personally solicited wealthy alumni, but they were more interested in constructing a building that would bear their own name.

His only remaining option would be to reduce faculty, staff, and programs to save money. That idea broke his heart, but he had to do it. He was not prepared to lose another employee or student to crime that he could prevent. He would use the savings to improve the security of the campus.

The Chief Financial Officer stuck his head into the president's office door and knocked on the doorframe.

"Busy?"

"Ah, you read my mind. You are *exactly* who I want to see. I want to talk about funding for the garage upgrades and additional police. We're just going to have to reduce staff and bite the bullet. But these security issues *must* be fixed."

"Well, actually, I did come by to talk to you about money."

"Oh no, another crisis?"

"Not exactly."

"Well, what then?" He stood and walked around his desk, unsure if he wanted to hear what was coming next. Lately the CFO delivered only bad news.

"We just received a $62 million dollar grant from an anonymous donor. The grant is for infrastructure improvement, security lighting, security measures, law enforcement, memorials, and medical research. So we have a great deal of latitude with it."

The president sank back against his desk, his mouth agape. "Anonymous?"

"Yes, it was transferred directly to the university from Bangkok Bank in Thailand. I reached out to the bank to verify that there was no error, and to try to find out who the donor was. The bank verifies that the money was legally transferred by the account holder, but they don't know who that person is. It's a numbered account."

"My God, then it's real?"

"It certainly seems so. The money *is* in our general account. Our bank verifies that the funds are there and available."

The president felt a little lightheaded. "Memorials? That's an odd thing to list in a grant."

He looked to his desk and picked up the paperwork he had just signed for Dr. Lynn Elliot's plaque. He decided on a whim that her plaque would now be a marble pedestal worthy of her service, and her sacrifice, to the university.

"Jenny," he called out to his secretary in the outer office. She instantly appeared in the doorway.

"I want a staff meeting today at 4:00 p.m. I want finance, contracting, procurement, HR, engineering, and law enforcement. Meeting subject is the installation of a new garage lighting system and the hiring up of our law enforcement staff to patrol it properly."

"Yes sir," she replied smartly, vanishing as fast as she had appeared.

Author's Note

Dear Valued Reader,

Thank you for reading The Bombs Bursting in Air. I hope you enjoyed it.

One learns by doing. Writing novels is no different. I learned a lot developing and writing this second Mike Elliot thriller.

I hope to put that knowledge to good use in future stories. I have to admit, the second one was a little easier than the first. Still, most readers don't realize the blood, sweat, and tears required to arrive at a written project of this size.

If you liked this yarn, please be so kind as to leave a review. It will only take a second and will be greatly appreciated. I am eager to hear your feedback. It will guide and shape my future writing, and frankly, it can't succeed without your help. So please leave a review on Amazon, Goodreads, or both.

And if you haven't read The Dawn's Early Light yet, you should. It will give you more background on Mike Elliot's past. Besides, it's a dynamite thriller you don't want to miss. You can find all of my books and stories on my Amazon Author Page (https://www.amazon.com/-/e/B01DEALAEW). Or just search Lee Duffy on Amazon. Enjoy.

Thank you,

Lee Duffy

www.ingramcontent.com/pod-product-compliance
Lightning Source LLC
Chambersburg PA
CBHW021953170626
46808CB00001B/137